DAVID ROBERTS worked in publishing for over thirty years before devoting his energies to writing full time. He is married and divides his time between London and Wiltshire.

Visit www.lordedwardcorinth.co.uk to find out more about David and the series.

Praise for David Roberts

'A classic murder mystery with as complex a plot as one could hope for and a most engaging pair of amateur sleuths whom I look forward to encountering again in future novels.'
Charles Osborne, author of
The Life and Crimes of Agatha Christie

'Roberts' use of period detail … gives the tale terrific texture. I recommend this one heartily to history-mystery devotees.'
Booklist

'*Dangerous Sea* is taken from more elegant times than ours, when women retained their mystery and even murder held a certain charm. The plot is both intricate and enthralling, like Poirot on the high seas, and lovingly recorded by an author with a meticulous eye and a huge sense of fun.'
Michael Dobbs, author of
Winston's War and *Never Surrender*

'The plots are exciting and the central characters are engaging, they offer a fresh, a more accurate and a more telling picture of those less placid times.'
Sherlock

The QUALITY of MERCY

DAVID ROBERTS

ROBINSON
London
—————
CARROLL & GRAF PUBLISHERS
NEW YORK

Constable & Robinson Ltd
3 The Lanchesters
162 Fulham Palace Road
London W6 9ER
www.constablerobinson.com

First published in the UK by Constable, an imprint of
Constable & Robinson Ltd 2006
This paperback edition published by Robinson, an imprint of
Constable & Robinson Ltd 2007

First US edition published by Carroll & Graf Publishers 2006,
this paperback edition, 2007

Carroll & Graf Publishers
An Imprint of Avalon Publishing Group, Inc.
387 Park Avenue South, 12th Floor
New York, NY 10016

AVALON
publishing group incorporated

A copy of the British Library Cataloguing in
Publication Data is available from the British Library

UK ISBN: 978-1-84529-316-1 (hbk)
UK ISBN: 978-1-84529-661-2 (pbk)

US ISBN-13: 978-0-78671-998-3
US ISBN-10: 0-7867-1998-2

Printed and bound in the EU

1 3 5 7 9 10 8 6 4 2

For Krystyna

I am grateful to Dr Madeleine Campbell and to Brigadier Arthur Douglas-Nugent for advice on matters equine. I am also grateful to Wera Hobhouse who checked my German and Commander John Roskill for advice on naval matters.

Truth will come to light; murder cannot be hid long.
. . . . . .
The quality of mercy is not strain'd.
It droppeth as the gentle rain from heaven
Upon the place beneath: it is twice bless'd;
It blesseth him that gives and him that takes . . .

Shakespeare, *The Merchant of Venice*

What, is't murder?
. . . . . .
Mortality and mercy in Vienna
Live in thy tongue and heart.

Shakespeare, *Measure for Measure*

March and April 1938

1

Lord Edward Corinth swung the Lagonda Rapier on to the Romsey road and pressed down the accelerator. The six-cylinder four-and-a-half-litre engine responded magnificently. A similar model had won Le Mans three years earlier in 1935 and, since then, refinements had vastly improved its ability to hold the road at speed, even in the rain. He glanced at the dog in the passenger seat beside him. Basil, Verity Browne's curly-coated retriever, seemed to be enjoying himself. The wind smoothed the hair on his head to felt. Teeth bared, he appeared to be grinning although, Edward had to admit, it might be fear. Reluctantly, he slowed down. He did not relish the idea of having to tell Verity that her beloved dog – with which he had been entrusted while she was abroad – had been catapulted out of the car by his rash pursuit of some notional speed record.

It was fortunate that he reduced his speed. As he negotiated a sharp bend, he came across a stationary yellow Rolls-Royce straddling the road, steam rising in wisps from its magnificent-looking radiator. He gritted his teeth and pounded the brakes. The Lagonda came to a halt inches from the Rolls. A uniformed chauffeur was standing at the side of the road, cap in hand, red in the face, soundlessly opening and closing his mouth like a gaffed fish. Edward raised his goggles, prepared to berate him for endangering his life and the dog's. Basil had slid off the seat into the footwell, a bundle of umber fur, too bewildered to bark a protest. Edward breathed again as Basil scrambled out of the car and shook himself vigorously, seemingly none the worse for his brush with death.

'For goodness sake, man,' Edward said testily, 'what the hell's going on? Get this car off the road before someone gets killed.'

Before the chauffeur could answer a tubby, dark-skinned little man with a baby face decorated with a neat moustache bounded out from behind the Rolls, perspiring though the wind was cold.

'Don't blame Perkins. The damn thing suddenly stalled – overheated or something. You're not hurt, are you? I'm most frightfully sorry.'

The owner of the Rolls, dressed in tweeds – heather mixture, Edward thought – Burberry raincoat and soft felt hat, looked as overheated as his car. He spoke Eton-and-Harrow English with a charming Indian lilt. The expression on his face – at the moment anxious – was, Edward knew, normally good-natured to the point of imbecility.

'Sunny! It is you, is it not?'

'M'dear fellow, I . . . Good Lord! Edward? Can it really be you? What an extraordinary thing!'

Sirpendra Behar, Maharaja of Batiala, known to his friends as Sunny, had been in Edward's House at Eton. He was a year older than Edward and they had become great friends – a friendship cemented by a mutual love of cricket. Even at Eton Sunny had been plump but that had not prevented him being a first-class bat. Edward and he had been in the Eleven and, in Sunny's last year, they had scored a century apiece in a memorable third-wicket stand that secured Eton the match in their annual tilt with Harrow. It was an innings still talked of – his nephew Frank had informed him – a generation later. Sunny had gone on to help establish the Ranji Trophy in 1935, playing for Baroda. His moment of triumph, however, was scoring a century on the Nawab of Pataudi's tour of England in 1936 after which he had more or less retired from first-class cricket.

Edward had not seen much of him after they left school – Edward going up to Cambridge and Sunny returning to rule Batiala, his father having died unexpectedly. They

4

shook hands warmly and Edward had an idea that Sunny would have embraced him but restrained himself knowing it to be 'unEnglish'.

'I say, Sunny, there's going to be the most awful pile-up unless we can move your car pretty speedily. I was deuced close to killing myself and, more importantly, killing the dog. I'll reverse the Lagonda back round the corner to warn any car that comes along that something's not right. I'll leave you beside it to wave people down. If I can't get the Rolls started, your chauffeur and I can at least push it out of the way.'

Edward was no mechanic but he did know a bit about cars. However, his engineering expertise was not required. When he got into the driving seat and pressed the self-starter the engine roared into life. He drove the Rolls a few yards and parked it safely off the road. Sunny's chauffeur explained that though it was only three months old, it had been plagued with mechanical problems – as were other Phantom IIIs. In fact, instead of having made the best car in the world as they had promised, Rolls was in danger of losing its reputation for engineering excellence. The chauffeur said it was going back to the workshop as soon as they returned to town but the Maharaja had insisted on taking it to Broadlands for the weekend to show Lord Louis Mountbatten who had particularly asked to see it. He loved fast cars and owned a Rolls himself – a Phantom II – a wedding present from his wife. It famously bore on its bonnet a silver signalman in honour of Mountbatten's connection with the navy.

'There we are!' Edward said, relieved. 'I've read somewhere that they have had problems with the Phantom overheating, particularly on those new German *Autobahnen* where one can drive at high speed for long distances. You haven't been driving the Maharaja on autobahns, have you, Perkins?'

'We have just returned from the Continent, sir . . .'

At that moment Sunny reappeared looking flustered and slightly ridiculous with his tie askew. It came back to Edward that if his friend had a fault it was that he wanted to be more English than the English.

'Well done, old boy. I heard the damn thing start. What did you do?'

'Nothing. Just my magic touch.'

'Look, old chap,' Sunny panted, 'it's most awfully good to see you again and I'm terribly grateful but I daren't stop to chat. I promised Dickie I would be there for lunch and it's after twelve now. Do you know the Mountbattens?'

'You're staying at Broadlands?'

'Yes. Ayesha's there already. She refuses to come in the Rolls until I get it fixed. She went down by train yesterday. But you've not met her, have you?'

'No, but I would very much like to.' Edward had been invited to the wedding but he had been in South Africa at the time. He heard it had been a tremendous affair and regretted missing it. The Maharani was said to be very beautiful and when, on her wedding day, she had paraded through Batiala on a milk-white elephant her poorest subjects had taken her for a goddess. She, like Sunny, had been educated in England, at Benenden, an exclusive boarding school for girls in Kent. Sunny's father had understood how important it was for a state like Batiala that the Maharaja and Maharani should be able to deal with the British on their own terms. 'I'm spending a few days with my brother at Mersham – you remember the castle, don't you? You came down for the annual cricket match once, I seem to remember.'

'And I was out first ball,' Sunny said ruefully. 'I was so humiliated but your mother was very kind and comforted me.'

'She was a good woman,' Edward said with feeling. 'I miss her very much.'

'I don't mind admitting – I was scared of the Duke.'

'My father scared me on occasion,' Edward laughed, 'but my brother is a very different man. I know he and my sister-in-law would be delighted to invite you over – both of you.'

'That's very good of you, Edward, and we should be very pleased to come, but there are four of us. My son, Harry, is with us. He's at Eton, you know.' Sunny could not hide his pride in his son. 'That's really why we are here in England – for the Easter holidays. And my daughter, Sunita.'

'Well, we would be delighted to see them as well. How long did you say you would be at Broadlands?'

'Four or five days – perhaps longer. Dickie seems very taken with Ayesha,' Sunny giggled nervously. 'Should I be jealous, do you think? He has a reputation as a ladies' man.'

'I am sure Lady Louis keeps him in order,' Edward said, unwilling to speculate. What he could not say to Sunny was that his brother regarded Mountbatten and the 'fast set' in which he moved as beyond the pale. The Mountbattens were always in the newspapers, usually pictured with an expensive new car or some American film star. The Duke thought no gentleman should see his name in print unless *The Times* or the *Morning Post* carried a brief formal announcement of the birth of a son, a marriage or a death. Lady Louis – Edwina – was rumoured, no doubt unjustifiably, to have 'affairs'. Paul Robeson, the black American singer and actor, had been mentioned as one of her admirers.

'But Edwina's not there – not yet anyway. She is supposed to be arriving tomorrow.'

'But there are other guests?'

'Yes indeed.' It was Sunny's turn to sound shocked. 'I wasn't suggesting . . .'

Edward suddenly felt the conversation had become prurient, if not vulgar, and hurried to end it. 'I must be off, too. I will telephone. Goodbye.'

'Thank you so much, Edward,' Sunny said, sounding almost pathetic.

'Glad to have been of assistance, old chap, but for God's sake get that car checked over. It ought not to be seizing up like that. We all might have been killed. Here, Basil, it's no good you looking at me like that. You'll be quite safe.' He pushed the reluctant animal into the car and patted him. 'I'll not drive above forty, I promise you.'

Basil gazed at him reproachfully and sank down on the seat and hid his head in his paws.

Verity was lonely and miserable. She had often been scared when reporting the civil war in Spain, notably at the siege of Toledo and then again at Guernica when she was wounded and her friend, Gerda Meyer, was killed but she had seldom been lonely. She had been surrounded by comrades-in-arms whose cause was her cause and that made it easier. Here in Vienna she was alone. Her lover, the young German aristocrat, Adam von Trott, had been kidnapped by Himmler's thugs in front of her eyes. She had imagined Adam in some terrible prison camp but in fact it appeared that he had been bundled off to the Far East where he could cause no trouble.

She was holding in her hand a letter – the first news she had had of him for over a month and it ought to have made her happy. He was in Japan, he told her. He was well and sent his love but it was not a *love* letter. She did not know what to make of his breezy descriptions of the beauties of the Orient. He described climbing Mount Aso, the largest volcano in the world, but he didn't say he thought of her when he reached the summit. Instead, lamely, she thought, he wrote that 'it might seem strange that I should idle in this wilderness while the face of Europe is being changed'. He wanted 'to cut loose from all attachments that are not essential'. She could only read that as referring to herself and it hurt. She dropped the letter on the table. Of course, she told herself, she wanted him to be happy but what had happened to make him forget what they had meant to each other just a few weeks earlier? She tried to be reasonable. She guessed he must believe that his mail would be read by Himmler's agents and he probably wanted to protect her by distancing himself from her, but still . . . She picked up the letter again. He spoke of having started work on political philosophy which might take 'longer than anticipated' and that he might go to India and Turkey.

He was studying political philosophy in the East! Surely he should be here in Vienna where he could study the brutal reality of German political philosophy at first hand. It was rumoured that any day now the Germans would march into Austria and it would become part of Hitler's new German Reich. It occurred to her that Adam had no reason to lament the *Anschluss* any more than the vast majority of Austrians who waited eagerly to greet their Führer. Adam hated the Nazis but he was a patriot.

Tears pricked her eyes. She wanted to talk to someone about Adam but who was there apart from Edward – and he was far away in England. In any case, why should he be sympathetic, she upbraided herself. She had hardly been fair to him when she threw him up for a good-looking German. It was right that she should pay for her cavalier treatment of the one person who loved her unreservedly. He would understand her feelings of betrayal and rejection because she had made him suffer as she was suffering now.

To cap it all, she was finding it difficult to make any headway with the job she had wanted so much. She did not yet speak good German and she had trouble with the soft, almost slurred Viennese vowels, so different from Adam's. The Viennese who spoke English seemed to treat her with amused contempt which made her angry with herself as much as with them. She had had to stifle the criticisms she longed to make of their comfortable acceptance of their country's absorption by Nazi Germany because she knew that, if she paraded her Communist beliefs, she would be deported as a troublemaker, or worse. Every day enemies of the Nazi Party 'disappeared'. The corpses of some were washed up on the banks of the Danube. Others simply vanished.

Of the other foreign correspondents in the city, she found most to be unfriendly and unwilling to introduce her to people who could help her discover what was going on. It was understandable. Over months and even years journalists based in Vienna had painstakingly developed their own lines of communication with the powers-that-be and saw no reason why they should share them with the newcomers now flooding into the city. These established correspondents seemed, for the most part, to share the prejudices of the people among whom they worked and lived. That was another reason why it would have been so wonderful to have had Adam with her. He could have opened doors for her to sources of information every journalist would have envied – but it was not to be.

She had hoped that at least among the Jews she would have found friends. They, she thought, must see the reality of what would happen when German tanks paraded through the city centre, along the Kärntnerstrasse and stood in the Stephans-Platz outside the cathedral. And yet so many did not. They seemed to believe that Austrian Jews would be granted privileged status – that they would be spared the Nazis' venom.

There were exceptions, she reminded herself. She had a date that evening to accompany a young Jew to a ball and she had gone to some trouble to ensure he would not be disappointed in her. They had met – rather absurdly – a week before at a *thé dansant*. It was fashionable in Vienna to go to the park at five o'clock to take tea and listen to the military band. This was the charming face of Vienna foreigners always fell for – *Gemütlichkeit*, they called it. When the music began, the young men would rise from their tables and invite ladies to dance. Verity had been surprised but not displeased when Georg had stood before her, bowed solemnly, almost clicked his heels, and invited her – in excellent English – to foxtrot.

Thinking back, she realized that he knew who she was and had decided she might be able to help him reach England but, at the time, she thought he had merely liked the look of her and she was flattered. By the end of the afternoon she had promised to help him obtain a visa and, that evening, had wired Edward for the necessary letter of welcome. She had seen enough of refugees in Spain prepared to promise anything – to do anything – to get to England to be almost inured to hard-luck stories, but this young man had not asked for her pity and she admired that. She could do very little to ameliorate the situation in which so many Jews now found themselves but what little she could do she would. Georg Dreiser was still in his twenties. He had done well at the Piaristen-Gymnasium and was now studying law at the University of Vienna and at the Konsularakademie, a diplomatic college with an international reputation.

Verity gathered that he had a foot in both political camps. He was a member of a Jewish student fraternity, politically active for the Zionist cause. He told her that he had found he had a talent for public speaking and soon had a reputation as something of a rabble-rouser. Each member of the fraternity took a so-called 'drinking name'. Georg's was D'Abere, a French version of the Hebrew word for 'talker'. On the other hand, he had many friends among the Catholic nationalists. He would walk in the Vienna Woods with a group of non-Jewish friends and discuss Wagner, Karl Kraus and Nietzsche. He was highly intelligent and spoke English, French and some Italian in addition to his native Yiddish and German.

He was not conventionally good-looking. His limbs seemed all over the place and, though he was tall, he was not strong. His face was as soft and puffy as one of the Viennese cream pastries he loved so much. His nose was squashed, like a boxer's, and his eyes set too close together but they were very bright and somehow knowing. He had what Verity could only describe as 'grown-up eyes'. He had seen much unpleasantness in his short life and understood that there was worse to come. He was quick to tell her about himself and his family. His father was a director of an insurance company and it was a paradox that, as anti-Semitism became more pronounced, he was protected by colleagues who were supporters of Hitler and *Anschluss*. However, the previous year his father's luck had run out and he was now in prison waiting to be tried on trumped-up fraud charges.

'It has some advantages,' Georg said drily as they attempted an Argentinian tango. 'As a prisoner of the civil court, he is protected from being sent to a concentration camp.'

'And you?' Verity had inquired. 'Are you safe?'

'Only until Hitler walks into Austria, which could be any day now.'

'But why didn't you leave before?'

'Why should I? I am an Austrian. Who has the right to tell me to give up my home, my family, my education and go into exile?' he demanded. 'Would you leave England if someone suddenly decides they do not like the look of your face?'

'No, of course not, but . . .'

'But now, yes, I must leave, but to leave I need a visa. I wondered . . . is there anyone you know in England who

11

could write and say there is work and a little money to support me for the first few months? We are not allowed to take money out of the country and the British Embassy requires that refugees prove they will not be a burden on the state.'

It made Verity boil with anger as she imagined some starched-shirt bureaucrat deciding on a whim whether or not to allow Georg to avoid death in a concentration camp.

'Of course!' she said abruptly. 'I'll do what I can. Meet me this time next week and I will try and have something for you.'

'You are most kind,' Georg said, bowing over her hand. 'You may say I shall not come quite empty-handed.'

'What do you mean?'

'I can't say any more. I am being watched but I have information which might be useful to your government.'

Verity looked at him with disbelief. 'Why should they watch you? Because you are a Jew?'

'I told you, I have a somewhat – *wie sagt man?* – unsavoury reputation as a political activist and I have friends who interest the authorities . . .'

Verity hesitated. She wondered if Georg was a fantasist. What could this young man know which would make him dangerous to the Nazis? He saw her look and changed the subject. 'Miss Browne, let me show you Vienna as it used to be,' he said eagerly. 'Let us have one last night of "Old Vienna" before it vanishes for ever.'

She looked doubtful. 'I've been to the Spanish Riding School if that's what you mean.'

'No, no! Not that – I hate horses anyway and they hate me – nor the Hofburg – not even Schönbrunn, though I would like to take you there sometime. No, I mean an old-fashioned Vienna Ball where we can waltz to music by Strauss. There are balls and dances every night until Lent. This year,' he added wryly, 'it will indeed be a time for penitence. Next week is the Konsularakademie ball which the diplomatic corps and members of the government attend. It is what I think you call a "glittering occasion".'

'And you can go?'

'That is part of the paradox! As a Jew I may not be welcome in certain bars and clubs but at the ball I shall be treated like any other gentleman. Nothing unpleasant – *Da gibs koa Sünd*! as we say here. Everyone knows my father and they know why he is in prison. I have no doubt they will do what they can to protect him.'

'It's a mad world!' Verity exclaimed.

'It is indeed. Until I am thrown into a camp I am quite acceptable in society, at least until our government surrenders to the Nazis.'

'You think they will?'

'There can be no doubt of it. Chancellor Schuschnigg is a good man but he cannot go against the vast majority of Austrians who wish to be part of the new German Reich. *"Und ist kein Betrug in seinem Munde gefunden worden."*'

Verity furrowed her brow so he translated: '"And out of his mouth there came forth neither deceit nor falsehood."'

She had not liked to snub the young man by refusing his invitation and it certainly promised to be an interesting occasion. She might glean information from people of influence, people whom, up to now, she had singularly failed to meet. But there was a problem: what was she to wear? Georg would, he said, borrow his father's white tie and tails. There was nothing for it, she told herself, but to buy something especially for the ball. On the face of it, it was absurd to spend money on a dress she would probably only wear once but she owed it to Georg not to look out of place. And it wasn't only a dress. She would need gloves, shoes and an evening bag and she would have to have her hair done. She suddenly felt more cheerful. She would give this young Jew something to be proud of.

She went to Spitzer for her dress. Fortunately, the manager spoke good English and, when she had explained her predicament, he was most helpful. An hour later she came out with a gown of shimmering moiré, the colour of 'lake water' as the manager put it, and a black evening cloak. She wished Edward was there to reassure her but the dress looked all right, she thought. Gloves she bought from Zacharias – long white kid gloves so sensuous she wanted to stroke her face with them. She found shoes at Otto Grünbaum and an evening bag – so small it would hardly take a handkerchief – exquisitely decorated with hundreds of tiny pearls. Flushed with success, she also bought a fan made from peacock feathers, which she practised opening and closing with a twist of her wrist.

Georg had said he would pick her up from her flat at eight o'clock but the hour came and went with no ring at the bell. At first she was anxious and then angry. Here she was all dressed up with nowhere to go, as the saying went. She had been made a fool of and she was not someone to take that lying down. Just as she was about to tear off her finery and go to bed in a sulk, there was a violent knocking on her door.

It was Georg, unusually flustered and almost bedraggled. 'I am so sorry – forgive me, please – I was delayed – unavoidably delayed,' he added as though grabbing at the phrase for support.

Verity's anger dissipated. He had obviously been in a fight. His evening dress was stained with mud and his tie was all awry. He had a cut on his cheek and his hair was mussed up. 'Have you been attacked?' she demanded.

'I . . . I met some youths . . . I will tell you later.'

'Wait a minute – before we go anywhere, let me tidy you up.'

She made him take off his coat and sponged the mud off it. She brushed his hair and gently bathed the cut on his face. As Georg calmed down he seemed to see Verity for the first time.

'You are so very kind and beautiful, Fräulein Browne . . .'

'You may call me Verity,' she said graciously, 'if we are to enjoy the evening.'

The ball was in full swing when they arrived and she was relieved to find that she was dressed correctly. As Georg said – whatever the prejudices of the Viennese, they were certainly not going to spoil the ball by exhibiting them. He introduced her proudly to several distinguished-looking elderly men as 'my English friend, the journalist, Verity Browne'. By no means all of his friends – to judge from their names – were Jewish and she met and danced with diplomats and government officials who urged her to come to them for information on the political crisis. On the whole, they seemed complacent. They would muddle through – they used the verb *fortwursteln* – Austria always did. Britain would support the Chancellor. Hitler would not prevail. Verity was triumphant. This was just the breakthrough she had been looking for. Virtue, she told herself smugly, was its own reward but if helping Georg led her into Viennese society she would not complain.

Panting, Georg and Verity polkaed to a halt. She was suddenly aware of a buzz of conversation around them and she asked him what was the matter.

'There's a rumour that Chancellor Schuschnigg has been summoned to meet Hitler. Here's Manfred Schmidt. He's an old friend of my father's – not a Nazi, you understand. He'll tell us what's happening.' He grabbed by the sleeve a bearded man with a worried frown on his face. 'Onkel Manfred, what's the news from the Ballhausplatz?' The Ballhausplatz was the Austrian foreign ministry.

'Ah, Georg, my boy, it is time you and your parents left for England. I hear that your father will soon be released from prison but the Nazis . . . who knows . . . ?' He hesitated. 'Hilter has ordered Schuschnigg to cancel the plebiscite' – this was the popular vote on whether Austrians wanted to become part of a greater Germany.

Suddenly, to Verity's horror, she heard outside the building a rising chant of *Sieg heil*. They went on to the balcony and looked out over the square. It was cold and wet but the *Platz* was illuminated by hundreds of torches borne aloft by young men wearing the white stockings and lederhosen of the outlawed Austrian Nazi party. They wore swastikas on their arms, which until then had been illegal, and chanted, 'Germany awake, Judah perish.' As Verity watched, the crowd swelled and began to sing '*Deutschland, Deutschland, Über Alles*' and then, lifting their arms, the '*Horst Wessel*', the Nazi Party anthem.

Georg turned to Verity and said grimly, 'It was youths like these who beat me up on my way to your apartment. It is as I feared. *Osterreich ist kaputt.*'

2

'You can do what you want, Ned, but I flatly refuse to go anywhere near Broadlands and nor will Connie.'

It was breakfast and Edward had just read aloud a note from Lord Louis Mountbatten, delivered by hand, inviting them all to lunch that very day. Connie studied her eggs and bacon, refusing to look her brother-in-law in the eye. His nephew, Frank, was still in bed. He had arrived the day before, exhausted after a punishing week of dancing and flirting on the *Normandie*. Edward looked at his brother with dismay. He knew Gerald could be obstinate but his refusal to consider being Mountbatten's guest seemed ridiculous.

'It's not like you to be discourteous,' he chided. 'I agree that from all accounts the man is rather too pleased with himself but he's said to be a good naval officer. He's not just a playboy.'

'I'm sorry, Ned, I don't want to be rude to your friends but there it is. I don't wish to discuss it.'

'He's not my friend but Sunny is and I certainly can't refuse him. What about Frank? Surely he can go? You know he will be bored here. This will give him something to think about.'

'I would rather he did not go but he's not a child any more. He can make his own decision.' The Duke looked even sulkier. 'I hate that word "bored",' he said suddenly angry. 'Most people are bored but they have to earn their living as best they may in "boring" jobs. They don't gad around the world picking up unsuitable girls. I am very much afraid my son is turning into a spoiled brat. He seems to think life is just one long party. Well, it isn't and the sooner he finds that out the better.'

'I say, Gerald, steady on! There's a war coming sure as eggs is eggs and we'll all have our duty to do but young men like Frank will carry the worst of it. You shouldn't begrudge him the chance to sow a few wild oats.'

'I'm not against the boy sowing a few wild oats . . .' He caught the expression on the faces of his wife and brother. 'Well, I'm not,' he said stoutly. 'Being a duke is a damn dull business. You'd agree with that, wouldn't you, Connie?'

She hardly knew how to answer him. She had indeed felt constricted on occasion by what was expected of her and, if she were honest, she did think her husband had become dull but she was well aware that most women would give their souls to be where she was.

'We have Frank and we have Mersham,' she said diplomatically. 'We have no cause for complaint when I think of what some people have to put up with.'

Edward looked at her with affection. Connie was not one of those indolent, whining women he met sometimes who could talk of nothing but how difficult it was to get good servants.

'You still haven't told me why you don't like the man,' Edward demanded, a trifle plaintively.

The Duke said nothing but opened *The Times* noisily and pretended to read. He hated gossip but what he had read about the Mountbattens had shocked him.

Lord Louis Mountbatten, known to his family and close friends as Dickie and to other friends and acquaintances as Lord Louis, was Queen Victoria's great-grandson. There was a photograph to prove it in an ornate silver frame on a side table in the drawing-room at Broadlands of him as a baby sitting on her lap. It was the hinge upon which his life swung and never for one moment did he forget his position as a member of the Royal Family or allow anyone else to. He was tall – over six feet – with a ramrod-straight back, a fine head and a strong jaw. He had very little imagination and no intellectual curiosity. When he went to the theatre it was to admire the actresses and – some spiteful gossips would add – good-looking young actors. He had no sense of humour, which occasionally made him ridiculous, but he was by no means stupid. He possessed one of those highly focused minds which, when presented with a problem, worry at it until it's solved. He had suggested several technical improvements to his naval superiors on subjects such as wireless telegraphy and gun aiming.

He was ambitious both in his chosen career and in his determination to be treated not just as a minor royal but a leader in high society. He was not particularly interested in politics but, when he thought about it at all, saw himself as a liberal. He loved sport – particularly dangerous sport in which he could prove himself to be a man among men. He drove fast cars and fast boats and played polo with only two things in mind – he must win if at all possible but above all he must put on a 'good show'. His vanity led him to make mistakes. He was not a good judge of character and preferred to be surrounded by men who would not criticize or challenge him. His closest friend was a man called Peter Murphy who supplied him with girls while making no effort to conceal his preference for his own sex.

Mountbatten had made himself a boon companion of his cousin David, the Prince of Wales, and it seemed a moment of personal triumph when the Prince became Edward VIII. The triumph was short-lived, however, and when the King was forced to abdicate to marry Mrs Simpson, Mountbatten dropped his cousin with, some felt, undue haste and went to considerable lengths to assure the new King of his loyalty.

Mountbatten was well connected but not rich so in 1922 he married Edwina Ashley. She was beautiful, intelligent and fabulously wealthy. Her grandfather was the millionaire financier Sir Ernest Cassel and, through her father, she was descended from the Earl of Shaftesbury, the nineteenth-century philanthropist, and the dashing Lord Palmerston, Foreign Secretary and later Prime Minister to

Queen Victoria. The marriage brought him two fine houses: Brook House – a huge mansion on Park Lane – and Broadlands. In every respect it was a brilliant match and, if Edwina chose to take lovers from almost the moment they were married, it did not seem to affect their mutual affection. On their honeymoon they had gone to Hollywood where they were treated as royalty which, of course, Mountbatten considered himself to be. He adored the shallow glitter of the world of movies which appealed to his exhibitionist side. The glamorous young couple were fêted by stars such as Charlie Chaplin and Mary Pickford. Cecil B. de Mille taught Mountbatten how to use a 35mm cine camera and, it was said, how to satisfy a woman.

It was hardly surprising that the 'old guard', personified by Edward's brother, loathed him.

When the Duke had left the breakfast table, Edward eyed Connie quizzically. 'Aren't you even the least bit curious to meet the man?'

'Of course, but Gerald's right – it's not our world and we would stick out like sore thumbs. Take Frank by all means but I wonder . . .' She hesitated.

'You wondered?' Edward prompted.

'I wondered if . . . Oh, I know it sounds silly . . . if the Mountbattens won't steal him away. You said yourself he will be bored here with just us.'

She sounded bitter and Edward looked at her with concern. Her only son and the light of her life had left Cambridge without taking his degree and, under the influence of an American woman Edward had detested on sight, went to America to work with Dr Kinsey, an American academic with an interest in codifying sexual preferences. Edward was profoundly grateful that neither his brother nor, he believed, his sister-in-law had any notion of the nature of the 'research' in which their son was involved.

Frank had returned without his American so Edward guessed – and certainly hoped – that his nephew, who was a sensible boy at heart, had had enough of such people. He told himself that at Frank's age he too had wanted to shock his father and prove his independence. In his case, his rebellion had never even been noticed. The old Duke was only concerned to see Gerald properly educated to take over the title and the estate. As the second son, Edward was of no importance and his father ignored him.

'I didn't mean that he could ever stop loving being at Mersham. How could he?'

'I know! He's a good boy. We're so proud of him.'

'You think Frank might be drawn into the fast set of which you so disapprove?'

'Yes, I do. It would be quite natural if he found it . . . alluring.'

'Look, don't worry,' Edward said comfortably. 'I'll keep an eye on him. Don't you trust me? The fact is, I have a scheme. Frank wrote to me a couple of weeks ago and mentioned in a PS that, if he had to join the armed forces, he was quite taken with the idea of the navy. If Mountbatten noticed him it might be no bad thing. Now, if you'll excuse me, I'll go and dig him out of bed.'

Connie was not quite sure she approved of 'pulling strings' but all she said was: 'Of course I trust you, Ned. Do what you think is right.'

Although Mountbatten's life was the navy, he never lost his taste for film stars and, as they were ushered into the drawing-room at Broadlands a few hours later, Edward noticed a glamorous woman standing by herself clasping a glass of champagne who 'reeked' of Hollywood. Frank saw her too and whispered stagily, 'Tell me, Uncle, isn't that Garbo?'

It was not, but she was obviously making an effort to be taken for her. She was smoking a cigarette through a long holder and staring vacantly into space. Like Greta Garbo, she possessed the type of face that the camera loved. It was beautiful – indeed it was one of the most beautiful Edward had ever seen – but it was completely blank. She had either learnt to hide her emotions or she was so bored she was almost comatose. Before he could decide which, he was greeted by Sunny who, beaming away, introduced him to Mountbatten.

'My brother and sister-in-law were so sorry they could not come,' Edward lied smoothly. 'This is my nephew Frank. I wondered if you might have a moment to talk to him about the navy. He's a great admirer of yours and is thinking about volunteering.'

Mountbatten looked at Frank speculatively and seemed to like what he saw. 'Be glad to,' he said abruptly. He tended to talk as if he were barking out orders. Before he could say more, he was distracted by a woman he obviously knew well, wearing an alarming amount of jewellery with a décolletage revealing – unwisely, Edward considered, given that she was not in the first flush of youth – an acre of heavily powdered flesh. Seeing his opportunity, Sunny, hopping around uncle and nephew like a schoolmistress gathering up her charges, shepherded them over to meet his wife and children.

Ayesha proved to be a classic Indian beauty, fine-boned, with large lustrous black eyes. She wore an exquisite sari of the most delicate silk with the natural grace of a princess. She was not tall but she towered over her husband. Edward liked her immediately. She was quietly spoken for one thing, which Edward appreciated in a woman as he had often told Verity. What was more, she had an enchanting smile. Frank was buttonholed by Sunny who was telling him all about the Phantom III's unreliability. Out of the corner of his eye, Edward saw that the boy was hardly listening. Instead, he was taking in Sunita. It was not long before Sunny also noticed that Frank was finding his story of the accident that did not quite take place less than fascinating.

Taking pity on Frank, he summoned Harry and Sunita over to be introduced. Harry was a good-looking, though rather sulky, sixteen-year-old. Sunny's daughter was seventeen and took after her mother. She was long-limbed, dark with thick glossy hair that hung down almost to her shoulders. She was blessed with her mother's fine bones and clear, black eyes. When she raised them modestly and smiled, Frank was suddenly bereft of speech. He gaped, then recovered himself and started asking questions which she laughingly answered.

21

Harry mooched off looking disconsolate, obviously familiar with the effect his sister had on young men. Edward sighed to himself. He had seen that look in his nephew's eyes before. He was smitten and, for the moment at least, everyone else was invisible.

Sunny called his son back to shake hands with Edward who asked him how he was enjoying Eton. Harry was at first monosyllabic despite his mother's prompting. However, Edward persevered and was rewarded. He knew two or three boys at the school – sons of friends of his – one of whom turned out to be Captain of Cricket and Harry's hero. Edward soon discovered that Harry was a typical schoolboy with a love of all things sporting – particularly cricket – and a fascination with cars. Inevitably, they discussed the embarrassing technical faults of the Phantom, the strengths and weaknesses of the Lagonda, which Edward rashly promised he might drive in the grounds if Lord Louis did not object. Harry, by this time, had lost his sullen expression and Edward saw that Sunny and Ayesha were grateful for the trouble he was taking with their son.

'Gosh, may I really, sir? That would be wizard! I'm a bit of a nut over cars. In fact, I'm building one myself.'

'You are *what*?' Frank broke in, momentarily distracted from his admiration of Sunita.

'At home, in India. My father's got lots of cars, you know,' he said earnestly. 'Some he's never even got round to driving.' Sunny looked embarrassed but proud of his son. 'I'm taking one of his old Rolls-Royces apart and building something else with the bits. I'm going to call it the Batiala Bullet.' Frank looked impressed. 'I say,' Harry continued excitedly, 'Lord Louis was showing me his collection of motorbikes this morning. Would you like to see them?'

He looked at Frank appealingly. Frank hesitated and Edward thought he was going to refuse but he caught Sunita's eye and her message was clear. 'Of course, I'd love to see the bikes, Harry. You'll come, won't you?' he asked the boy's sister, his admiration so naked Edward winced inwardly.

Harry again looked annoyed that his sister might spoil things but when she said to him gently, 'If you don't mind, Harry,' he relented and smiled his assent.

'Don't be long, Baby,' Sunny said anxiously. 'You mustn't be late for lunch.' He looked at Edward with a half-smile of apology. 'We call her Baby at home but she made me promise not to call her that in public so now she'll be cross with me.'

When the three young people had departed, Edward looked over to the other side of the room. 'Who is that woman over there? She must be a film star. I almost feel I recognize her.'

'She is beautiful, isn't she,' Ayesha said, smiling. 'All the men keep looking at her, have you noticed? But I'm not sure it gives her pleasure. She has hardly spoken a word, even to Dickie.'

'But who is she?'

'Joan Miller. She's married to that man over there, Helmut Mandl.' Edward saw a coarse, heavily built man smoking as if his life depended on it.

'He looks a nasty piece of work,' he whispered. 'Is he German?'

'Austrian, like her. Joan Miller's just her stage name.'

'And Mandl?'

'He's very rich – the owner of Hirstenberger Patronen-Fabrik, so Dickie tells me.'

'The arms manufacturer? Of course! I've read about him. It comes back to me now. Joan Miller's the girl who cavorted naked in that film everyone was talking about. What was it called?'

Ayesha giggled. '*Last Night in Vienna*. Now you see why the men are gawping at her.'

Before Edward could comment, Mountbatten brought over a young man.

'Lord Edward, I want you to know Stuart Rose,' he said in his commanding bark. 'Stuart's over from Noo York.' Mountbatten's attempt at an American accent was pitiful. 'I think we should keep him here. I gather you have a friend in common.'

Mountbatten turned to talk to Ayesha and Edward saw

him briefly take her hand. She tried to look angry but
Edward had the feeling there was something between
them and felt sorry for his friend. He decided he disliked
Mountbatten. He was one of those men who must have
what they wanted whatever the cost – like a small boy
demanding another child's toy.

'You know that lady?' Rose said, seeing his face.

'The Maharani? I have only just met her,' he answered
abruptly and then, feeling he was being rude, added, 'I
was at school with her husband.'

'Ah, you English and your school friends!' Rose said,
laughing. 'Cigarette?' He proffered a silver case. Edward
took one and Rose lit it for him with a florid-looking
lighter decorated with a camel. 'I have studied at St Paul's
Concord, Harvard, Yale and Columbia and picked up a
few friends on the way but, damn it, we Americans never
label our friends by their education the way you do.'

'I don't believe that,' Edward said, smiling. 'What about
your fraternities? Aren't you loyal to your "frat house" for
life?'

'Touché!' The young man grinned engagingly. 'I guess
you're right. The friends of our youth have a special place
in our affections.'

Edward thought Frank might like him and said as
much.

'It would be an honour. Does he like art?'

'Not that I've ever heard,' Edward replied drily.

'Well, with your permission we'll change all that.'

Edward was taken aback. The man was presumptuous
but he supposed it might just be his American frankness.
'You don't need my permission and his parents will be
pleased if you take him off their hands,' he offered, giving
him the benefit of the doubt. 'But didn't our host say we
had a friend in common?'

'Bernard Hunt.'

'Hunt? I wouldn't say he was a friend – more an
acquaintance. We met on the *Queen Mary*. He knows a
great deal about Poussin, I recall.'

'He's a first-class critic. It's what I want to be,' Rose
added ingenuously. 'I worked at the National Gallery of

Art in Washington and Bernard's going to introduce me to Kenneth Clark and get me a research job at the National Gallery.'

'You sound as if you have your future mapped out,' Edward said with a touch of envy.

'I guess. There's a war coming so I need to get my education before the shooting match starts.'

Hunt was a predatory homosexual and Edward was pretty sure Rose was also that way inclined. Should he warn Frank, he wondered? No, the boy was old enough to look after himself. He glanced over at Mountbatten who was still talking to Ayesha and wondered about *his* proclivities. Was he rather too obviously a ladies' man? Was flirting with his friend's wife just a cover for his taste for young men? He was angry with himself for indulging in cheap cynicism but he was beginning to share Gerald's instinctive distaste for the man. He caught Sunny's eye and read pain, embarrassment and shame in that quick glance. His friend was the most peaceable of men but, in the last resort, he would not allow himself to be made to look a fool. Sunny was happy when his wife was admired but he would never countenance infidelity.

Edward thought the best thing he could do was to interrupt the tête-à-tête. Making his excuses to Rose, he joined Mountbatten. If the latter was annoyed, he did not show it but courteously involved him in a discussion of polo. Apparently, Ayesha was an accomplished player.

'Do you play, Lord Edward?' she inquired.

'I never have.'

'It's not too late to learn,' Mountbatten said with genuine enthusiasm. 'You and your nephew must try it.'

'Yes, you must,' Ayesha urged him. 'There's no game like it. If you have a good eye and you can ride . . . It's more exciting than hunting.'

After a moment, Mountbatten drew Edward to one side and told him there was someone he particularly wished him to meet.

'Who is that?' Edward asked, looking round.

'He's waiting for you in the Gun Room. I wanted to say . . . to warn you, he's not like Stuart, say, immediately likeable. He's austere – even cold – but he's able . . . very able and he's . . . he's a patriot.'

Edward was curious. It was not like Mountbatten to sound uncertain. 'What's his name? Why does he want to see me?'

'His name's Guy Liddell. He's a great-nephew of Alice-in-Wonderland, if you follow me. I have known him for many years but I'll let him tell you why he wants to meet you.'

'But *who* is he?'

'Well, he's a gifted cellist and a superb dancer. He won an MC in the war serving with the Royal Field Artillery. Afterwards, he joined Scotland Yard and liaised between Special Branch and the Foreign Office. Will that do?'

'He's a policeman?'

'I can't tell you any more but, believe me, he's one of the best men we've got. He's like me in one respect – he doesn't suffer fools gladly.'

Mountbatten showed him where to go but did not offer to accompany him.

The Gun Room was smaller than Edward expected. There were Purdeys locked in the gun cabinet, rods in some sort of basket, fishing tackle including nets and gaffes, walking sticks piled in a corner, wellington boots, a few stuffed birds – in other words the type of room found in every country house including Mersham Castle. The head of what Edward thought might be an elk grinned at him from just above one door. On every wall, nondescript sporting prints competed with photographs of Mountbatten at play – standing in heroic pose over a, presumably, dead tiger, on a polo pony swinging a stick, and at the helm of a yacht.

A row of heavy leather-bound volumes, no doubt recording the game killed on the estate, filled a bookcase. The sole window was shuttered and it took a moment for his eyes to adjust to the gloom. The pool of light spilt by the table lamp did not extend beyond its immediate environs but he could just make out a cheap clock on the wall behind the battered table on which so many guns and rods, not to mention dead animals, had been thrown over many years.

'Lord Edward, how good of you to spare me a few minutes. Forgive the cloak-and-dagger stuff but I try to keep in the background as much as possible. I have heard very good things about you from the people at Special Branch and I gather you sorted out a nasty little problem for the FO. Van said you cleared up the mess with the minimum of fuss.' Van was Sir Robert Vansittart, until recently the Permanent Head of the Foreign Office. 'In fact, you seem to have made your mark with a number of people whose opinion I value, without drawing attention to yourself. Not something Dickie would understand.' Liddell chuckled mirthlessly.

There was something cold and even repellent about his manner which made Edward glad Mountbatten had warned him not to rush to judgement. His clipped, patrician accent sounded as though it had been marinated in lemon juice. He was of average height, with receding hair and an officer's obligatory toothbrush moustache. As his eyes got used to the gloom, Edward saw he had the upright posture of the professional soldier and the expressionless face of a man with too many secrets.

'Sir Robert is a remarkable man. I was sorry that he felt he had to resign,' Edward ventured.

'Hmm,' was Liddell's only comment. His eyes seemed never to leave Edward's face and he found himself having to look away at a photograph of Mountbatten with Errol Flynn.

'I wondered if you'd be willing to help your country once again?'

'Would I be working for Special Branch?' Edward found himself asking.

'You'd be working for me.'

'May I ask who you are, sir?' Edward persisted. 'I mean, Lord Louis told me a little bit about you but not who you work for.'

'I work for a government organization preparing for the next war with Germany. We are particularly concerned with subversive activity in this country by agents of foreign powers.'

'Does it have a name – your organization?' Edward asked daringly.

Liddell looked down his nose and coughed. 'It does not exist so how can it have a name?' A thin smile indicated that this was a joke. He hesitated and then said, 'You took an oath of secrecy when you were working for Special Branch so I suppose I can tell you this much – I run a section called MI5. It is never to be referred to nor its existence even hinted at. You understand me?' Edward, intimidated by the man's steely authority, nodded his head in assent. 'If at any time your authority is questioned, you can, as a last resort, imply that you work for Special Branch but that is only when you have no alternative. I should perhaps say, however, that we in MI5 have no powers of arrest. We make use of the police when we need to use brute force. By the way, what does Miss Browne know of your – what shall I call them? – your activities on behalf of the government?'

Edward was taken aback though he ought not to have been. Verity was always seen as his weak link, at least as far as secrecy and his patriotism were concerned. As a Communist and a journalist, she would always be suspect but Edward would never contemplate giving her up on that account. In his book, loyalty to one's friends stood above any other loyalty.

'She knows I undertook an investigation for Special Branch.'

'Did she give you her blessing?' Liddell asked sarcastically.

'She understood that I had to do what I could to defend my country. She *is* a patriot but her idea of what is good for this country may not always be the same as the government's.' He knew he sounded pompous but it was the truth. 'She takes the view that Special Branch has a particular bias against Communists while ignoring the danger from the right.'

Liddell coughed. 'It is true we needed to combat subversive Bolshevik activities in Britain – still do for that matter. I had better tell you, in the strictest confidence of course, that we have just arrested Percy Glading, the CPGB's National Organizer. He was working directly for the Kremlin. You know the Communist Party has a clandestine wireless station in Wimbledon? No? Well, believe me when I say that the Party is acting under direct instruction from Moscow.'

'But . . .'

'I know. I am sure Miss Browne is quite unaware of it. It's for you to decide whether you want to open her eyes to what the Comrades are up to but, of course, there must be no mention of your source. Anyway, you can tell her that for the last three years most of our energies have been devoted to preparing for the war with Germany.'

Edward cheered up. 'Why has it taken so long? Why has Mr Churchill been a lone voice warning of German rearmament?'

Liddell shrugged. 'The politicians posture but our duty is to plan for the worst.'

Throughout the conversation, Edward realized, Liddell had assumed that he would do what he was asked to do and it came to him that he was no longer an amateur – a dabbler – choosing what he would or would not investigate but a government agent. His orders might be phrased as requests but they were in reality commands. The knowledge pleased him as much as it surprised him. Quite without meaning to, he had drifted into a line of work for which he had a taste and, he was beginning to think, a gift.

Liddell was still talking about Verity. 'Did you know that she will be back in England by the end of the week?'

'I didn't but, from what I hear on the wireless, the situation in Austria is very tense. I assumed her days in Vienna were numbered. I mean,' he corrected himself, 'as a known Communist she will be in considerable danger when the Nazis take over and the sooner she is back in London the happier I will be.'

'Lord Weaver has ordered her to leave, at least until her safety can be assured.' Lord Weaver was the proprietor of the *New Gazette* and Verity's employer. 'As soon as the Nazis establish themselves in the city, the Jews will be rounded up and sent to camps and the Communists with them, if they are not shot.'

Liddell sounded so matter-of-fact it chilled Edward's blood but not for one moment did he doubt that what he said was true.

'I'm told she's bringing an interesting young Jew with her – a man called Georg Dreiser. Find out if he has anything of interest to tell us. I rather doubt it, but you never know.'

'Yes, Miss Browne asked me to write a letter promising to support him financially until he could support himself. You know that thousands of Jews are being condemned to death because the British Embassy won't give them visas without such letters?'

For the first time Liddell looked uncomfortable. 'We could be swamped if we let in everyone who wanted to come here.'

'If by some miracle we win this war, we shall not easily be forgiven for our indifference.'

'We are doing our best,' Liddell said coldly. 'Relief measures are being discussed.'

'So, that's all? You simply want me to find out what Miss Browne's Jew knows?' Edward spoke scathingly but he was angry and ashamed – for his country and for himself. He would continue to live his comfortable life while men, women and children were thrown into concentration camps and murdered. It was intolerable. He had to do more but he felt so impotent.

'Not quite. There's someone else I want you to get to know. I want you to find a way of meeting a German called Heinrich Braken. He was until recently one of Hitler's intimates but he seems to have disgraced himself and is now in London – at Claridge's.'

'Braken? I've never heard of him.'

'He was a friend of Hitler's back in the twenties and although he has never been given any political power, for a long time he was intimate with the great man.' Liddell's voice was acid. 'You might say he was Hitler's court jester. Then he was put in charge of the foreign press. He spent time in America and speaks perfect American. But now he has fallen out of favour. We don't quite know why. He could be useful and it would certainly annoy Hitler if he were to come over to us.'

'I see. How will I meet him?'

'That's up to you but he has friends in London – the Mitfords, Harold Nicolson, Randolph Churchill – that set. Oh, and that young American, Stuart Rose, knows him.'

'And what exactly do you want from me that you can't ask Rose to do?'

'Rose is American, homosexual and a Communist. To be any one of those rules him out,' Liddell reproved him. 'Find out Braken's intentions. Make him feel safer in London than he would be in Berlin. He could be very useful to us. He knows – if anyone does – what makes Hitler tick.'

'What can I promise him?'

'You can tell him we'll look after him. Find out what he wants.'

'How do I report to you?'

'You don't. I will make myself known to you when I want to.'

'But in an emergency . . .?'

'There won't be an emergency but, if you have to, ring this number.' Liddell scribbled on the back of an envelope and gave it to Edward. 'Just say "Putzi" and then ring off without waiting for an answer. Someone will contact you.'

'Putzi? Why Putzi?'

'Didn't I say? It's Braken's nickname. By the way, how's your German?'

'Not fluent yet.'

'Putzi's not.'

'Not what?'

'A little fellow – that's what it means – Putzi. He's built like a carthorse.'

'Is there anything else I ought to know about him?'

'We know for a fact that he slept with Joan Miller – but who hasn't? You've met her?'

'I've seen her but we've not yet been introduced.' Edward was puzzled. 'She was Putzi's mistress in Vienna while she was married to Mandl?'

'Yes, do I shock you?' Liddell sounded amused. 'But it was in Berlin, not Vienna.'

'Does her husband know?' Edward thought it might account for Mandl's look of discontent.

'Mandl permitted it, I think. I'm not sure why. Perhaps because he wanted to get close to the Führer.'

Edward shook his head in mock concern. 'What will it do for my reputation if I befriend Putzi? I don't want to shock my friends. They think it's bad enough . . . Well, be that as it may . . .'

'No, you are right. It is important you do not act out of character. You mustn't "like" Putzi too obviously. You've got to make him want to know you. Show him you despise him. He's the most awful snob so it shouldn't be difficult. Whatever you do, don't act "furtive". The mysterious manner engenders distrust. A frank, open approach gains confidence. You can joke and talk a great deal and still say nothing. Now you must get back to the party before you are missed.'

'May I ask how much Mountbatten knows?'

'Dickie's a good man but he likes to talk. Tell him nothing. Tell no one anything. The curse of this job is that you are on your own. It's a lonely life.'

After lunch, at which Liddell did not appear, Edward slipped out of the drawing-room and went on to the terrace to smoke. The air was fresh but there was some warmth in the sun. He leant on the balustrade and contemplated the scenery. Beyond the lawn, the Test shimmered in the sunshine decorated with several pairs of swans. It was a sight, he thought, to calm the most troubled soul. 'Capability' Brown had laid out the grounds and in the process had altered the course of the river so that it would flow closer to the house. For a keen fisherman the Test was holy and Edward was wondering if he could ever get himself invited to take a rod when he caught a glimpse of a figure in a fur coat at the other end of the balustrade. It was Joan Miller. She, too, was staring at the view but, Edward guessed, seeing nothing of it. Her beautiful face was expressionless but for some reason he pitied her. Maybe it was her almost palpable loneliness.

She was smoking a cigarette through a long white holder and the faint scent of Balkan Sobranie wafted towards him. She ignored him. He had no wish to break into her reverie and, tossing away his cigarette, prepared to go back inside. A husky, dark voice redolent of the soft Austrian of her native land halted him.

'How do I escape this world?' she demanded of no one in particular with all the drama of Garbo.

For a moment Edward wondered if she was considering suicide. 'Escape? Why do you need to escape? Most women would envy you and most men . . .'

'Lust after me? Is that what you would say?'

'You are very beautiful,' Edward found himself admitting.

'But you did not know who I was? I saw you asking your friend.'

'I'm afraid I rarely go to the pictures, Miss Miller.' He knew he sounded sententious if not censorious. The actress gave a little shrug of dismissal as if to say this was his loss not hers.

'What right have I to be sad, you ask?' Though he had not. 'It is true I am not rich but my husband is. My jewels belong to Madame Mandl the hostess, not to me. My husband does all his business at the dinner table – that is why he is here, making himself pleasant to Lord Louis. He thinks that even now – on the eve of war – he can sell armaments to the British navy. Have you heard of the Oerlikon gun?'

'No.' Edward was surprised to find her so communicative.

'It's Swiss. Mandl says it's much superior to the half-inch Vickers. I tell him the British navy will never buy from him and, if they did, the Führer would not be best pleased but he is so greedy. Apparently the Oerlikon fires a shell which can penetrate the armour of a U-boat and it fires at a rate of five hundred rounds a minute.'

'You seem to know a lot about it.'

'I'm not a fool, Lord Edward,' she said sharply.

'I never thought you were but . . .'

'I've had to listen to him trying to sell it at so many dinner tables, I could repeat his whole spiel word for word but I'll spare you.' She smiled thinly.

'Is it your husband you wish to escape? Does he treat you badly?'

'If you mean does he hit me, no, he does not. He could not afford to have his beautiful wife appear with a bruise on her cheek. The bruise is on my heart.'

33

Despite the drama in her voice, Edward was surprised to find that he believed her.

'He keeps you captive?'

'Yes. He wants me to return with him to Austria – or rather the new German Reich. Mandl is useful to Hitler.'

'But you don't want to go?'

'When I was in Hollywood last year, Mr Mayer . . . you have heard of him . . . ?

'Louis B. Mayer – the MGM mogul?' Edward was rather pleased to recognize the name.

'It was Mr Mayer who changed my name to Joan Miller. He promised me a film contract but Helmut insists I return with him to Vienna. He hopes I will fascinate Herr Hitler but I hate the lot of them. Do you know, in Vienna we eat off solid gold plates? But the food tastes of dust and ashes.'

Edward was tempted to laugh, but he again felt that, behind the language of some cheap Hollywood film, a genuine passion lurked. She turned on him for the first time the full force of her beauty. He thought he understood why she so rarely looked directly at a man because, when she did, there was something in her eyes which transfixed him. He was not in the least attracted to her sexually but he would, he knew, do anything he could to please her.

'So, why not leave him? Walk away.'

'I cannot. My little girl is in Vienna. You understand? She is surety for my good behaviour. If I walked away, as you put it, I would never see my baby again.'

'Why are you telling me all this, Miss Miller – I mean Frau Mandl?' he demanded, a trifle resentfully.

'You can call me Joan,' she commanded him with regal benevolence.

'Why tell me all this, Joan? You don't know me. I might report this conversation to your husband.'

'I don't know you but I know of you. I know you are a friend to my friend Georg Dreiser . . .'

'You're a friend of his? I have never met him but I was happy to support his application to come to England. I repeat, why tell me all this?' Edward was suddenly angry. He did not need to hear this strange woman's sob story.

34

'I saw you and knew you were an English gentleman,' she answered coldly. 'Was I wrong?'

He relented enough to say, 'I promise I'll think about what you have told me and how I can help. I suppose you can't go to Lord Louis?'

'No, he and Helmut are business associates. I could not expect him to help me. I don't imagine he will want to – what is it you say? – rock the boat.'

'No, quite. By the way, before you were married, what was your name?'

'Hedwig Kiesler.'

'You are sure your husband does not love you? Before lunch I saw him looking at you. His gaze was so intense.'

'He does not love me. He loves to *possess* me. He has mistresses but I don't mind that. He hates me. He uses me to impress his friends and business colleagues. I am – what do they call it? – a trophy of his success and if I humiliated him by running away . . . I think he would hunt me down and kill me. I could not leave my baby in his care. You understand?'

'When you get back to Vienna you must hire a lawyer . . .'

'He *owns* lawyers . . . I could never get away that way. But you are right, what can you do? An English gentleman . . .' The scorn in her voice made him wince.

'Let me think about it . . .' Edward repeated, not wanting to get involved in what was by no stretch of imagination his business but compelled against his will to do her bidding. 'Tell me – how did you meet him?'

'I was in a play about Elizabeth of Austria and he came backstage. I was young. Each night he filled my dressing-room with flowers. He went and saw my parents and asked permission to marry me. He was already divorced but he was very rich and my parents thought it would be a good match. You think he's what the French call *mal baisé* but *I* found him attractive. At least I did then. He was so . . . so *fervent*. We were married in the Karlskirche in Vienna. He loved me then – or at least that was what I thought. He called me "Hasi", his little bunny, but things went wrong almost immediately. I quickly realized he wanted to own me. I was one more beautiful object in his collection. Then, while I was pregnant with Heidi, the film I had made just before I met him came out.'

'*Last Night in Vienna*?'

'Yes. There was a terrible scandal. I was seen running naked in the woods. At the time it was being made, it seemed not very shocking. I was merely the spirit of freedom at one with nature. I was naive. The film was a *succès de scandale*. Helmut said I made him look a fool – that I was nothing better than a whore.'

'So why did he not divorce you?'

'He thought about it but then he began to be proud of my – what is the word? – my notoriety. Instead of shunning me, his friends and business acquaintances wanted to meet me. Then, when we went to America, we met Mr Mayer on the boat and he offered me a film contract. I saw this as a way of escape but, as I told you, Helmut won't let me go.' She shrugged and, for no good reason, Edward felt himself condemned as a failure. In that little gesture she conveyed that she had sought a 'parfait gentil knight' and found instead a man of straw.

At that moment there was a noise and Harry burst through the french windows.

'Come on, sir. Frank says you must watch us ride the motorbikes. We're going to have a race. Lord Louis has a wizard new Kodak cine camera. He's going to film us.' He dashed off in high excitement without waiting for an answer.

'We're coming. Let's go downstairs, Joan. I must make sure the boys don't kill themselves. My brother would never forgive me. He thinks I'm irresponsible enough as it is.'

On the gravel the boys stood beside two motorcycles. Edward began to feel apprehensive. These were not little pop-pop machines but something much more serious. Frank was standing beside a Harley Davidson, gleaming red and black and promising all kinds of trouble.

'I say, Frank, old lad, is this wise? This looks a powerful animal. Are you sure you can ride it?'

'Don't worry, Uncle. I rode bikes at Cambridge and in America. Anyway, we're only going a few hundred yards, just to give Harry a bit of excitement. He's a nice boy and he's determined to have a go.' Frank tried to sound superior but failed.

'You're not just showing off in front of . . .' Edward indicated Sunita with a nod of his head.

'Uncle, you can be so patronizing sometimes,' Frank said sharply. 'I'm not a child.'

'Sorry,' Edward mumbled, ashamed of himself.

Frank smiled and forgave him. 'I'm so glad you introduced me to Lord Louis. He's a man I could follow, if you understand me. He says I ought to join the RNVR. He's told me who to go and see in London. He says the navy needs people like me. Do you think he means it?'

For a blessed moment, Frank had forgotten his pose of the languid man-about-town bored with everything and become an eager boy again.

'I'm sure he wouldn't say it if he didn't mean it.' Edward prayed he was right.

Everyone was milling about admiring the machines and offering unwanted advice. Mountbatten came up to them. 'Ready then, boys? Just to the end of the drive, but be careful.' He tapped the saddle of the Harley Davidson. 'This beauty can do ninety miles an hour.'

'I say, is it safe?' Sunny inquired, meaning his son's machine.

'Of course it's safe,' Mountbatten said forcefully, misunderstanding. He stood back and admired it. 'It's called the Knucklehead because of its bulging rocker boxes and I think it's the handsomest machine they've yet built.'

'He meant Harry,' Ayesha corrected him.

'You mean the Rudge? Don't you worry, my dear. Safe as houses.'

Harry was astride a Rudge Ulster – an altogether smaller machine than the Harley Davidson but still capable of doing seventy miles an hour on the flat – and his parents had every reason to look anxious.

'You will be careful, won't you, Harry,' Ayesha was

saying. 'Promise me not to go fast or I'll tell Dickie you can't ride at all.'

Edward noted her easy use of Mountbatten's nickname.

'Oh, don't fuss, Mummy,' the boy said impatiently. 'I've ridden it a bit already. It's no more difficult than riding a bike.'

'Right, boys,' Mountbatten said. 'I'm going to the end of the drive in the car so I can film you coming towards me. When you pass the car, that's the end of the race. And, Harry, you get a hundred yards' start because Frank has the more powerful machine and much more experience than you. Good luck! Herr Mandl will start you when I wave to say I'm ready.'

The drive was no more than three-quarters of a mile but to Edward it seemed quite long enough.

With a little help from Mandl, the boys started their engines and waited for the signal. When it came, Harry wobbled away, gaining confidence as he gathered speed. They wore no helmets because the distance was hardly great enough for a serious accident but, as Frank accelerated and passed Harry, only just avoiding the Rudge Ulster as it swerved like a shying horse, Edward began to think the boys ought to have been encased in armour.

Frank roared past Mountbatten, shouting and waving one hand in the air in triumph. Harry was only a few seconds behind, but, while trying to avoid the Harley Davidson which was now stationary in the middle of the drive, he veered off the road and bumped over the grass before coming to a halt some hundred yards away. Although he toppled over, there was no danger and Frank was soon helping him untangle himself from the bike. They both saw the man at the same time. He was lying on his back with one arm above his head as if he had been waving and had fallen to the ground with his hand still outstretched.

'I say,' Frank said, going over to him, 'are you all right?'

'Is he asleep?' Harry asked doubtfully.

'His eyes are open,' Frank pointed out as he knelt beside the man. He tried to find a pulse but the flesh was cold and lifeless. 'I think he's dead.' Lord Louis walked over to see what the matter was and Frank indicated the body. 'I think the poor chap's had it,' he said, looking up at Mountbatten.

'You mean . . .?' Mountbatten, too, knelt beside the body. 'He's dead all right. Frank, ride back to the others and tell them to telephone for the police. We'd better not touch anything.'

'Shouldn't we try to revive him?' Harry asked doubtfully. This was the first corpse he had ever seen.

'Not even the Good Lord could raise this one,' Mountbatten said abruptly.

'Who is he?' Frank asked. 'Do you recognize him?'

'Haven't the foggiest. Never seen him before,' Mountbatten replied. 'I wonder what he died of. I can't see any wound or anything. Must have had a heart attack.'

'Perhaps if we turned him over,' Harry said, excited now the initial shock was fading.

'No, Harry, Lord Louis's right,' Frank said, grabbing his arm. 'We can't do anything for the poor chap so we'd better leave him for the police doctor to examine. I'll buzz off back to the house. Golly! This'll need some explaining.'

3

'Thank God you're safe! I've been worried sick about you.'
They were in Edward's rooms in Albany. Verity had
refused to let him meet her off the train. She wanted first
to go to her flat and compose herself – wash and lie on her
bed staring at the ceiling, luxuriating in being free from
fear for the first time in weeks. She had roused herself with
some difficulty and thought about eating something but
the idea made her feel sick and she lit a cigarette instead.
Still in something of a daze, she opened her suitcase. She
looked at the crumpled contents with loathing and
considered throwing the whole thing out of the window.

In the end she found a dress that she had left behind in
her cupboard when she packed for Vienna. She showered
and, feeling better, went out into Sloane Avenue, hailed a
taxi and told the driver to take her to Fleet Street. When
she left the *New Gazette* two hours later, the adrenalin
which had enabled her to make a full report of her
activities to Lord Weaver, her employer, was exhausted
and she felt weak and desperately tired. She looked at her
watch. It was six in the evening. She decided she needed a
strong drink and a shoulder to cry on. She hailed a cab and
had it take her to Piccadilly.

'Have you, Edward?' Verity asked, looking at him sadly.
'I don't know why you should. I treated you so badly but
now I'm punished for it.'

'Adam . . .?'

'Gone! I don't think I'll ever see him again.' To his amazement, she burst into tears.

'V . . . ' he pleaded, 'dearest V – don't take on so.'

'Oh God. . . ' She gulped away her sobs. 'Don't be kind. I can't bear it. Why don't you hate me?'

'I never could. Now, please, stop weeping. You have streaks of black running down your cheeks. Here, let me.' He took out his handkerchief and tried to mop up her tears. Instead of meekly letting him, she threw herself into his arms, clutching at him like a drowning man hanging on to a lifebelt. 'I do love you, Edward.' She blinked blearily up at him. 'I'm so tired. If you hold me, I can rest.'

'You're safe – that's all that matters.'

She tore herself away, angry not at him but at the world, at herself. 'I'm safe but hundreds, perhaps thousands are *not* safe.'

'Tell me what happened,' he said gently. 'You were arrested. Did they . . . did they . . . hurt you?'

'They roughed me up but they weren't serious about it. If they had been, I would be dead.'

'What happened exactly? I only know what I read in the *New Gazette.'*

She steadied herself. 'I think it would do me good to tell you.'

'I *need* to know. I love you, V, and I want to know how it has been for you. Everything.'

'Well then, let me think. You heard that Hitler ordered Schuschnigg to cancel the plebiscite? That was last Friday. On Saturday Schuschnigg resigned and the Nazi, Seyss-Inquart, replaced him as Chancellor. On Sunday the "Reunification of Germany" was decreed and Austria ceased to exist. All day long huge bombers roared over our heads. I watched it all with Georg Dreiser. He was so sad. It was as if someone he loved had died.

'I went back to my flat to listen to the wireless while Georg went off to pack and say goodbye to his family. It was so strange listening to history being made on the wireless. They played military marches between accounts of German troops being welcomed by the grateful people of Austria. According to the man describing events, Hitler was met by thousands of people raising their arms in homage to their Führer and I am sure he wasn't lying. It was everything I had dreaded. And it all happened so fast. The Führer's Mercedes was crossing the border . . . the Führer was in Linz . . . Then, unaccountably, there was a delay. Linz is only two hours from Vienna but Hitler did not come. The crowds gathered. The Vienna Nazis, their numbers swelled by thousands imported from the provinces, waited tensely for their hero but all they could do was wait. Shout, march, threaten and wait. Apparently, I learnt afterwards, Police Chief Himmler had rejected the security precautions designed to safeguard Hitler. One shot from a maddened Jew or an Austrian patriot might have led to a bloodbath.

'On Monday the Brownshirts began to round up Jews in Leopoldstadt – that's Vienna's Jewish district. Anyone carrying a suitcase was in danger of being arrested. I hardly dared go out because gangs of Nazi thugs were roaming the streets looking for "enemies" but I had to see Georg off. The trains were still running to the Swiss border and, thank God, no one stopped him at the station. It was not until Monday evening that the Führer entered Vienna. I prayed, though you know what I think about religion, that Georg had got across the border but I knew the rest of his family was still in the city. Himmler, they said on the wireless, was already preparing the "great spring cleaning" to rid Vienna of its Jews . . .

'I went out to see for myself. Don't let anyone tell you that the Viennese – I can't speak for the rest of Austria – did not welcome Hitler. They did. The church bells were ringing as first the tanks and then the soldiers marched through the centre of the city. In the Heldenplatz the crowds were screaming and crying out, "We want to see our Führer," "*Ein Volk, ein Reich, ein Führer!*" "*Juda verrecke!*" "Death to the Jews!" Everyone had put on their best clothes as if it was some sort of national holiday. The men were in green suits, lederhosen and white stockings – a ridiculous outfit at the best of times and this was not the best of times – or in Nazi uniform. Women in frocks or dirndls threw flowers at the soldiers marching past.

You've no idea how terrifying it is to see rank after rank of soldiers goose-stepping through the streets of a city. The sound of marching boots on cobbles . . . I'll never forget it as long as I live. And the noise of thousands of ordinary people shouting themselves hoarse over the coming of a tyrant – I kept thinking that soon this awful noise might be heard in Whitehall and Trafalgar Square.

'Then there was Hitler himself in the brown uniform of a storm trooper. He was standing in an open car saluting and smiling. If I had had a gun, I would have shot him. Instead, they threw flowers and I saw at least one woman crying tears of joy. It was a kind of frenzy. I found it pathetic that the crowds which greeted Hitler along the Ringstrasse – delirious with joy – were old enough to know better. They were not young fanatics. I mean, *they* were there as well, of course, but for the most part the crowds were Viennese bourgeois – small shopkeepers – roused out of their normal stolidity. They seemed convinced that the Saviour had come to them in the form of a little man in a brown uniform dwarfed by the enormous military car in which he stood gesturing. Pathetic but sinister. Behind and in front of the Führer in thirteen police cars – I counted them – Gestapo SS in black uniforms with skull and crossbones on their caps scanned the crowds for enemies. And suddenly I realized how I must look, skulking around, not waving or screaming for my Führer. I saw some men in uniform scowl at me so I scurried back to the flat to type up my report.

'The saddest thing, Edward . . . the irony of it all is that I'm convinced the Jews in Vienna would quite happily have joined in the welcome if they had not, for reasons they could not understand, been proclaimed enemies of the new German Reich. I'll never forget what I saw. Never!'

Edward saw tears in her eyes but knew better than to say anything.

'I heard later that Hitler had briefly appeared on the balcony of the Imperial Hotel and General Krauss had thanked him for uniting the German nation. I suppose I ought to have been there but I was too frightened. On

Tuesday, when things had quietened down a bit and Hitler had rushed back to Munich, I went to see what had changed. The city was eerily quiet. The Simpl. . .'

'The Simpl?'

'The Simplicissimus – Vienna's most famous cabaret. It's run by two Jews, Karl Farkas and Fritz Grünbaum. Grünbaum was a refugee from Hitler's Berlin and one of Vienna's favourite comedians. You know who I mean?' she said, seeing he did not recognize the name. 'He's appeared in countless UFA films. Anyway, the cabaret is – or was – the gathering place for all the enemies of Fascism – not just Jews but Communists as well. I went several times. My German – or rather my Austrian – isn't good enough for me to understand all the jokes but it was the one place in Vienna I felt at home. The Communists were the only people actively to oppose the Nazis but there weren't enough of them.

'I thought that if there were any friends left in Vienna they would meet at the Simpl but when I got there it was boarded up and deserted. At last, I found an old man – a caretaker or something – and I asked to speak to Herr Grünbaum. He told me that he had been taken away to prison. He did not know what had happened to Farkas.

'I trailed round the bars and cafés – starting with the Reiss-Bar, a chic place off the Kärntnerstrasse, all chromium and glass. No one I knew was there so I went on to the Künstler, the Landtmann and the Arcaden near the University. The Künstler and the Landtmann were trying to pretend nothing had happened but at the Arcaden a group of Brownshirts were sitting where the students used to gather.

'I stopped because they were singing. The Germans love to sing. *"Heute gehört uns Deutschland, Morgen schon die ganze Welt"* – "Today Germany belongs to us, tomorrow we'll own the whole world". Before I knew what was happening, one of the brutes seized me. I told him I was English and a journalist but they did not seem to care. I thought I was going to be raped. Instead, they took me to the Rossauerlaender police station – since the previous day the headquarters of the Vienna Gestapo.

'I was questioned by the most frightening man I have ever seen. He said his name was Eichmann – Adolf Eichmann. He was quite polite to begin with but icy cold. He said I was a known Communist and Jew-lover. I said I was an accredited journalist and I demanded to talk to someone at the British Embassy. I mentioned the names of everyone I could think of who might protect me. In the end, I was so desperate I said that I was a friend of Adam von Trott. Eichmann said I was a notorious liar, an incompetent journalist and in the pay of Moscow and that I would be hanged.

'They put me in a cell with half a dozen Jews waiting to be shipped off to God-knows-where – to their death probably.'

'*In carcere et vinculis*!' Edward exclaimed.

'Just when I had given up all hope, I was called by one of the guards and saw . . . the face of an angel – a plump, middle-aged, balding angel but an angel for all that. He turned out to be Mr Barker from the Embassy. He was almost as nervous as I was. Anyway, he said I was to go with him. I was to be deported and he was charged with seeing that I left the country. You can only half-imagine what it felt like to be out in the street again. I had the awful feeling that, even if I could have saved the lives of all the Jews in my cell by staying behind, I would still have gone with Mr Barker. I was plain terrified.'

'And that night you were in Switzerland?'

'Yes, but I'm going back,' Verity said fiercely. 'They can't get rid of me that easily. Joe Weaver says he can get me new accreditation papers. He's spoken to Ribbentrop. The Germans are still keen to keep the British press sympathetic to their cause so they don't want a noisy quarrel with the *New Gazette*. Oh, Edward, I can't describe what it was like to be in that awful place. I knew it was a prison from which people never escape. But somehow I had. And yet part of me is still there in that ante-room of hell. Never tell me that the Nazis are people whom one can make treaties with or talk to as though they were human beings. They are evil incarnate.'

'What do you mean, you're going back? You can't go back. I won't allow it.'

'I've got to. It's what I need to do. I need to bear witness. Does that sound insufferably pompous?'

'But they know you will report what you see. They're never going to allow that.'

'Joe told Ribbentrop that his newspaper would kick up a fuss if I wasn't allowed back. He told him the *New Gazette* would do everything possible to rouse the British people to the threat Hitler poses if they treated his journalists like criminals.'

Edward grinned. 'I can just imagine Joe blowing his top but, seriously, wouldn't it do more good if the treatment you received in Vienna convinced him to do what he threatens and turn against appeasement?'

Verity shook her head. 'He told me that, in reality, he could not do it while the Prime Minister still thinks he can negotiate a peace. Apparently, Chamberlain believes that Hitler is a sated beast and, now he has Austria, he will digest his new empire at leisure.'

'But he won't.'

'No, of course he won't. They say in Vienna that he's already got plans to take over the Sudetenland.'

'The German part of Czechoslovakia?'

'Yes.'

'I still don't like the idea of you going back to Vienna,' Edward said gravely.

'I'll be safe enough,' Verity smiled wanly, 'but it'll take a few days – two weeks at the most – to sort my papers out so if you can put up with me . . .'

'Of course! You must come to Mersham. Connie's expecting you.'

'That would be wonderful. I'm always able to *sleep* there and that's what I need at the moment – sleep.'

'I've heard from Dreiser,' Edward said after a pause. 'He sent a telegram from Geneva. He had to take a roundabout route. He'll be in London on Saturday. I thought we might pick him up from Victoria though I've given him my address if we miss him.'

'Thank God!' Verity smiled for the first time. 'That, at least, is one thing worth doing but it isn't enough.'

'You mean, we should do something to help the others . . .?'

'I do. I used to think that, as a reporter, I ought to stand above events – not get involved, remain impartial . . .' Edward, remembering her partiality to the Republican cause in Spain, had to hide a smile. 'Now, I think I must *do* something. I must intervene.'

'But do what, exactly?' he asked, his heart sinking. 'What can we do that matters, living under the shadow of war?'

'The Nazis have decided to expel as many Jews as they can. They can't fit them all in the camps. The trouble is that not many countries will take them – South America, Palestine of course. Joe says Chamberlain is talking about allowing at least the children into Britain. There are people organizing trains to bring out Jewish children from Berlin and Vienna – the Committee for the Care of Children. We must help.'

She looked up at Edward with bright eyes, wide with appeal. 'We must,' he agreed.

Verity was too tired to rest so Edward suggested they had dinner at Gennaro's 'for old times' sake'. The restaurant was crowded but Freddy, the head waiter, found them a quiet table and they ordered champagne 'to buck you up', as Edward put it. Verity nibbled nervously on a bread roll but said she wasn't hungry. She had the same look of inexpressible weariness and despair she had when she came back from Spain that last time. There were black stains under her eyes and she looked thin and slightly grubby, as though she needed to soak for an hour in a hot bath. It was a shame, Edward thought, that girls could not go to hammams. Of course, there was always a spa – perhaps Harrogate or Cheltenham.

He must have smiled at the idea of Verity at Harrogate because she said sharply, 'Have I got a smudge on my nose?'

'No. Why?'

'You were smiling while I was talking of jackboots . . .'

'Sorry. I was listening, I promise.'

'Well, let's change the subject. What have you been up to while I've been away? Seen anything of Maggie

Cardew?' This was a woman whom Edward had liked but whose brother he had helped prove a murderer.

'No,' he said, shortly. 'She won't see me. I bring more pain than pleasure to my relationships with women, I've decided.'

'Poor didums!' she said, patting his cheek patronizingly. 'Feeling sorry for ourselves, are we?' She sighed and played meditatively with her *Velouté de tomates*. 'We don't seem to be very successful with our love affairs, do we?'

'No. Are you going to eat that?'

'What? Oh, this. No, I don't think I am. Do you think Freddy would mind if I ordered a plain omelette? My stomach's so . . . so tight, somehow, I can't seem to digest anything.'

Edward looked worried. 'I'm going to make you see my doctor. You need a thorough check-up. You're much too thin and . . .'

'Stop it. I'll be all right in a few days. I don't know . . . I felt so alone in Vienna. I had no friends there and I missed Adam dreadfully.'

She looked so pathetic that Edward put out a hand and laid it over hers.

'Have you got a cigarette?' she asked. Reluctantly, because he thought she smoked instead of eating, he proffered his cigarette case and she took one. He leant forward and lit it for her and she took a long drag on it. 'That's better,' she said appreciatively. 'How's Basil? I was hoping to see him in Albany.'

'He's at Mersham. They don't allow dogs at my place. He lodges with the Hassels when in town. Do you want him back? I hope not. He loves Mersham. Gerald's rather taken to him. They go on long walks together.' He saw she wasn't really listening. She was crumbling a bread roll to pieces with one hand while holding her cigarette in the other. He knew it was pointless but he could not prevent himself saying, 'You live on your nerves. You smoke too much and eat too little. No wonder you can't sleep.'

'Distract me then,' she said with an effort. 'You still haven't told me what you've been up to. Mixing with the nobs, I'll be bound – toadying up to Mr Churchill, I expect.'

Verity had taken a strong dislike to Winston Churchill, whom she had never met, having decided that he was the enemy of the working class. Edward, to her fury, had fallen totally under his thrall and had undertaken a couple of investigations at his bidding.

'As a matter of fact, I have been mingling with the nobs – as you put it – nothing to do with Mr Churchill though.' He took a deep breath and began to tell her about meeting Sunny, his visit to Broadlands and the boys' macabre discovery.

'Mountbatten, eh?' He was glad to see that he had her attention. 'He's just a playboy, isn't he? These minor royals ... well, they'll be the first to go in the revolution.'

'I think Mountbatten's more than that. He's not a drone. They say he's a good officer. He's very ambitious.'

'Huh! So whose was the body Frank found?'

'Well, that's the odd thing. I telephoned the local chap – a man named Inspector Beeston – rather a dunderhead, I fear. I met him when we found the corpse. Anyway, the dead man turns out to have been an artist – a man called Peter Gray. Adrian Hassel knew him. They were at the Slade together though he was older than Adrian – late forties. He had a show at the Goupil Galleries in 1931 which was judged to have been a success.'

'What was he doing at Broadlands?'

'That's what no one knows.'

'And he died of a heart attack?'

'That's what the doctor thought at first but the post-mortem has thrown up a much more exotic cause of death.'

'Which is ...?'

'Ergot poison.'

'Never heard of it.'

'Nor had I but I did a bit of research. Ergot's a fungus that lives off rye and other grasses. Apparently it has been used as a country recipe since at least the Middle Ages to combat depression, hasten childbirth and, intriguingly, enhance sexual performance.'

Verity laughed and it did Edward good to see her. 'So, what ...? He went too far and his love life ...'

'V, please, keep your voice down if you're going to be

mucky. It's more likely that he was prescribed it for depression. He had had a bad war – shell shock. Adrian said that after the war, he was in and out of hospital but gradually seemed to get over it.'

'So, he was taking ergot and took too much?'

'The problem with ergot is that it's not very exact in its effects. It's quite easy to poison yourself.'

'What happens? What are the symptoms?'

'Well, according to the books it can cause gangrene by constricting the blood flow to the extremities – fingers and toes. It's sometimes called Holy Fire because it feels as if your feet or hands are on fire.'

'How horrible! But does that necessarily kill you?'

'It can do but in this chap's case, according to the doctor who examined the body – they haven't yet talked to the doctor who prescribed the ergot – Gray may have taken an overdose. Then he would have been ill – you get vomiting, diarrhoea and stomach cramps – but he might have thought he'd recovered. You start to feel better but later you can suffer kidney or liver failure and die. Oh, and too much ergot can give you hallucinations. '

'Before you die, presumably. Could it have been murder?'

'Bloodthirsty little thing! It *could* have been but it's much more likely to have been an accidental overdose.'

'Has . . . what's-his-name? . . . Gray, got any relatives?'

'A niece, Adrian says. Apparently she was an orphan he took in when she was a baby.' Edward saw Verity's interest flag and hurried on. 'And another thing – a beautiful film star asked me to save her from her husband.'

Verity laughed. 'Tell me another one!'

'No, it's true, honest Injun.' He told her all about Joan Miller.

'So what are you going to do?'

'Don't know yet. Nothing, probably. It's not my business, though she is very beautiful,' he teased, but Verity was too exhausted to rise.

When the taxi drew up outside Cranmer Court, Verity was sleepy and rather drunk. He almost had to carry her up to her flat and had to dig around in her handbag to find the door key which was, as he put it to her later, in 'deep litter'. He was taken aback by how bleak the place looked. Verity had never got round to hanging pictures on the walls. There was a layer of dust on the table and no milk in the refrigerator. He had been thinking of making a cup of tea to sober her up. She had all but collapsed on the sofa and he wondered if he dared leave her in her present state.

He decided the best thing he could do was to put her to bed. He carried her into the bedroom, removed her shoes and stockings and then heaved off her dress. He looked at her with compassion. She seemed as vulnerable as a child and he wanted more than anything in the world to have the right to look after her. As he pulled the sheet over her, she half woke and to his alarm started weeping.

'Don't leave me, Edward,' she muttered. 'I'm so cold. Hold me.' And she put out her arms to him.

With a sigh, he took off his tie and dinner jacket, lay beside her and held her in his arms. Within a few moments, she began to breathe deeply and regularly. After half an hour he thought he would see if he could disentangle himself and sneak out without waking her but, when he tried to move her arms from round him, she stirred and burrowed her face in his chest. He resigned himself to an uncomfortable night. Her weight on his arms, light as she was, was giving him pins and needles. In the end he did sleep and, though he opened his eyes several times during the night, Verity was still in the deep, unfathomable sleep of the exhausted.

The next morning Edward woke up early and lay beside Verity, not wanting to wake her, thinking about the tasks Liddell had set him. He had no idea how he was to get to meet 'Putzi' – Heinrich Braken – short of turning up at Claridge's and asking to talk to him. Of the people Liddell had suggested might introduce him, he had met only Harold Nicolson and they had disliked each other on sight. Unity Mitford he had heard was mad and Randolph Churchill . . . well, much as Winston loved his son,

Randolph had the alcoholic's unpredictability and Edward knew enough about him not to want to get involved if he could possibly avoid it.

In the end, as so often happens, there was no difficulty. He didn't know whether they had been put up to it by Liddell or, more likely, Mountbatten, but he received an invitation from Joan Miller and her husband to dine at Claridge's, where they also were staying, to meet Braken.

Claridge's was Edward's favourite of the grand hotels. Charles Malandra, the king of maîtres d'hotel, was an old friend and he was warmly welcomed when he strode into the restaurant. The surroundings were austere but sumptuous, the chairs comfortable and the food excellent, but what Edward particularly liked was the quiet. There was no floor show and Geiger's Hungarian Orchestra played in the foyer, where guests sipped their aperitifs before going in to dinner, not in the restaurant itself. The atmosphere was, Edward thought, choosing the word after due deliberation, episcopal.

He had wondered how he could break it to Verity that he was having dinner with a Nazi in preference to her but, before he had to explain anything, she told him that she had been invited to dinner by her boss, Joe Weaver, and he was not to be refused. In any case, there were to be politicians and other influential people whom she wanted to meet and possibly harangue. Verity was never one to pass up an opportunity of making her views known to anyone who would listen and the more important they were the better.

So it was with a clear conscience that Edward entered the hotel restaurant and looked about him. He saw Mandl at once. He seemed less coarse and objectionable than when he had seen him at Broadlands. Joan still looked melancholy but this was, he thought, something to do with the way her eyes never seemed to light up even when she smiled. As usual, she was smoking a Sobranie in a long white cigarette holder. Putzi appeared to be a classic 'lounge lizard' with smooth, brilliantined hair and eyes black as ink. He was a big man with a heavy 'stupid' face but he obviously was not stupid if he had first entranced Hitler and then escaped from him.

It was not the way of diners at Claridge's to show that they noticed famous guests. It would have been odd if there had been no one in the room who was notorious for one reason or another. However, Joan's extraordinary beauty – and no doubt her notoriety as the naked star of *Last Night in Vienna* – meant that she attracted some quick glances and one or two more deliberate stares. Neither of the men rose to greet Edward. A waiter pulled out a chair for him and, as he sat down, Mandl introduced Putzi with a wave of his hand which was almost contemptuous. Putzi smiled half-heartedly, like a schoolboy who knows he's done wrong but hardly knows how to admit it. Edward guessed Mandl had been doing his best to persuade him to return home. Joan acknowledged him with the slightest of nods. They were drinking champagne and Edward had the feeling they were already on the second bottle. He decided this was not going to be an evening at Claridge's he would look back on with any pleasure.

'Am I late? You said eight, Herr Mandl.'

'You're not late, Lord Edward. There were some things I had to talk to Putzi – Herr Braken – about before you came.'

'He was trying to get me to return to Berlin,' Putzi bleated, sounding already half-drunk. 'They are putting so much pressure on me. Last week Colonel Bodenschatz – Reichmarschall Goering's personal adjutant – was trying to make me believe that all was forgotten and forgiven. Isn't that what you English say?' He spoke with an American accent the English he had learnt at Harvard and less salubrious institutions where he had played piano. 'But I don't believe it. I think I will be walking into a trap. The Führer used to love me. You see, Lord Edward, I knew him before he was . . . before he became our beloved leader. Did you know Herr Himmler's father was my schoolmaster?' He giggled. 'But now . . .' He shrugged expressively. 'Bodenschatz threatened that, if I do not return to Germany, my family will suffer but I told him I did not care. My wife does not love me . . . there is only my son Egon, God bless him. Herr Hitler loved my wife. Did you know that, Herr Mandl? She was the first – before Eva or Geli. I played the piano and he danced with my wife.'

'You should not say such things,' Mandl rebuked him.

'You were responsible for the foreign press?' Edward asked.

'I knew how to deal with them. I told them what they wanted to hear – Germany rehabilitated, part of the family of nations once again – you understand. The Führer decisive, responsible, a new Bismarck . . .'

'But . . .?'

'But it all went wrong . . . the Jews . . .'

Mandl tried to hush him. 'Lord Edward does not want to hear about all that, Putzi.'

'No, I am interested. We cannot make out whether Hitler wants war or . . .'

Putzi embarked on a long, ill-thought-out monologue on the Führer's political ambitions at the end of which Edward was beginning to wonder what this wreck of a man had to offer Liddell even if he did decide to remain in England. He drank and smoked cigars while still making time to wolf down caviar, a steak and a very sweet pudding. Edward hoped he was not going to be asked to pay for the meal – Liddell had said nothing about expenses – but in the end Mandl picked up the bill.

Putzi was lonely, Edward gathered. He wanted to be invited into high society but so far he had received no invitations of any consequence. Unity Mitford had taken him to one or two parties but, reading between the lines, Edward gathered that he had not been a success. He had wanted to meet Unity's parents, Lord and Lady Redesdale, but, apparently, they did not like the look of him and had refused to invite him to stay for the weekend. Harold Nicolson had taken him to the House of Commons and he had lunched with three or four Members of Parliament on the right of the Conservative party but that wasn't enough. He seized on Edward as a means of cracking his social isolation and Edward began to realize that he would get nowhere until he procured him an invitation to one of the great country houses. He knew that Gerald would never have him at Mersham and he decided he would get Liddell to put pressure on Mountbatten to invite him to Broadlands.

It was a considerable relief to Edward when the meal ended. He tried to get away but this proved more difficult than he had imagined. Putzi had been introduced by Harold Nicolson to a cabaret club called Murray's which Edward had heard of but never visited. It had a dubious reputation but was popular with some of the young men about town who liked 'slumming'. It was in this Soho basement that Edward now found himself about eleven thirty when he would much rather have been at home in bed or, better still, with Verity.

Putzi – apparently already a temporary member – was made welcome and, to Edward's embarrassment, they were given a table on the edge of the dance floor. Percival Murray, the owner, whom Putzi addressed as 'Pops', was unctuous and signalled two scantily dressed 'dancers' to come over to the table. Edward, feeling very out of place, watched as Mandl and Putzi fondled them. Mandl seemed quite unconscious of the impropriety of behaving in such a way with his wife present. It showed a contempt for her which made Edward angry and ashamed.

He saw him stuff banknotes into the pocket of the waiter who reappeared with what passed for champagne. Edward took one sip and almost choked. It wasn't long before Joan was recognized as the star of *Last Night in Vienna* and she was applauded by several of the men sitting with girls at other tables, two or three of whom demanded autographs. She obliged, looking gloomier than ever but this did not seem to bother her admirers. In the end, Joan told Edward they should dance, solely in order to free herself from the mêlée she said, unflatteringly.

'I know this sort of place,' she growled in his ear. 'We have them in Vienna. It's little better than a brothel.'

'I can't stand much more of this,' he responded, ungallantly. 'Would you like me to take you back to Claridge's?'

Mandl seemed not to care that Edward was taking his wife back to the hotel and his pride was stung that the possessive husband did not see him as a threat. He hoped it was because Mandl imagined English gentlemen did not behave badly, which he knew to be untrue.

As they were leaving the stuffy little basement, he caught sight of a face he knew. It was Stuart Rose. He was sitting alone staring at Mandl and Putzi. As Edward started to climb the narrow stairs up to street level, Rose turned and looked at him. He was smiling but it was not a pleasant smile. He raised a glass to his lips as though drinking a toast. Edward nodded but did not feel like making conversation. It had been a long evening and it might not yet be over.

He found a taxi in Soho Square and they were driven to Claridge's, neither saying more than a few words to one another. It was almost two o'clock when they reached the hotel but the bar was still open. Joan begged him to have a nightcap and he did not feel he could leave her without being sure she was all right.

'What about your husband?' he asked when they barman had given them cognac in ridiculously large balloons. 'When will he come back?'

'Not tonight. He and Putzi will take a couple of whores back to their rooms.'

Edward was shocked. 'Does he often do that?'

'He's not interested in sex with me,' she said flatly, her voice cloudy with cigarette smoke. 'I told you before, I'm just a useful possession. Anyway, it makes him feel good which means he leaves me alone. He thinks himself a *Teufelskerl* – the devil of a fellow.'

'I could find you a place to stay,' he said uncertainly.

She smiled for the first time that evening and raised a hand to stroke his cheek. 'That is good of you but it would not be sensible. It would cause trouble for you, for your government perhaps, and certainly for me. I have to get my child out of Austria – or must I now say Greater Germany?'

'Have you got anyone at home who would help you? Is there a nanny or a servant you trust?'

'My little girl's nanny would do anything I asked but she's seventy-five – she was my nanny also, you understand. She could not do anything that needed . . .'

'I understand.'

'Have you an idea?' she inquired, sounding almost eager.

'I have the beginnings of one – a wild scheme but it might just work.'

'Tell me.'

'Not yet. I have to think things through. Are you to be at Broadlands next weekend?'

'Yes. Mandl is to meet some navy friend of Lord Louis' – something to do with selling the gun I told you about.'

Edward noticed she almost always referred to her husband as Mandl, as if she did not know him well enough to call him by his first name.

The bar was closing so he said goodbye, shaking hands formally as though a kiss might alter their relationship.

He got back to Albany after three and went straight to bed. 'I'm much too old for late nights,' he told himself as he brushed his teeth. The following morning he said it again feeling the fur on his tongue and the ache in his head.

4

One of the few disadvantages of being single, Verity
decided as she twirled in front of the mirror, was that she
had no one to tell her she looked good in a new dress.
Although she went for months not thinking about what
she wore, in London she tended to splurge in all her
favourite shops. It was true that Vienna had its temp-
tations, unlike war-torn Madrid. For a start, taxis were
cheap – just fifty groschen for most journeys. At Zwieback's,
the department store in the Kärntnerstrasse, you could
buy almost anything. The shoes were particularly seduc-
tive and she had bought several pairs at Coyle and Earle
in the Karlsplatz, while for the hats she loved she went to
Habig's . . . but all these were still in her apartment in
Vienna so, of course, it was incumbent on her to buy more
in London.

She could hardly go to dinner in Eaton Place in some
old thing she'd bought a year before, she said to herself.
As she had often argued – though never fully convinced
herself – you didn't need to be dowdy just because you
were Communist. In London, she liked the restrained
luxury of Bond Street. She loved Schiaparelli but this time,
feeling rather guilty, she bought one of Coco Chanel's
classic black dresses and though she had hitherto never
worn scent, was persuaded into buying Chanel No. 5. Its
soft, flowery, almost powdery scent was voluptuous and

made her feel alluring. She also bought an irresistible pair of Daniel Green evening shoes – ivory silk satin with rhinestone buckles, open-toed and with heels to give her some of the height she lacked.

Verity had dined with Lord Weaver on several occasions but this particular evening was one she would always remember. As the butler showed her into the drawing-room she stopped short in surprise and consternation. Winston Churchill was talking to her host in the slurred, almost melancholy growl that was already familiar to her and many thousands of others who had heard his wireless broadcasts or attended the public meetings he addressed. Here was her *bête noire* – the man she held to be the enemy of the working class. The man who had broken the General Strike, who had praised Mussolini and who had repeatedly attacked the Communist Party as nothing more than Stalin's cat's paw.

As Weaver turned to greet her, Verity almost gave way to her strong desire to make a run for it. Then she noticed the wicked gleam in the newspaper proprietor's eye. He wanted to see how she would comport herself. He had a reputation for enjoying bringing together at his table inveterate enemies – 'to see what would happen', he had once told her – and he must have known from what Edward had told him that she considered Churchill to be an enemy of everything she held sacred.

Silently she shook Churchill's hand and, unable to do anything else, tried to smile as he said how much he had looked forward to meeting her. 'Lord Edward tells me that you find my views objectionable, Miss Browne. I do hope we discover that we have some opinions in common. I particularly admired your reports from Vienna. I confess I shed a tear for Kurt von Schuschnigg. I was informed today that he has been incarcerated in one of those damnable Nazi gaols.'

Verity was surprised into speech. 'I had not heard that but, as you know, I was deported immediately after Hitler entered Vienna. There's no news, is there, Joe, of when I will be allowed back?'

'Soon, I hope,' was all Weaver could say.

Verity's surprise at his guests was increased when she was introduced to Unity Mitford, a large blonde with bad teeth and an expression – permanent, she thought – of resentment tinged with frustration. Verity had met her sister Jessica, an active Communist, but she knew Unity was of a quite different persuasion. She was obsessed with Hitler, whom she had first met in 1933, and Jessica had told her that she had made up her mind to become Hitler's lover. Jessica had also confided to Verity that she believed her sister to be mad. Unity was a cousin of Mrs Churchill's, which was something of an embarrassment to Churchill.

Still reeling from shock at being thrust into such company, she was reassured to see she had an ally of sorts in another guest, the young American art critic, Stuart Rose, whom she knew to be a Communist sympathizer, if not a Communist. Weaver seemed suddenly aware of the combustible nature of the party and, perhaps wondering if he had gone too far in bringing enemies together, signalled to the butler to announce that dinner was served.

During the soup and well into the fish course, Verity was able to talk to Lady Weaver about trivialities but then, inevitably, the conversation turned to what was happening in Austria.

Unity started by telling what she considered an amusing story. She had joined the Council of Emergency Service which had been formed to train women to take over men's jobs in the event of war. Its chairman was Dame Helen Gwynne-Vaughan, Professor of Botany at London University.

'I was told to present myself to Dame Helen,' Unity said in her rather high voice. 'She said she had heard I was trying to become a German citizen and, if this were true, I could not remain a member of the Council. I tried in vain to persuade her that, though I spent a lot of time in Germany, I had no plans to take German citizenship. The old bat had it in for me from the beginning,' she ended sulkily, 'so I had to resign. My friend Putzi, Herr Braken – Stuart knows who I mean – said it was sheer jealousy, nothing more.'

Verity was surprised to find that Rose was on familiar terms not only with Unity but also with this other Nazi whom she had heard Edward mention. She bit her tongue and said nothing.

Rose opened his mouth to say something but seemed to think better of it.

Unity continued to lecture the dinner table. 'I gather you were in Vienna, Miss Browne, when Herr Hitler entered the city. Wasn't it the most wonderful day? I was there with my friend Mrs Cochrane-Baillie. I was heartbroken that I did not see *mein Führer* when he arrived at his birthplace, Linz. I believe it was most affecting. You know he's going to make it the capital of the new province? He told me so himself. I strained my voice shouting for that great man outside the Imperial. We cried, *"Was! Ihr beide hier!"* as we did when he occupied the Rhineland. He is a great patriot, is he not, Miss Browne? I was allowed ten minutes with him after he appeared on the balcony – an interview I shall never forget.'

Unity spoke affectedly, hoping for a reaction. Verity knew she ought not to respond but was, in the end, unable to restrain herself.

'I'm afraid, Miss Mitford, that I cannot share your enthusiasm for seeing a country raped and good men thrown into concentration camps.'

Unity pretended to look surprised. 'Oh, but that's nonsense. You must have seen! The Austrians are happy and full of hope at being united with the mother country. How can you call it rape when I witnessed, as I am sure you did, the people going mad with joy shouting *"Heil Hitler! Anschluss"* at the top of their voices and waving swastika flags. Did you see, when night fell, the bonfires in the shape of swastikas on the hills round the city? It was inspiring.'

'And were the Jews cheering too?' Verity inquired coldly.

'The Jews, the Communists . . . who cares about them? Oh, but of course,' she smiled sweetly, revealing her bad teeth and opening wide her baleful blue eyes, 'I forgot that you and Stuart share my sister's sympathies for those evil people.'

Before Verity could reply, Churchill broke in.

'My friend Georg Franckenstein, the Austrian Ambassador, tells me that just thirty-five per cent of the population supported *Anschluss*. He tells me that there are great numbers of Austrians who are vigorously opposed to having a regime forced upon them which is alien in aims and methods to their traditions. Why else did Hitler forbid the plebiscite which would have shown the level of support he had? I consider Hitler's rape – yes, I too use that word – his rape of Austria a dastardly outrage. Tens of thousands of liberals, democrats, socialists and Jews will now try to leave the country and I very much fear that many of them will not succeed. Their fate can only be imagined.'

Churchill pugnaciously leant across the table like an old bulldog whose snarl could easily become something worse but Unity seemed unperturbed. Stuart Rose tried to lighten the atmosphere by asking Unity about her painting. 'I remember particularly a picture of yours of Hannibal crossing the Alps – most striking. You had an exhibition at the Brook Street Gallery, did you not?'

'Oh, I have no time for that now,' Unity said brusquely, 'but I have started on a portrait of the Führer . . .'

Unity Mitford was so much of a monster that Verity could not feel her own dislike of Churchill as she might have done in other company. What was more, he asked her intelligent questions about the situation in Austria and, which was even more surprising, listened to her answers. He treated her with charm and courtesy but never patronized her or talked down to her as so many men, particularly politicians, were prone to do. Weaver seemed amused by the trouble Churchill was taking with her and absolutely refused to let his wife take the ladies out when the port and brandy were circulated. It was a courtesy Verity appreciated – as she also appreciated Churchill's restraint in not mentioning Edward. He was sensitive enough to know that she would resent the least hint that he was being polite to her out of consideration for her friend.

She was enthralled by Churchill's estimate of how badly the country was doing in its efforts to catch up with

Germany. 'A stolen march indeed,' he said, taking the cigar out of his mouth and breathing smoke like some benevolent dragon. 'It can hardly be doubted that the Germans have laid new types of fighters and bombers upon their mass production plants. As they order whole-sale from a unified industry, full supplies of these should be available by next April. Perhaps Miss Mitford is able to furnish us with more detail?'

Unity refused to admit that there was any threat to Britain. 'The Führer has often expressed to me the friendship he feels for us. We are Aryans and the natural allies of . . .'

Without seeming to hear her, Churchill continued to talk about the *Anschluss* and what it meant to Britain. 'The gravity of what has happened to Austria cannot be exaggerated. Europe is confronted with a programme of aggression, nicely calculated and timed, and there is only one choice open – not just to us but to other countries in Europe. We either submit, like Austria, or take effective measures while time remains to ward off the danger and, if it cannot be warded off, to cope with it.'

His measured phrases and deep seriousness impressed Verity profoundly. 'And will the next victim of Hitler's mad aggression be Czechoslovakia, do you think?' she asked.

'I do. Czechoslovakia manufactures the munitions on which both Rumania and Yugoslavia depend for their defence. Isolated on three sides by Hitler's annexation of Austria, her fate is sealed. No doubt to English ears the name Czechoslovakia sounds outlandish,' he continued. 'It is just a small democratic state with an army not much larger than ours. I have hopes that they will stand firm but can they hold out in the long run without our support and the support of the French? I very much doubt it. Some people have called me a warmonger but I must remind them – remind you all – that force and violence are, alas, the ultimate reality.'

'Why are you not in the government, sir?' Stuart Rose asked.

'That is the question,' Weaver said, pouring himself another brandy. 'That is indeed the question – where is the only man with the strength of purpose and moral authority to stand up to Hitler?'

Unity stood up to leave. 'I cannot listen to any more of this nonsense,' she said with a touch of hysteria. 'Why cannot any of you understand that we must stand as a friend to Germany? Herr Hitler is not the enemy. The Jews and the Communists – they are the enemy.'

When Unity had gone, Stuart Rose looked round the table and said drily, 'A year or two back, I spent a few days in Styria in a little inn at Aflenz. Burnt into the beams of the ceiling was this couplet, *"Wer ehrlich denkt und handelt recht, Er bleibt im Dreck, es geht ihm schlecht,"* which I would roughly translate as "He who thinks honourably and behaves justly gets left behind and has no success."'

Churchill harrumphed and Weaver grinned his tiger-smile.

'You speak good German, Mr Rose,' Verity said in surprise. 'It's better than mine.'

'Not at all,' he replied, almost too quickly. 'I just happened to remember those lines. I have no idea who wrote them.'

With the departure of Unity the conversation became less political and more relaxed. Rose and Churchill discussed art and how painting was worth doing even if, as Churchill modestly admitted, one did it badly. Verity asked Rose what he thought of Frank. Edward had told her they had met at Broadlands and seen a lot of each other since.

'An admirable young man. He thinks highly of you, Miss Browne. Told me so himself. Said he would like to have fought in Spain.'

'He did for a few days.'

'And you and Lord Edward hauled him back by the scruff of his neck. He told me that too.'

'You seem to have talked a lot,' she said, caustically.

'As a matter of fact, we did. I like young people and I like Frank. He may not know much about art but he knows about life. He knows who to trust and that's always half the battle.'

'He trusts you?'

'You mean that might not be a good idea?' Rose seemed amused.

'I wouldn't trust you,' she said, emboldened by the wine she had drunk.

'You may have to,' was his surprising and somewhat enigmatic response.

As they were putting on their coats, Churchill offered to drop Verity at Cranmer Court and she accepted. For the first time, in the car, the scent of Havana cigar heavy about them, Churchill did mention Edward.

'Forgive me for saying so, Miss Browne, but I think that man of yours, Lord Edward Corinth, is to be reckoned with. He tells me that you don't share my views on many social issues but you must grant that I have seen more of life than you and I know a good man when I see him. There are not so many of them around that they can be squandered. You should hold to him. He will be an anchor in the coming storm, as Clemmie is for me.'

It was disconcerting to have advice on so personal a matter from a man she had met for the first time just a few hours earlier. She ought to have resented it but she did not. Whether it was the lateness of the hour, the wine she had imbibed, the mad girl who had spoken of Hitler as though he were a god or the comfortable car lulling her into a false sense of security but all she could think of was that this man sitting beside her saw the world for what it was. He recognized the danger and had prepared himself to overcome it.

She roused herself to say, 'I agree with everything you said at dinner, Mr Churchill, but you must allow that we Communists are your only true allies. We alone have steadfastly stood up to Fascism since Hitler came to power in 1933 while the politicians have procrastinated and . . .'

'Miss Browne, I grant you that the Communist Party has stood against Fascism while other parties – my own most culpably – have courted and appeased it but I have the profoundest misgivings concerning the Soviet Union. I do my best to suppress them in the crisis we now face. The Soviet Union may be our ally in the coming conflict but we must not close our eyes to who these people are and what they really want. You must have seen in Spain how ruthless were those who took their orders from Moscow. They were not interested in the Spanish Republic but in extending the influence of the Russian Bear into Europe. Regardless of the political colour of the government of that great empire, that has always been Russia's design.'

Without waiting for her to object, he went on, 'We know very little of what is happening in Russia but we know enough to see the terrible repression, the starvation, the terror, the fear that permeate that vast country. We know that the Soviet prison camps are as full of innocent men and women as those in Germany. The power of the executive to cast a man into prison without formulating any charge known to law and to deny him the judgement of his peers is in the highest degree odious and is the foundation of all totalitarian government, whether Nazi or Communist.

'From all I have heard of you and learnt from your reports, which I have read in the *New Gazette* since the beginning of the war in Spain, I know you speak the truth as you see it. However, in my opinion, you shut your eyes to the faults of your comrades when to recognize them might seem to undermine the good fight. I understand that and I fully expect to have to do the same if, as I hope, the Soviet Union joins the coming fight against Nazi Germany, but we should not let that blind us to what we know is the truth behind the façade.

'When you return to Vienna – or perhaps, as I gather from Lord Weaver is now more likely, you go to Prague – I would ask you to write to me when you have time and give me your appreciation of events as they unfold. Hitler knows that whoever is master of Bohemia is master of Europe.'

Verity was flattered to be asked to help form the opinions of this opinionated man and unable, sleepy as she was and under the influence of Churchill's overpowering personality, to defend the Soviet Union as she might later wish she had done, said, 'There is a young Austrian Jew – Georg Dreiser – whom we have managed to bring over to England. He should be in London tomorrow. I think you would find him interesting. His friends are not just Jews but all sorts of Austrians. He claims to have information about new bombs . . . I don't really know if he is fantasizing but you might be interested.'

Churchill rolled down the car window and threw out his cigar end. 'Accurate information is my greatest weapon. I believe Hitler only listens to those who agree with him. I like listening to you, Miss Browne, just because you don't.'

The following morning, in stark contrast to Eaton Place, she wended her way to Covent Garden for a meeting with a senior figure in the Party, Owen Coombs. The head office of the CPGB was at 16 King Street – an ironic address, she had always thought – and, although she had often been there for meetings and rallies of one kind or another, on this occasion her heart was troubled. It was all so different now from those heady days in 1936 when young men had flocked to King Street to enrol in the International Brigade. Alone among political parties, the CP had declared unequivocally for the Republicans and, for anti-Fascists, there could be no alternative to joining the Party.

But Verity's experience in Spain had left her disillusioned. She would never have admitted it to Edward, let alone to Churchill, but she now realized that the Party always had to give the impression that Communists were the only ones who really fought when, in reality, Party leaders were interested solely in expanding its sphere of influence at the expense of all other left-wing groups. It was not simply that the war in Spain was all but lost and Franco would soon march into Madrid at the head of his army – that was bitter indeed – but much more bitter was the knowledge that she, and many like her, had been manipulated – quite cynically – by the Soviet Union. Stalin used the Party – and the civil war – to undermine the democracies. She had to acknowledge that Stalin had as much interest in restoring the Spanish Republic as the arch-enemy, Franco. It hurt her to have to admit it but, in this respect at least, Churchill had the right of it.

Verity had been very reluctant to accept the reality even when Edward and other observers she respected pointed it out to her. It was only with the horror of Guernica – whose destruction at the hands of the Luftwaffe she had witnessed – and its aftermath that she had begun to see what was happening. She, and many others fighting in Spain, had unwittingly participated in a giant publicity stunt for a Communist Party totally under the control of Moscow. She strongly suspected that the Party had had warning that Guernica – the undefended capital of the Basque region – was to be razed to the ground but had quite deliberately passed the city no warning in order to maximize the horror. The Party was not interested in any of the shibboleths to which it paid lip service – freedom, equality, independent thought. It asked just one thing of its members – obedience – and it was unquestioning obedience that Verity had never been able to give to anyone.

As she entered the warren of rooms and staircases which almost seemed to reflect the tortuous thinking of the people who occupied them, she permitted herself to think the unthinkable: how different was the CPGB from the Nazi Party? They both used terror to achieve their ends. Both were indifferent to personal aspiration and individual suffering. Alarming rumours had reached her of the terror in the Soviet Union where loyal Party members disappeared without explanation and were never seen again or were summoned to appear before courts to recite 'confessions' obtained by blackmail and torture.

As she knocked on the door of Coombs' office, she was still wrestling with her conscience. Should she resign? *Could* she resign? She had a feeling that resigning might not be an option and, in any case, how could she face Edward and tell him that he had been right all along?

She had met Coombs only once before and had not known quite what to make of him. He was not one of the hectoring sort she might have found it easier to stand up to. He did not bully. He sounded perfectly reasonable, even understanding. But what was he *thinking*? After the last interview – almost a year before – she had told herself he had no idea what he wanted or what he thought of her.

At her knock, he called for her to come in and she found she had forgotten his boyish smile and untidy shock of brown hair. His eyes were brown and nondescript and his hand – when he rose from his desk to grasp hers – was firm and dry. It was only then that she remembered how tall he was. He seemed to uncoil himself from behind his desk and re-coil as he sat down. Verity was not quite sure of his position in the Party but she had a feeling that he was a senior figure.

'Comrade – Miss Browne – Verity!' he intoned. 'May I call you Verity? I feel we know each other well – both of us having been Party members for so long.' The implicit appeal to her loyalty drew from her a nod of recognition.

'We have all – all of us here – been very pleased with your work for the cause. Your reports in the *Daily Worker* and the *New Gazette* show how right we have been to oppose the Fascist threat here and in Austria. We have been pleased with the way you have – what shall I say? – insinuated yourself into circles in which you can meet our enemies. We will of course require a full report on your dinner last night in Eaton Place and what Mr Churchill said with reference to the world situation and the Soviet Union in particular.'

Verity was no longer surprised that Coombs knew precisely whom she had seen and when. She hated the thought of being spied on but had grown to accept it as inevitable. The gentle inquisition continued, taking her through everything she had done in the past year. It was thorough and Verity, who was not good at dissembling, hid nothing, aware that – had she tried to – Coombs would have known. There was no hint of criticism unless it was of her relationship with Edward. It was odd, she thought, that the Party applauded her affair with the German aristocrat, Adam von Trott, and sympathized with her that he had dropped her so precipitately, but found Lord Edward Corinth sinister – a threat to her loyalty to the Party. Of course, if she were honest about it, the Party was quite right to be disturbed. Edward had indeed undermined her faith – not in Communism but in the Communist Party.

'Just so long as you always bear in mind Lenin's famous question: "Who? Whom?" You must ask yourself who is doing what to whom. Social justice and capitalism are incompatible. But why am I telling you what you already know?' Coombs smiled and Verity tried to smile back but failed.

When the questioning came to an end, Coombs sat in silence, watching her for several minutes. Fortunately, she was familiar with the technique and remained silent herself. Any interrogator worth his salt knows that silent expectation is hard for an interviewee to deal with. The urge to break the silence with an unintended confession, or at least an admission, is very difficult to resist.

'Well,' he said at last, 'you want to know what the Party requires of you.' Verity was not sure that she did but . . . 'It is our belief that Mr Churchill will, at the outbreak of war, become Prime Minister. He will be rewarded for having seen the Fascist menace for what it is when most of his colleagues closed their eyes to it. We do not object to this in principle but it is important we know exactly what he is planning and, most particularly, what his attitude is to the Soviet Union. We know he distrusts it, of course, but will he see reason?'

'I'm not a spy,' Verity said sharply. 'I'm a newspaper correspondent.'

'We know that,' Coombs said soothingly. 'We have spies. What we need from you is exactly what you pride yourself on – honest reporting. Not too much to ask, surely?'

Verity nodded dubiously. It seemed very like spying to her. But was she being naive? Edward would say so. She had to choose sides and in this dirty, dishonest decade there were no Queensberry rules. The end justified the means.

'Oh, by the way,' Coombs said as he uncoiled himself to say goodbye, 'that young Jew of yours – Georg Dreiser – has something we would like.'

'What is that?' Verity asked, surprised.

'Don't you know?' he inquired with gentle irony. 'He has access to people – scientists – working on Germany's new bomb. We want him to bring them over to us. It is very important, you understand?'

'To us?'

'To the Party, to Moscow,' Coombs clarified. 'I understand you are taking him to Mersham Castle at the weekend. One of our people will ask you for an introduction. That is all. You will facilitate this. Not too much to ask, I think.'

'A Comrade will be at Mersham . . .?' Verity asked in surprise bordering on alarm.

'There or in the neighbourhood. Someone will be in touch. No need for you to do anything. You will get your instructions.'

'How will I know him?'

'He will mention my name.'

As Verity left King Street, she did not notice a man at the corner writing in his little notebook but Coombs, looking out of his window, did and smiled. He was aware that Special Branch kept constant watch on the comings and goings at Party Headquarters. Cat and mouse – it was a game two could play.

Verity went from King Street to have lunch with Adrian Hassel, one of her oldest friends who had seen her through bad times in the past and whom she knew she could trust absolutely. They were to meet at the Slade in Gower Street and walk to Bertorelli in Charlotte Street. Adrian always ate there when he was working at the Slade because it was quick and cheap. The bill never came to more than two and sixpence with lamb cutlets and peas at a shilling and *Spaghetti à l'Italienne* eightpence.

Adrian took her into the Slade's cavernous interior and showed her the picture he was working on, a vivid – Verity was inclined to think lurid – study of Waterloo Bridge at sunset – bright reds and yellows, a homage perhaps to Whistler. She said the right things but Adrian knew she hated it and laughed wryly.

'Don't pretend, Verity. You're not a good liar. You'll be surprised to hear,' he added defensively, 'that I have begun to sell. I've got an exhibition coming up – at the Goupil, no less – in October. You must come.'

'I will if I can, Adrian, but I expect to be in Vienna or perhaps Prague.'

'Of course,' he said suddenly serious. 'You must think we are all ostriches – unable to see what's right in front of our noses. The fact of the matter is that we know a war is coming but each day which passes without war being declared leaves us profoundly grateful.'

'You don't worry about what compromises are made in your name to delay the war, then?'

'I'm afraid not. We are just happy to be able to go about our normal lives.'

Verity pursed her lips and would have said something had Adrian not pointed to an elderly man walking towards them in the company of a young woman. 'Look, there's Professor Schwabe. He's talking to Vera Gray. I'd like you to meet her. Her uncle was a very good painter, you know – much better than me. When I was a student here just after the war I got to know him quite well. He could have been a great painter but the war did for him. I thank God I missed it by a couple of years. He had one of those breakdowns, like so many who saw and suffered so much carnage.'

Before Verity could protest, Adrian had taken her arm and introduced her as 'the famous war correspondent', which made her squirm with embarrassment. Vera Gray was, she guessed, in her mid-twenties. She wasn't pretty but she had a strong face and a pleasant smile. She wore not a scrap of make-up. Her hair, which was thick and brown, was untidy and spattered with paint, as were her overalls. She recognized the look in Vera's eyes – the look of someone recently bereaved – vulnerable and naked.

'I'm so sorry about your uncle, Miss Gray,' Adrian said. 'I was proud to know him. We were students together here at the Slade after the war though of course he was five or six years my senior. I feel badly that we rather lost touch. I don't know when I last saw him. Two years ago, perhaps – yes, at least that,' he continued, thinking aloud.

'Thank you,' she said, a trifle breathlessly. 'I know who you are, of course, although for some reason I don't think we have ever met, but my uncle talked of you. He wasn't very sociable, particularly recently.' She hurried on. 'Are you able to come to the memorial meeting on Friday? It's down near Romsey, where he died. Tarn Hill was a favourite place of his — do you know it? It's a well-known beauty spot. He painted it – and the view from it – time after time but never got tired of it. I'm glad that, if he had to die, he died there, not in some London hospital.'

'I remember it from his pictures. I don't think I have ever been there. He's not being buried . . .?' Adrian inquired.

'No, no. He was an atheist, I'm afraid. There's a cremation at Putney on Wednesday, after the inquest, and then we are going to scatter his ashes on Friday where he was happiest.'

'I see. There has to be an inquest?'

'Yes. It's just a formality but the way he died . . .'

'It was ergot poisoning, wasn't it?' Verity chipped in.

'How did you know?' Vera Gray looked rather put out.

'The fact is my friend, Lord Edward Corinth, was there when his body was discovered . . . I'm so sorry, perhaps I shouldn't have . . .'

'No, please don't worry. Lord Edward's a friend of yours, is he? I have heard of him, of course. I gather it was his nephew and a friend who actually stumbled on . . . It must have been a terrible shock for them.'

'Do you know why your uncle was on the Broadlands estate?'

'I told you, he liked to paint . . .'

'He was two or three miles from Tarn Hill, wasn't he?'

'He liked to walk . . .' she said uncertainly.

'But in his state of health?'

'That was the odd thing. He had been feeling so much better in the last year or two. He had – at least I thought he had – quite given up taking ergot. His depressions had become so infrequent . . . That was why I thought it safe to move out and get my own flat. I have one of those "cabins" in that new, modern block – you know the one I mean? It's built like an ocean liner in Lawn Road in Hampstead. It's only two or three stops on the Underground from Mornington Crescent. I used to look in on him almost every day.'

She sounded, Verity thought, as if she were defending herself against unspoken charges of neglect.

'Painting is very therapeutic,' Adrian said, trying to be soothing.

'Yes, it is, but it was simpler than that. I think, as time passed, he began to forget. He was beginning to forget everything.' She laughed nervously. 'I mean,' she seemed to correct herself, 'he began to forget the past. That was good, of course. To tell the truth, I'd heard enough of his war memories.'

Verity looked at her curiously and, catching her glance, saw that she thought she had revealed rather too much.

'I was very glad for him, of course. The horrors of the war, which had almost unhinged him, faded. He stopped having nightmares. There were so many nights when I heard him screaming. When I was younger, I put my fingers in my ears and hid under the bedclothes but later on I used to go into his room and try to soothe him.' She shuddered. 'The sight of him writhing in a tangle of sheets, sweating like a . . . It almost broke my heart.'

'It must have been awful,' Verity said with feeling. 'Adrian said you were an orphan . . .?'

'Yes. It was very Victorian. *Bleak House* is a favourite of mine. I can so easily identify with the Jarndyce children. You remember the wards of court who went to live with their cousin?'

Verity had not read *Bleak House* and looked puzzled. Seeing she had to explain a little more, Vera continued, 'My parents died in a railway accident when I was a baby. My uncle and aunt, who had no children of their own, took me in.'

'I see, but your aunt . . .'

'She died a year or two after. I don't remember her. I wish I did.'

'So your uncle had to look after you alone? That was brave of him.'

'Yes, wasn't it? He ought to have put me in orphanage. For a time, he had an old woman to look after me – a cousin of his – but we didn't really get on. I must have been a very tiresome child.'

'But you repaid the debt to your uncle a hundred times,' Adrian said. 'You were the light of his life. You looked after him and kept him sane.'

Vera looked surprised at his vehemence and he started to apologize. 'Perhaps I shouldn't have said that but he told me so himself.'

'Did he really? I wish he had told me,' she said wistfully.

'But you must have known?'

'Yes, of course I did,' she said, pulling herself together. 'But it is nice to be told,' she could not resist adding, her voice regretful, almost bitter.

Verity felt she knew what Vera had suffered.

'My mother died when I was born,' she said in a low voice, 'and my father was so busy – he is a lawyer, you know, a very fine one – that I hardly ever saw him when I was a child and I see him even less now that I'm so often out of the country. I think I know what it must have been like for you to be an orphan.'

'I'm sorry,' Vera said. 'I'm still so upset. You mustn't think I did not love my uncle. We adored each other. It was just that he could be a bit of a burden. And now, of course, I regret we didn't talk more about important things.'

Verity looked at Vera with pity. She had been entrusted to a succession of nannies and had been lonely but that was surely preferable to being a sick man's nurse. It suddenly came back to her like a sharp pain how much she had wanted a mother when she was a child – how much she had envied other children. She shook herself mentally. It had given her strength to do the job she was doing – at least that was something to be thankful for.

'He began to forget the war and his . . . his injury?' she prompted Vera.

'Of course, when he was reminded of it – when he saw a friend from those days or read a book about the war he started to . . . I don't know . . . to have that look I recognized. I particularly dreaded November the eleventh.

He refused to parade at the Cenotaph. He said he wasn't worthy.'

'What would he do if he did feel depressed?' Verity asked, perhaps tactlessly.

'After I moved out, you mean?'

Verity nodded.

'He'd telephone me. I made him put in a telephone when I moved to Lawn Road so I could check on him.' She laughed. 'He made such a fuss. Said he didn't need new-fangled instruments and that he had managed quite well without one but I insisted and he was glad of it, I know. When he felt down he would ask me to go round . . .' she hesitated, 'or he'd take off for Tarn Hill. He had an old Bullnose Morris in which he travelled about the country . . .'

'I am very sorry, Miss Gray,' Adrian put in, seeing that she was becoming distressed. 'It must have been an awful shock for you. We would very much like to come to the memorial meeting if we won't be intruding.'

'Not at all. Everyone is welcome.'

Verity thought she was about to say something else but had checked herself.

Over lunch, Verity passed on to Adrian what Edward had told her about the discovery of Peter Gray's body at Broadlands.

'Gray was a very good painter,' he said, after a moment's thought. 'Very dark, in the manner of Paul Nash. As Vera was saying, his war experience had left him . . . what shall I say . . . ?'

'Shell-shocked?' Verity suggested.

'Yes, but that's not the half of it. Or rather it's not very helpful to say he had shell shock. It's as vague as saying he was mad. I was going to say his suffering made his paintings more powerful. They have a depth to them which I can never hope to achieve.'

It was one of the things Verity liked about Adrian – his genuine modesty. She had an idea. 'Mersham isn't very far away from Tarn Hill and I know Edward will want to come and pay his respects. Why don't you and I spend the night there and the three of us can go to the memorial meeting together? Would Charlotte like to come?'

It amused Adrian that Verity was sure enough of Edward not to have the least doubt that she and her friends would be welcome guests of his brother. It seemed not to occur to her that she might be overstepping the line.

'I would be very pleased to come if the Duke doesn't mind but Charlotte is trying to finish a novel and the publishers are chasing her. I think they fear that any novel published just when war breaks out will sink like a stone.'

'You think war is that close?' Verity asked, interestedly.

'I don't know – probably. Isn't that what you think? Despite what I said to you about being grateful for every day of peace, we have been expecting it for so long now that I really think it will be a relief when it's finally declared.'

Verity's mind went back to Gray's death. It didn't somehow *smell* right to her.

'Do you know what happened to him to drive him . . . well, mad?'

'What sent Gray off his rocker? He told me once – he didn't like talking about it . . . understandably. He said he had refused officer training because he wanted to be with the men. He had been in France from September 1916. In October 1917, when they were being very heavily shelled, two of his officers were killed in front of him. He remembered helping to pick up the bodies, or rather the pieces he could find, but nothing more. He had some sort of fit. He had no recollection of being sent down the line or being in hospital in France. He was shipped back to England. In the military hospital in Brighton, he was alternately depressed and violent. On one occasion, he attacked a doctor and twice tried to kill himself. He felt rage at having been so abused, he told me, by events he could not control. I also got the feeling that he felt guilty for having survived when so many of his friends had been killed.

'He was lucky enough to find a doctor – Captain Hubert Norman, his name was – who traced the source of his madness back to before the war. As a child, he had suffered a bad bout of pneumonia and had pains in his head and felt that life was not worth living. Anyway, thanks to Norman, he recovered after a fashion and found in painting a way of overcoming his depression. Every now and again though he would have another attack. He was very angry at the Ministry of Pensions which defined people like him – ordinary servicemen, not officers, of course – as "post-war inefficients". He was labelled a "psychiatric casualty of war". One forgets but people like Gray were officially termed "harmless lunatics". He, at least, was spared being "segregated" – in other words locked up in an asylum where the mentally ill would be "free of all responsibility", as the authorities put it. You can imagine that the condition of most of those shut up in institutions away from their family and friends quickly deteriorated.'

'Gosh!' Very exclaimed. 'It makes me feel quite ashamed. So, after the war . . .?'

'Gray had a bad knock in 1919 when his wife died of influenza like so many millions of others. He was left without his strongest support and with the responsibility of bringing up Vera on his own. An old aunt or cousin of his came to help but he hinted that she wasn't much use. He had a bad relapse in 1921 and was sent to Storthes Hall Asylum in Yorkshire for "Insane Ex-Service Men". I visited him there once. It was an awful place. If you weren't depressed when you went in, you certainly were when you came out. What he saw there made Gray a bitter opponent of locking people away without proper psychiatric care just to get them out of the way. I remember he said he was frequently punished for not showing due deference to the doctors and for "putting on airs".

'I don't know what the rights and wrongs of it were. No doubt he was a difficult patient. Vera says she's sure everything was done with the best intentions. I think the truth is that Storthes Hall was a kind of failed Craiglockhart – that excellent hospital where they did pioneering work on shell-shocked troops. Sassoon's written about it. Now it was different. Gone was the urgency of the war but the patients were still treated as failed soldiers. There was now no battlefront to which these men were to be returned. Anyway, Storthes Hall was eventually wound up in 1931 and the inmates sent to other asylums or hospitals.

'I know Gray regularly visited friends from Storthes at a place called Brookwood in Surrey. It was one of the mental hospitals to which patients from Storthes were sent. I knew when he had been because he always came back sane but very depressed. It was very hard for Vera. She hardly had a life of her own. That was why it was such a wonderful thing when she was able to move away – not far but the physical separation was the important thing. There was never much money – Gray had a tiny pension from the army – but Lawn Road is a sort of co-operative and she pays very little rent.'

'Did Gray sell his pictures?' Verity asked.

'Not many. They were too repetitive. The view from Tarn Hill doesn't have quite the same fascination for others as it has . . . had for him. Just recently, however, I gather he was being "discovered" and getting quite good prices.'

Verity had been listening intently as she chewed at her lamb chop. She suddenly started and looked at her watch. 'Oh God! I must go. I'm meeting my refugee at Victoria in half an hour. I almost forgot.'

'Would you like me to come with you?' Adrian said gallantly.

'Would you really? I'd be so grateful. Edward was going to come but he telephoned this morning to say he couldn't make it. I don't know why but I feel a bit nervy about the whole thing. I'm not used to having someone to look after.'

'I thought he was going to stay at Mersham?'

'Yes, in due course, but he's staying with me in Cranmer Court for a day or two at least. He has to get a job and that means being in London and he can't afford to stay anywhere half decent. He wasn't able to take any money out of Austria. He's been staying with a Jewish refugee group in Switzerland while his papers to come here were finalized.'

'How good's his English?'

'Very good.'

'I've got a friend at the BBC. I think they are looking for people to broadcast to Europe in the event of war. I could put him in touch.'

'Oh, would you, Adrian? That would be marvellous. He's very intelligent.'

Adrian paid the bill and they got a taxi in Charlotte Street. 'I'm so jumpy,' Verity confessed. 'What if he doesn't find a job? What if he hangs around and I can't get rid of him?'

'Hold on, Verity. You've done a good thing and there's no point in getting jittery about it. From what you tell me, he'll find his feet soon enough. Think of the thousands of Jews who don't speak English or French and don't have friends abroad to guarantee them. They won't find it easy to reach safety.'

'You think I did right? I always said in Spain that, as I was a reporter, I ought not to get emotionally involved. I mean, I saw so many poor starving people – children as young as three begging in the streets. I had to harden myself against all that suffering or I could not have done my job.'

'I understand but this is different. Your reporting has convinced us – most of us, anyway – that Germany is doing what no civilized country has ever done. The murder of hundreds of thousands of innocent people means we have to do what we can, however little, to help. Am I wrong?'

'You are right but it's so difficult to think clearly. I'm so selfish. I want to help but I can't bear the idea of having my liberty circumscribed. That's why I know I would be a bad mother. I'd abandon my children and be destroyed by guilt.'

'Don't torture yourself.' Adrian laughed. 'You're no monster. You just have what most people would say are male priorities.'

The train was late, of course, and they sat in the tea-room at Victoria drinking watery coffee. They considered going to the news cinema in the station but Verity said she had had a bellyful of bad news and did not want more.

'By the way, Adrian, how's Basil? I gather that toad of a man lodges my dog with you when he's in London.' She laughed to show she was joking 'I'm so grateful. I hope he isn't too much of a handful.'

'Well, he is rather large for London. He spends most of his time at Mersham which is what he needs – somewhere to romp around. Our little house isn't nearly big enough but I must say I've grown rather fond of him.'

'Why Adam had to give me such a large dog! Maybe he thought it had to be big to fill the gap he would leave.'

'Oh Verity!' Adrian exclaimed, seeing her distress. 'Look, it's against all my principles but may I give you some advice?'

'As long as you don't expect me to take it,' she replied, managing a smile. 'Anyway, I know what you are going to say – forget Adam and appreciate what I've got in Edward.'

'That's just it. It's got through your thick skull at last, has it? Anyone with half a brain can see you love him so why not accept it and make him happy? He doesn't deserve to be messed around and if he gets fed up and you lose him . . . well, you'll regret it for the rest of your life.'

'Golly, Adrian, I've never heard you so serious.'

'I *am* serious. The fact is I care about you – we both do – and it makes Charlotte cross to see you looking elsewhere for something which is staring you in the face.'

Verity made a moue and said, 'Point taken. I've been thinking along the same lines if you must know. Now, let's change the subject. You don't want me to cry, do you? I've noticed that the one thing guaranteed to embarrass a man is for him to be seen making a girl cry in public.'

At last the train was signalled and they congregated with a crowd of other anxious-looking people on the platform.

Georg was one of the last passengers to alight and, when he saw Verity, he smiled with relief. She was shocked at his appearance and had difficulty in returning his smile. He seemed to have lost weight. He was very white and his face had an unhealthy pallor. His eyes were bright but set in dark circles and his voice was gentle yet resonant. He had with him only a small suitcase which he refused to let Adrian carry. His overcoat was shabby and had evidently been slept in. He was deferential and, though obviously relieved to be at his journey's end, clearly fearful and homesick. Adrian, for the first time, began to understand what it was to be a refugee – dependent on the charity of strangers.

Georg bowed and made to kiss Verity's hand but changed his mind at the last moment. He merely said how grateful he was that she had come to meet him. Adrian, listening to his dark velvet voice, decided he might indeed be a natural broadcaster.

Verity, dismayed and a little scared, was glad Adrian had come with her. In London, this shabby, lost soul was nothing like the confident young man she had met in Vienna and had pictured striding down the platform to meet her. Her heart sank as she realized what she had taken on and she fussed over Georg to hide her anxiety, which made him all the more embarrassed as he sensed her unease.

The next couple of days were difficult for both of them. Georg, as Verity had feared, was rather a burden despite making every effort to be invisible. He slept in her spare room and did not wake up – or at least get up – until she had left for the *New Gazette* but she was always aware of his presence which irked her though she knew she was being unreasonable.

His presence was just one of the things which made her fretful. It was taking more time than she had hoped for Lord Weaver to secure her papers of accreditation so she could return to Vienna. It made her restless and irritable to be stuck in London while history was being made. Adrian took it upon himself to take Georg about and show him the sights. He had never been to London and together they went to the Tower, the National Gallery and the Zoo. This last proved to be a mistake because the animals in their cages seemed to depress him. He was worrying about his parents and wrote to them though without much hope of a reply.

On the Friday they were to go to Mersham, Georg became visibly agitated. He told Verity that he had some important information for the British Government which he would exchange for help in getting his family out of Vienna. He wouldn't expatiate on the nature of this information except that it concerned weaponry. Verity informed Edward who tried to get him an interview with a Foreign Office friend who, he thought, might be able to help. The friend had already left London for the weekend and it was agreed that the meeting would take place the following week. She remembered what Owen Coombs had said about wanting to capture Georg for the Party but decided that her first loyalty was to her country. If Georg had anything of interest to say, he must say it first to one of Edward's friends in the Foreign Office.

Georg professed himself satisfied with the plan but he remained on edge, reading the papers avidly and listening to the news on the wireless whenever he could. He could not understand why the British seemed so uninterested in the *Anschluss* and complained to Adrian about British complacency.

'You believe the English Channel will protect you from invasion. It won't.' Angrily, he smacked his copy of *The Times*. 'You are worried about the flood of Jewish refugees – I notice it is always "a flood" – instead of taking it as a warning of what is to come. And you are not really interested in what is happening to the Jews in the new Reich.'

It was not easy, Adrian explained, for ordinary English people to understand what it meant to be a refugee. Quite simply, they had no experience of it. The French, the Russians, the Czechs and the Poles all knew what it was like to have their country invaded and to have to run for their lives leaving everything behind. The English did not.

Georg's anxiety about his parents was fuelled by guilt. He was safe in England and they were in imminent danger of being sent to a concentration camp. He had to get them out before it was too late and to ignore what he knew in his heart to be the truth – his parents would never leave their home until they were removed by force. When he had gone to say goodbye to his mother and father it was a final leave-taking. His father was frail after his time in prison and seemed fatalistic about the future.

'Your mother and I are too old to start a new life in a new country. You go, my boy. You have your whole life in front of you. We shall stay and hope to be ignored.'

Georg's mother wanted to give him money but he knew he would be searched at the frontier and, if he was found trying to smuggle money out of the country, he might be turned back or sent to a prison camp.

'Well then, take this,' she said and pressed into his hand a small parcel – not more than three inches square and an inch thick.

'I can't take this,' he protested.

'Yes, you can . . . you must. It will be stolen or destroyed if it stays here. You can sell it when you get to England. It is all we have to give you.'

Georg knew very well what it was – a tiny drawing by Albrecht Dürer made on his visit to Venice in 1505. It was a sketch of a woman of exquisite beauty with melancholy eyes dressed in Venetian costume – unquestionably a preliminary sketch for a famous painting in the Kunsthistorisches Museum in Vienna. Georg's father had been given it by his father at his bar mitzvah and it had hung over his desk as long as Georg could remember. In the end, he was prevailed upon to take it. Hitler hated Vienna and the Viennese Jews in particular. It was in Vienna that he had failed as an artist and had been laughed out of the Academy of Fine Arts. The first thing he intended to do was to strip the Viennese Jews of every art treasure they possessed. He would begin with the Rothschilds but Himmler's long arm would search out even the humblest Jew with treasures to seize.

With tears and prayers, Georg had finally parted from his parents and he was still dazed and grief-stricken. He knew he should look ahead and not dwell on the past. Of course, he could never forget his life in Vienna but he could at least make a future for himself in England as his father had begged him to do. So now, in London, he looked about him but he did not much like what he saw.

London was so drab and the people so smug. He went to two Jewish refugee centres and came away determined to have nothing to do with them. He was not one of those poor lost souls. He could make it on his own. If only English cooking wasn't so bad!

5

It was a relief to Georg and to Verity when they departed for Mersham. As Verity had assumed, Edward had asked – or rather informed – his brother that Adrian was also to be a weekend guest and so it was arranged. Georg was to take the train with Fenton, Edward's valet, and the luggage. Edward was to drive Adrian and Verity in the Lagonda to the memorial meeting for Peter Gray and then go on to Mersham.

Edward had known Adrian as long as he had known Verity. It had been at a party in the painter's flat that he had tracked her down after their fateful meeting the night of General Craig's murder at Mersham almost three years before. Adrian had watched with concern Verity's refusal to accept Edward's love and return it. It was true they were an odd couple but he was convinced they belonged together. Both his friends were private and prickly and Adrian tried not to make the mistake of asking either of them when they were going to accept this. He had broken his rule and wondered if he had been foolish to allow himself to lecture Verity while they waited for Georg's train at Victoria. He comforted himself with the feeling that she had been receptive. She certainly had not told him to mind his own business as she might have done a few months earlier.

The Lagonda swept out of London and into a countryside already showing signs of spring. Daffodils and primroses coloured the hedgerows and, with the hood down and the wind blowing, Edward began to feel more relaxed. He liked Adrian, though it was a standing joke between them that he could not abide his paintings, and Verity seemed calmer and quieter. It was comforting to be with someone who knew what he felt for Verity – how complicated it was loving someone who rejected marriage on principle and always put her work before her affections. Had Verity not been in the car, he and Adrian might have had one of those terse but loaded exchanges which was the closest men of Edward's class got to baring their hearts to their friends.

When they reached the top of Tarn Hill, they followed an unmade-up track until they saw three or four cars and, just beyond, a small gathering of people wrapped in winter coats, collars raised against the wind and holding on to their hats.

'This must be where Gray parked his car,' Edward remarked as he brought the Lagonda to a halt beside an ancient Austin.

'He could quite easily lug his easel and so on over there,' Verity said, pointing to where the little group had gathered.

'I must say,' he shouted, removing his hat which the wind tried to sweep off his head, 'the view is stunning but it must often have been too cold to paint.'

'And how did he stop his easel blowing away?' Verity shouted against the wind, clutching her hat to her head.

'There must have been something about this view which made him want to be here whatever the discomfort,' Adrian agreed.

In fact, the memorial meeting was held in something of a hollow and some ragged trees gave further protection so at least they could hear what was said and read.

Rather to Edward's surprise, Adrian was one of three of Gray's friends who had been asked to talk of what they valued in him as a man and a painter. Edward was impressed and wished he had known the man Adrian evoked so vividly. Vera read a poem by Tennyson – 'Crossing the Bar', which had been a favourite of her uncle's – and an old friend of his, a man called Reginald Harman, Edward gathered from Adrian, read part of a sermon by John Donne. Then, making sure the ashes would not blow into the faces of the mourners, Vera tipped her uncle's remains into the wind and Edward was moved – despite not having known him – and felt that a spirit had been freed.

They stood for a minute in silence, heads bowed, and Edward thought how the war had wounded a whole generation – some in the flesh, many in the soul. Now, another war threatened and new wounds were being inflicted. He prayed for his nephew Frank who might soon be called upon to fight a second war against perverted Prussian militarism. Verity closed her eyes and thought of Georg Dreiser, exiled from his country by evil men, and asked that he might find peace in his new home.

As the three of them turned to walk back to the Lagonda, Vera came up to Verity and Edward to thank them for coming.

'I'm afraid my uncle did not have many friends. Adrian – you were one – but I think, if he had known both of you, he would have trusted you. By the way, may I introduce you to one of his oldest friends, Reginald Harman.'

'The painter?' Edward inquired eagerly as Vera turned away to talk to someone else. 'I have one of your seascapes.'

'I am so pleased,' Harman said gravely. He had the upright bearing of an old soldier but his goatee beard, unkempt grey hair and fierce grey eyes gave him the appearance of an Old Testament prophet. 'But, you know, Peter was the better artist. It was a misfortune that he never got the recognition his work deserved, though it never seemed to bother him. However, I have hopes that this new exhibition, which was planned before his untimely death, will remedy this neglect.'

He sounded pompous but Edward suspected it was the formality of an earlier generation not immediately at ease with strangers.

'His obsession with this place must have worked against any commercial success?' he suggested.

'It did but he painted other things – other places, people. There's a portrait of Vera as a child which is a masterpiece.'

'I did not know he was a portrait painter. Did he paint his wife?'

'Not to my knowledge.'

'Isn't that rather odd? She was the light of his life, I gather.'

'I suppose he thought he did not need to – while she was alive – and then it was too late. Who knows?'

'Where is the exhibition?'

'The Goupil, in September – just before yours, Adrian. I'll make sure you get invitations to the private view. I understand from Vera that it was your nephew and his friend who discovered poor Peter's body, Lord Edward?'

'That's right, close to the drive up to Broadlands. Do you know why he was there?'

'It's not far as the crow flies. You see over there – that farmhouse?'

'Yes. It looks as though work's being done on it. I wish I had brought my binoculars.'

'That farmhouse is on the Broadlands estate,' Harman said. 'At least I think so. I remember asking Peter about the view and who owned the buildings at the bottom of the picture.' He hesitated, as though he was going to add something. 'Perhaps he felt ill and was seeking help. He didn't like people very much so I can't think of any other reason why he would walk down towards the house. It's certainly out of character. He wasn't a great walker and getting back up the hill to collect his stuff . . .' He shook his head and the wind whisked his mane of hair into flickering white flames. 'I have to say I'm as puzzled as you as to what he was doing there.'

'Could he have been meeting someone?' Edward asked.

'It's possible,' Harman replied, after a moment's thought. 'He did say something to me about wanting to meet an American painter – or did he say a dealer? I don't remember – he seemed rather confused – but I assumed it would be in London. I only remember because it was so unusual. He'd almost become a recluse, you understand.

He hated meeting anyone new. On the other hand, his paintings were suddenly becoming rather sought after. I believe – and I told him this – that history will mark him out as one of the few English painters of his generation who'll last. I am so glad I *did* tell him.'

'How sad to think he won't be alive to enjoy it.' Adrian said.

'I don't feel sad on that account because he would not have enjoyed it. He truly lived for his art. He wasn't interested in money. I know people say that but, in his case, it was true. He was tortured by depression and only his painting brought him relief.'

'And the ergot he took to control it,' Edward added.

'I think he had more or less given up taking it. His depressions were nowhere near as severe as they used to be and he was afraid of the effect ergot had on him as a painter. It is a poison as well as a healer. Nature is never as simple as we would like to think. Many natural remedies can have deadly effects in certain circumstances.'

'That's what I told you when we met in London,' Vera said to Verity, coming up to Harman and taking his arm affectionately.

Verity nodded and said, 'But what do you mean, Mr Harman, when you say he was afraid of the effects on him as an artist?'

'Well, for one thing, he said that, after taking ergot, colour looked different to him. I don't quite know what he meant but obviously an artist has to trust his eye. He also said that if he took too much, it gave him hallucinations and made him forgetful which could be quite frightening.'

'Hallucinations! You mean he imagined there were snakes in the room with him or something?' Verity exclaimed. 'I remember reading something about someone eating hallucinogenic mushrooms and seeing snakes. Ugh! My worst nightmare.'

'I'm not sure what form they took,' Harman said, sounding as though he did not wish to continue the conversation. 'I just know they were very unpleasant. Now, Vera, shall we get out of the wind? My old bones are beginning to complain.'

'Of course, Reg. Let's take refuge in the car.'

'Miss Gray, could I come and talk to you about your uncle?' Edward said as she moved away. Vera looked surprised but said he could find her at the Slade most days.

'You have a flat in Lawn Road?'

'That's right. Do you know it?'

'Isn't it an artists' community of some kind? It's the building which looks like an ocean liner?'

'Yes, my uncle was a friend of the architect, Wells Coates. He and a friend, Jack Pritchard, designed what they hoped would be a Utopian community for single professional people who just wanted somewhere to sleep. I mean, people dedicated to their work and not interested in domesticity. You must come and see it but, be warned, my flat's more like a ship's cabin than anything else – very small but with everything I need. There's no kitchen – you order food from a central kitchen – but you don't want to hear about all this.'

She seemed eager to talk about something other than her uncle.

'Don't you remember, V? You took me to meet a young German artist who was living in Lawn Road. Not very good, I thought, and you were cross with me because I wouldn't buy any of his work. We ate in the – what is it called? – the Isobar.'

'Yes, I remember. It's a sort of club for artists.'

'The Isobar, yes . . .' Vera said. 'Fancy you having been there before. Somehow it's turned into a refuge, or at least a meeting place, for Jewish artists the Nazis have chased out of Germany. It's perfect for me. I love the feeling of having my own place but being able to find congenial company in the Isobar whenever I want it. But I must go. Reg is getting cold. Goodbye for now, then.'

When they had walked out of earshot, Adrian said anxiously, 'I hope we didn't upset Mr Harman.'

'Sorry,' Verity said. 'Was I too blunt? I didn't mean to be rude. I suppose I've just got used to asking perfect strangers quite intimate questions.'

Back in the Lagonda, Verity asked Edward what he thought of Vera.

'She's a good girl who has had a difficult childhood. In fact, you could say she never had one – not a proper one, anyway.'

Vera was not beautiful and she certainly made no attempt to make herself attractive but, when she smiled, her face lit up and Edward had decided he liked her. He would do what he could to help her – though she hadn't asked him to and he wasn't sure what help he could give. The last thing she would accept was charity and, if her uncle's paintings started to sell, she would have an income even if her own pictures failed to find buyers. He thought he would like to see them and decide for himself if they were any good. As for Gray's death – he wasn't altogether happy it was just an accident and wished Vera had not insisted on having his body cremated.

At Mersham, Adrian was warmly welcomed by the Duchess, who had met him in London with Edward. As she greeted Verity, she tried hard to look equally happy but Edward could see the effort behind her smile. Connie, perhaps unkindly, thought that any good deed of Verity's would always involve her friends having to take on most of the burden and Georg was rather a burden.

'Mr Dreiser's arrived,' she whispered. 'I hope he's all right. He doesn't say much.'

'I expect he's just shy. Gerald can be rather intimidating. I'm so grateful to you for putting him up. It means a lot to me.'

'Don't be silly, Verity. One only has to imagine oneself in the same position to want to make him feel at home. It's just he's . . .'

'I hope you understand why I had to get him out of Vienna, Connie. The Jews aren't allowed to come to England without an invitation . . . I had to do something, however little . . . If you only knew . . .'

Seeing she was genuinely upset, Connie repented of her irritation with Verity for foisting Georg on them and kissed her warmly. 'Of course I understand. You were quite right to help. We're too complacent.'

Verity did at least receive an unrestrained welcome from Basil who jumped up as though wanting to embrace her, in the process almost knocking her over.

'Basil, darling, how large you have grown,' she said, fondling him. 'I'm so sorry to have left you for so long but I can see you have been well looked after.' She smiled brightly and added, 'Connie, it's so kind of you to have taken him in – poor exiled hound.' She nuzzled him affectionately. 'I hope he hasn't been too much of a handful.'

'Not at all! Gerald loves taking him for walks. It gives him a reason to get out of the house – Gerald, I mean. And Basil has developed a bond with one of the grooms so he really is no trouble.'

They went into the drawing-room where tea was laid. The Duke, struggling out of his armchair, looked rather relieved that his tête-à-tête with Georg had been interrupted. Edward thought his brother was looking older. Basil, who had followed them in, knocked against the little table on which the Duke had laid his book and it fell on to the carpet. Verity picked it up for him. It was a recently published admiring portrait of Hitler by Lord Londonderry called *Ourselves and Germany*. Verity had not read it but she had seen reviews of it and hated what she had learnt of its message. This boiled down to advice to the Prime Minister to give way to Hitler on every issue in the hope that he would leave Britain and its empire alone.

With a huge effort, she bit back a contemptuous remark, remembering that Londonderry was a friend of the Duke's. If she got into an argument with him within minutes of entering his house, it would not be easy for her to stay. She knew he was suspicious of her at the best of times. She shook his hand and he mumbled something that might have been a welcome after which she sat down on a chair as far away from his as possible. Paradoxically, although she could hardly have a civil conversation with the Duke, she loved Mersham and thought it the most beautiful house in England.

Edward shook hands with Georg and patted his brother on the shoulder – the nearest they ever got to an embrace.

He had only met Georg very briefly that morning when he had come to Albany with Verity and Adrian before they had set off to drive to Tarn Hill leaving Georg, in Fenton's charge, to take the train to Mersham.

Edward had seen the battle raging in Verity and breathed a sigh of relief when he realized that she had managed to hold her tongue. It crossed his mind that his brother had deliberately set out to provoke her by displaying the book so obviously but, on balance, he thought him neither spiteful nor clever enough to plan such a provocation.

At first, Georg was either too shy or too homesick to make much effort at conversation but Edward turned on his charm and he was soon talking animatedly of the situation in Vienna. Verity was struck once again by Edward's easy authority and his gift for making the person he was talking to feel that he valued their views.

'How did the memorial meeting on Tarn Hill go?' Connie asked, thinking Verity looked sad.

'It went well, didn't it, Adrian?' She fondled Basil's ears. 'I liked Vera – Gray's niece.'

'Was Gray a well-known painter?' Connie inquired. 'I'm afraid I had not heard of him.'

'Well respected rather than well known,' Adrian said.

The conversation faded. The butler poured out the tea and Adrian did battle with a scone. Verity stretched luxuriously and let her hand fall from Basil's head. She gazed about her, contentment stealing over her. 'Oh Connie, I do love it here. I always sleep well at Mersham. In fact, I sometimes think it's the only place I can truly rest. I was thinking how right Vera was to scatter her father's ashes where he had been happiest. When I die, I would like my ashes to be scattered where I was happy.'

'Where would that be? Spain?' Adrian asked.

'Here, perhaps, under the copper beech, if it was allowed.'

Connie looked up in surprise. 'I'm so glad you feel happy here,' she said. 'Of course, I think it's the most beautiful place on earth and I always like people who share my opinion. But don't let's talk about death.'

'No, you're right, but I can't help thinking of my friends and comrades in Spain – many of them at this moment dying in defence of Madrid. I feel I deserted them when the cause was lost. I don't think I'll be forgiven for that if there is an afterlife.'

Adrian reached over and squeezed her hand affectionately, thinking how sad it was that Verity had no place to call home. Mersham was the nearest – a place she had visited only half a dozen times, owned by people she hardly knew and, he suspected, who did not much care for her.

'Where's Frank?' Verity asked, trying to snap out of her melancholy.

The Duke answered her. 'He's at Broadlands. He spends all his time there. He thinks the Mountbattens are – how did he put it, Connie? – "absolute humdingers".'

'You disapprove, Gerald?' Edward inquired mildly.

'He can do what he wants. If he prefers "humdingers" to old "fuddy-duddies" like us, who can blame him?'

'It's not that,' Connie said. 'It's natural that he likes being with amusing young people. He's mad about polo. It's his new passion. Did you know, Ned?'

'He's mad about that Indian girl,' the Duke muttered, petulantly.

'Sunita?'

'Yes. She and her brother play polo in India and they – and Lord Louis, of course – have started teaching Frank. Apparently, he's a natural,' Connie added proudly. 'But then he's good at all sports.'

'The boy's got a good eye,' Edward agreed. 'So, is he sleeping here?'

'Yes, but that's about all. He treats the place like a hotel. Mountbatten has lent him a motorbike and he drives back and forth at high speed,' Connie answered. 'I have told him to be careful but he doesn't listen.'

'Oh, I shouldn't worry, Connie, my dear,' Edward said comfortably. 'Better than moping about here with nothing to do.' He saw his brother bridle and tried to explain himself, making things worse if anything. 'You know what I mean, Gerald. He's got to be able to have a bit of fun.'

'Yes,' Connie backed him up. 'He spent yesterday in London with a man called Rose – an American, I think Frank said – an art critic?'

'It's the first I've heard that Frank likes art,' Verity said without thinking.

Edward scowled. 'I met the man when we went to lunch at Broadlands. I can't say I cared for him.'

'Well, he didn't get back here until the early hours so he must be having *some* fun,' Connie said defiantly. 'You know he's hoping to join the Naval Reserve? Of course, you do. Wasn't it your idea, Ned? Lord Louis has kindly arranged an interview for him. I wish he didn't have to join anything but I think the navy's safer than the army, don't you?' She had an idea that the next war would be like the last and, if her son could only be kept out of the trenches, he might survive. Edward was certainly not going to disabuse her. 'Tell me, Mr Hassel, about the man – what was his name . . .?'

'Peter Gray?' Adrian prompted her.

'Yes. The poor man! Does anyone know why he was in the grounds of Broadlands when he died?'

Leaving Adrian to talk to Connie, Edward suggested to Georg that he might care to take a stroll in the garden. 'The Knot Garden is supposed to be the oldest in England,' Edward informed him. 'Basil, will you come too?'

Clearly, Georg had no idea what a Knot Garden was, or why he should be interested in it, but welcomed the chance of escaping from the Duke.

'He's not getting too much for you – the Duke?' Edward asked when they were out of earshot.

Georg looked alarmed. 'No, please, Lord Edward, I am most grateful to him – to your family – for giving me shelter.' Seeing Edward's face, Georg relaxed. 'I am still worrying about my family, you understand? And I must find work. I do not like to live on charity. Mr Hassel has arranged for me to meet Mr Harcourt of the BBC World Service. There is some possibility I might . . . with my languages . . .' He seemed unable to continue.

Edward was concerned. 'What can we do about your parents? To get them out, I mean.'

'I have asked the Duke if he would offer my father a job – anything – it does not matter. A gardener,' he said looking about him. 'With such an offer, he might be allowed to come to England. He has been released from prison. Did Verity tell you? There was no case against him but he is an embarrassment to the authorities. He is well known in Vienna and this, I hope, means he cannot be sent off to a camp as he would be if he did not have – how do you say it? – friends in high places. The trouble is my parents say they want to stay in Vienna.'

'Stay? Don't they realize the danger they are in?'

'Of course, but they don't want to leave their home. They say they're too old to begin again in a new country.'

'I understand that. Still, you must persuade them it is not too bad here.'

'It's not that, Lord Edward. My father has a high opinion of England and the English though he has never been here. It's just that he wants to die in his own bed.'

'If the Nazis allow him to. God! What a world we live in!'

Edward was silent for a moment, watching Basil race round the garden enjoying his freedom. He wondered what he would do if he was told he had to leave everything and go, penniless, into exile. At last he said, 'What else worries you? I mean, that is enough but . . .' He checked himself. How fatuous it was to ask a Jewish refugee what worried him.

'This man at the Foreign Office you have so kindly arranged for me to see . . . will he understand how important my information is? He won't try to brush me aside? I have not come empty-handed but I do not think Verity believes me. I have friends in Germany . . . scientists . . .' He seemed to come to some sort of decision. 'Lord Edward, can I tell you or is there someone . . . someone in your secret service I should talk to?'

'Of course I can arrange for you to meet . . . someone in authority in our secret service.' He was thinking of Guy Liddell. 'But if you can tell me a little more about the nature of your information, I can judge who you ought to speak to.'

Georg looked at him gratefully. 'I trust Miss Browne – Verity – with my life, you understand? But she is a journalist and I must be secret. Other lives than mine depend upon it.'

'That sounds serious. I promise I will pass your message on to the right person and nobody else. You don't have to worry on that score.'

Georg nodded and took a deep breath. 'The simple fact is that you are going to lose the war. I have a friend . . .'

'You are thinking of how we have allowed the Luftwaffe to grow so much stronger than our own air force?'

'No, no. Worse than that. Much worse. My friend is a scientist and he is working on a bomb.'

'A bomb?'

'A very great bomb, using nuclear fission. Do you know what I mean, Lord Edward?' Georg waved his hands in the air for emphasis.

'I only know what I have read in the newspapers. I may be wrong but I understood there was no possibility of Hitler having such a weapon before 1950.'

'That is not correct, I fear. I only wish it were so. My friend – a physicist at the Friedrich-Wilhelms University in Berlin – has been working on it since 1927.'

'How do you know this?'

'Stefan Meyer, the director of the Vienna laboratory, is an old friend of my father. Two of his team – both of whom I have met – Hans Pettersson and Gerhard Kirsch, have made considerable progress. They are building a secret reactor in Gottow, a village outside Berlin. . . Should I stop there? How much can I tell you . . .?'

Georg looked suddenly anxious, whether because he doubted Edward's trustworthiness or because he did not know how much he would understand of what he was being told, Edward did not know.

'You can tell me anything but perhaps it is better if you talk to a scientist who can evaluate . . .'

Georg nodded. 'That would be good. You see my life is in danger.'

'But you are safe in England.'

'Not safe, not even in this Knot Garden,' he said, smiling. He seemed to relax a little. 'Let me tell you a little more in case . . . I'll put it as simply as possible but it would ease my mind to have told someone. In Berlin, Professor Otto Hahn and his colleague, Fritz Strassmann, have discovered that it is possible to split the nuclei of uranium, the heaviest of all the elements. This releases energy on a scale far greater than the splitting of lithium nuclei. They call it fission.'

'I don't understand,' Edward said helplessly. 'I wish I knew more science. What is "fission"?'

'I don't understand it all either but in a chain reaction a neutron fired at a uranium nucleus would cause it to split, releasing energy and other neutrons. These neutrons would immediately hit each other, split and the process would continue many millions of times within a fraction of a second. The end result is an explosion far greater than you could possibly imagine . . . greater than all the explosions of the last war added together.'

Georg stopped and stared ahead of him, seeing nothing. The sheer dread in his eyes meant Edward did not doubt for one moment that what he was being told was the sober truth. Such a bomb would mean that in the next war no one would be spared – not the soldier in the front line, nor women and children going about their normal lives. He had a sudden vision of Mersham and everybody in it reduced to ashes in a split second. It made him feel physically sick. Could such evil ever be overcome?

'At Cambridge, our people are also working on splitting the atom. Rutherford's team . . . there's been a lot about it in the press.'

'Yes, but too slow – much too slow. They don't believe this bomb can be made in our lifetime but they are wrong. It *can* be . . . it *is* being made.' He clutched Edward's arm.

'What can be done?' Edward asked, his voice thin and uncertain.

'Probably nothing,' Georg said brutally, 'but there is a chance . . .'

'A chance?'

'A chance of getting hold of two of the Friedrich-Wilhelms team – Arno Brasch and Fritz Lange. They don't like the Nazis and if their safety could be assured . . .'

'How do you know so much?' Edward said, suddenly suspicious. 'This isn't some sort of trap, is it?'

'On my mother's life it is not. When I knew I would have to escape from the Nazis, I went to see Professor Meyer. He has many English friends . . . He wanted me to warn you . . . to ask for help . . .'

On the Monday, the four of them – Edward, Verity, Georg and Adrian – returned to London. However, they had all been invited back to Mersham the following weekend. Adrian had demurred but Connie had been pressing and, since he knew Charlotte would want him out of the way while she finished her book, he accepted. He and Connie got on well together and she had suggested he might like to paint the castle or its grounds. Verity was relieved to have entertainment for Georg and accepted for both of them with alacrity.

6

Lord Louis made the announcement on the Tuesday, after the afternoon training session, and Sunita clapped her hands with glee. 'I have arranged a practice match next Saturday against some of my Bluejackets. The only way you can improve now, Frank, is by playing polo properly. You're better than I was when I began. You've got a good eye and you're born to ride. For me it was hard work but worth the grind. It's the best game in the world. It's a bit early to be playing polo but the field's in a good condition and we won't push the ponies too hard. By May, when the season proper starts, you'll be ready for it.'

Mountbatten was a good trainer. He was calm, never lost his temper but kept Frank at it until he dropped with fatigue. Harry told Frank that he could not be called a polo player until he could vault into the saddle but refused to show him how it was done. To Harry's annoyance, Mountbatten had insisted that Ayesha make up the fourth in the Broadlands Fencibles, as he had named them, along with Frank, Sunita and himself. Harry was to hold himself in reserve.

Frank adored this new game. It helped that Sunita was such a good player and he wanted to be as good as she. She teased and flirted with him without ever saying anything which might make him think she was seriously interested in him. Frank got frustrated when he ran his pony up and down the field but never seemed to get near the ball. When he asked Mountbatten what he was doing wrong, he was told not to worry and that it would all suddenly come right – like learning to ride a bicycle.

'I played my first game on the famous ground within the Maharaja's palace in Batiala,' Mountbatten recalled. 'In the first half, I never got near the ball, let alone hit it. Then in the last chukka, to my intense surprise, I actually hit the ball three or four times. I have been dippy about it ever since.'

This had been during his first visit to India in 1921 as ADC to the Prince of Wales. Sunny's father had introduced him to the game when they visited Batiala and it had quickly become a passion. The Prince had remarked much later that Mountbatten's interest in India's many problems was 'confined to that part of the country bounded by the white boards of polo fields'. Mountbatten continued almost wistfully, 'I remember so well my first visit to Batiala and your grandfather's great kindness to us, Harry. We shot black buck from a Rolls-Royce, twisting and turning over impossible country at fifty miles an hour. I have no idea how the car survived but it's why I have always bought Rolls-Royces.'

To Mountbatten's great joy, he discovered, when courting Edwina, that she had fitted Broadlands out with a golf-course, three tennis courts, and, most important of all, a polo field. That was in addition to eight hundred acres of shooting and a stretch of the Test known as a fisherman's paradise. For someone as sports mad as Mountbatten, it was everything he needed to be happy. His wife's affairs were a small price to pay.

He was captain of the Bluejackets, the Royal Navy team, and had twice carried off the Inter-Regimental trophy. 'I insist my team call to each other for passes using first names so, by the inflection of our voices, we can interpret what's in the caller's mind and act appropriately,' he told his young players as they gulped down long glasses of lemonade between sessions. Mountbatten proudly showed Frank the polo stick he had invented with its oval-shaped head to give 'loft and length' and presented him with a copy of the book he had written, under the name of Marco, called simply *Polo*.

The invitation Frank brought back to Mersham for his parents to come to Broadlands to watch him play in his first polo match put the Duke in a difficult position. It was breakfast – the only meal at which Frank saw his parents as he spent most of every day at Broadlands. What possible excuse could the Duke make without giving mortal offence to his son, let alone Mountbatten? Connie said little but pointed out that they would not be going into the house.

Frank backed her up. 'Come on, Pa, don't be so stuffy. Lord Louis has been very good to me. After all, he's arranged for me to go for an interview for the RNVR in London. With his backing, the navy's bound to accept me! You've got to come! Anyway, it'll be fun. There'll be lots of people there. There will be smoked-salmon sandwiches and champagne in a marquee before the match and tea and cakes afterwards. There can't be anything objectionable in that! And Lord Louis says you're to bring everyone staying the weekend. I particularly want Uncle Ned and Verity to be there. They are coming back at the weekend, aren't they? I say, what's going on with those two? Are they getting married or . . .?' he added as he forked sausages and fried eggs on to his plate from a silver chafing dish on the sideboard – all this exercise made him ravenous.

'Don't ask me,' the Duke retorted. 'We'd be the last to know and, frankly, I don't trust her . . . never have. Not since she came here pretending to be something she wasn't.'

'Oh, but that was ages ago,' Frank protested. 'I think she's a very good egg and I just wish he'd pop the question.'

'He has,' Connie told him, 'but she won't accept him while she's doing her reporting.'

'I don't approve of the way these young women pretend they're as good as men and . . .'

'Gerald, please!' Connie broke in. 'Ned will marry who he likes and as long as she makes him happy . . .'

'But will she? Can she?' the Duke demanded. 'The life she leads is coarsening . . . I'm sorry, Connie,' he said, holding up his hand to stop her contradicting, 'but it is. She's not a . . . well, she's not a lady . . . not as my father would have understood the word.'

'Oh, bother all that,' Frank said. 'I think she's got loads of pluck and she's just the sort of woman Uncle Ned needs. He'll not be bored with Verity. Still, I'm glad she seems to have broken with that German – what was his name? Von Trott. I thought she had really fallen for him when I saw them together at that cricket match.'

'And now you've dropped that American woman,' the Duke could not prevent himself asking, 'when are you going to find a nice English girl and settle down, Frank?'

'Gerald!' Connie protested. 'Frank's a sensible boy.' She put out her hand and stroked his cheek. 'He'll find the right girl but there's no hurry.'

Frank kissed his mother's hand and held it to his cheek. 'What girl could ever live up to you?' he said naively and she blushed with pleasure.

Frank's enthusiasm and the trouble Mountbatten was taking with his son made it impossible for the Duke to hold out and, with much huffing and puffing, he agreed to be there on Saturday at one o'clock to see him play in his first polo match.

Although the Duke would never have admitted it, even to himself, the idea of Frank joining the navy frightened him. The boy was everything to him and, besides, there was the question of who would inherit Mersham. What if Frank were to die without having married and had a son? Ned would – most reluctantly – inherit, if he outlived him, but what good would that be? His brother showed no sign of marrying and having babies. The title would become extinct and Mersham would belong to some distant cousin. It didn't bear thinking about. Perhaps, after all, it would be better if Ned did marry the Browne woman – better than nothing. No, the responsibility was Frank's. That Indian girl the boy was so mad about . . . she was the daughter of a maharaja . . . but to have a brown Duke of Mersham . . . Was that better?

'Champagne and smoked-salmon sandwiches!' harumphed the Duke. 'What's wrong with beer and ham sandwiches?'

Verity was glad to be back, although she knew the Duke might be less than pleased to see her two weekends running. She tried once again to put her finger on why Mersham appealed to her so much. There was something about the castle, honey-coloured with age, serenely unperturbed by the antics of those who inhabited and visited it, which put things into perspective. 'What fools these mortals be,' it seemed to say and the river, which made a placid moat about its ancient walls, echoed the sentiment. Even the swans floating on the shimmering surface seemed superior. Although it was not warm, Verity was sitting out under the copper beech in a deckchair. She had a rug over her knees and a book in her hand – a travel guide edited by Eugene Fodor – but she wasn't reading it.

Lord Weaver had telephoned to tell her that he had totally failed to get permission from Austria's new rulers to allow her return to Vienna as the *New Gazette*'s correspondent and it now seemed she would go to Prague instead. Accepting the inevitable, she decided she must now bone up on a country of which she knew next to nothing. According to Fodor, writing in 1936, 'Today the whole of Czechoslovakia is at peace and dominated by the desire to keep the peace,' and he had gone on to remark that countries are like women, 'the best are those which are least talked about.'

As she gazed unseeingly at the water, she found herself smiling wryly. Czechoslovakia's peace would soon be shattered – of that she was sure – and the country would soon be 'talked about', if that was what she wanted. Basking in his success at absorbing Austria into the Reich, Hitler was poised to gobble up one more country. Her thoughts turned to Georg. She felt guilty and irritated in equal measure. She knew he wasn't happy. He was worrying about his parents of whom he could get no news and, to put it brutally, he was becoming rather a bore. He was still staying with her in Cranmer Court but this could not go on for much longer. She needed her privacy and Georg, naturally enough, was always hanging about with nothing to do but mope. He had no friends except the Jews he met at refugee centres who had similar problems. He had no money and refused to take any off her. When she did force some on him, he took it with bad grace as if she were insulting him.

The only light at the end of the tunnel was the interview he had been offered at the BBC. They were looking for linguists to broadcast to the Continent. The government believed this to be a cheap and effective way of bolstering the morale of the oppressed peoples of Europe but Edward said – and Verity agreed with him – there was a danger these broadcasts would encourage the Czechs and the Poles to believe that Britain would come to their aid if they were attacked which, in reality, did not seem likely or even practicable.

Thinking of Edward made her think of Churchill. She always tried to be as honest with herself as she could and she was now beginning to accept that she might have been wrong about him. He could never be forgiven for his part in breaking the General Strike but his hatred of Fascism was as strong as hers. She sighed. And what about Edward? Churchill had told her she would be making a mistake if she refused him. Was he wrong? Adam was beginning to fade from her memory. Had it been real love? It had seemed so at the time but now she was not so sure. It had been a *coup de foudre* – a thunderstorm which had overwhelmed her and then passed, leaving her shaken but . . .

At that moment, Edward himself appeared. As she watched him cross the lawn, immaculate as always in jacket and tie with grey flannels creased to carving-knife sharpness, it was almost as if she was seeing him for the first time. The long beaky nose, the strong determined chin and, although she could not see them at this distance, the shrewd, gentle eyes. His purposeful stride quickly brought him to her side.

'V, I've been looking for you. I've just been having the most extraordinary talk with Georg. I really don't know what to make of it . . . Hey! Why are you looking at me like that? You're trembling. Are you cold? You ought not to sit out in April . . . V, my darling, what is it?'

It was the first time he had called her 'darling' and the word made the tears run even more freely down her cheeks. He knelt beside her and, rather awkwardly, put his arms around her.

'Tears? What are these for? The fate of nations or something nearer home?'

'Don't be an idiot,' she gulped. 'What do I care for the fate of nations? I care about us – about you. I can see you clearly now.'

'Not until you wipe away your tears, you can't. Here, take my handkerchief. It's quite clean. Is all this about Adam?'

'Yes, I mean no. I thought I loved him. I *did* love him but . . . but it's over. Oh, I'm such a fool! Can you forgive me? I can't forgive myself. It's *you* I love, I can see it quite plainly now. It has always been you – I have just been so caught up in myself . . . so utterly selfish. Can you love me even though I'm what the Duke would call "soiled goods"?' She tried to laugh through her tears.

Edward was taken aback. He took her face in his hands to see if she were serious. 'You mean it?' he said, almost afraid. 'This isn't just – you know – on the rebound? You won't fall in love with someone else at the polo?'

'Don't tease, Edward. I know I deserve it but please don't tease me. I'm serious. I've been thinking about it all week . . .'

'All week?' Edward pretended to be impressed.

'I've been trying to sort myself out. You know I've always loved you but I thought it was as a friend – as a loving friend – but I understand now that you're the only man who can make me happy . . . Am I making any sense?'

'A bit but, dearest V, are you sure? I don't think I could bear it if it turns out to be another mistake.'

'Oh God, how can I make you believe me? I know it's my own fault. I deserve it if you can't believe me ... It's too late, isn't it? You don't ... you don't care for me any more?'

'My darling ...' was all he could say. He half lifted her out of her deckchair and held her to him and, unresisting, she let him. When he began to kiss her face, she kissed him back fiercely, angry with herself for not seeing what everyone else had seen – that he was her man for now ... for ever.

Connie, glancing out of her bedroom window, saw them locked in each other's arms and sighed. So there it was, she thought. Ned had found his woman and won her. There was a tear in the corner of her eye. She had never felt that burning, jealous love – so uncomfortable and difficult to make room for in ordinary humdrum life – and now she knew that she never would. For a moment, she felt naked envy but it was soon replaced by happiness that in a world of violence and betrayal two people could still love one another. It must mean that in the end – the bitter end – human decency would triumph over hatred and despair.

Stuart Rose gazed at Frank enraptured as he swung off his pony, landing lightly on his feet, and took a long glass of lemonade from the silver tray which the butler held out to him. As he raised his head to drain the last drops, the melting ice slid over his chin and fell on to the grass. Rose wanted more than anything to spring up and embrace the boy – smell the sweat already cooling on his chest and lick the wet lips now parted in laughter. Fortunately, his will was much stronger than his lust and he merely smiled and asked Frank to sit beside him for a moment.

Frank had no idea of the emotions he stirred in the man in the deckchair and would not have believed it had he known of them. To him, Rose was a teacher, better than any he had come across at Eton, who had opened his eyes to art and culture. They had been to London galleries together, listened to Beethoven symphonies on the Broadlands radiogram and pored over art books in Rose's bedroom.

In short, Rose had set out to woo him and had been successful but, now that he had him literally at his feet, he did not know what to do. Frank had been chattering away but Rose had heard not a word he said. Perhaps, he thought, it was enough to know that he could make Frank do what he wanted. There was no need to prove it. It was clear that Edward Corinth – whom he had immediately identified as an enemy – had seen what he was about and distrusted his motives in taking on Frank's education. He had to give him his due, however. The uncle had not said a word of warning to his nephew. He was wise enough to know it would only make Frank fly to his mentor's defence. Rose smiled wryly. He had Frank in the palm of his hand and yet could do nothing with his power. Perhaps, after all, he was educating the boy from sheer good nature and his reward was to watch him blossom, quite unaware of the feelings he aroused in his new friend.

Rose, at Owen Coombs' bidding, had insinuated himself into the Mounbatten set and for the past few weeks had virtually lived at Broadlands. During one of his brief visits to London, he had taken the opportunity of going to Cranmer Court – not to meet Verity, whom he knew to be at the *New Gazette*, but to talk to Georg Dreiser. Coombs had told him of Georg's close contacts with a group of scientists working on the bomb which Hitler hoped might win him the war. Coombs had also told him that Georg had to be prevented at all costs from taking the secret of the atomic bomb to the Americans.

'Better Hitler keep his secrets than that. He has to be made to see that his scientist friends must transfer their allegiance to the Soviet Union.'

'And if Dreiser will not be persuaded?' Rose had asked.

'You *must* persuade him,' Coombs said, thumping the table. Verity would have been surprised to see her smiling, easy-going inquisitor so animated.

'But if he won't?' Rose insisted.

'Then you must get rid of him.'

Rose raised his eyebrows. 'I'm a loyal member of the Party,' he drawled, 'but I'm no murderer.'

'The Party decides what you are and what you are not,' Coombs had said flatly.

Georg had heard the knock on the door of the flat and had decided not to answer it. He knew enough about unexpected knocks on the door to be aware that they should not be answered. Then he reminded himself that he was not in Vienna. He was in England and there was no state police to haul him off to some cellar to be beaten into submission by men in black uniforms. He laid aside the precious Dürer drawing which he had been examining with wonder and delight. Cautiously, he opened the door, making sure that it was still on the chain.

Rose – speaking fluent German – was at his most affable and explained that he was a friend of Miss Browne's whom he had met recently at a dinner. He said she had mentioned him and he had dropped by to see if he could be of any help. He had many friends and perhaps he could put him in the way of a job.

Georg was disarmed and let him in. Ten minutes into the conversation, Rose casually mentioned the scientists at the Friedrich-Wilhelms University in Berlin, Pettersson and Brasch. Georg immediately understood why this man had come to visit him. The only mystery was his allegiance. He had already had a brief interview with a young man at the Foreign Office and been dismissed as just another hysterical refugee, not to be trusted or taken seriously, and Georg had left the meeting in despair. Although Edward had promised to put him in touch with someone in authority in the British secret service, his contact had proved elusive and no meeting had yet been arranged. It made Georg nervous and unhappy that he had such vital information but no one would listen. Poor Cassandra! Now he knew what she must have felt bringing news of Troy's doom to those who would not believe her.

For a moment, he had wondered if this man who had come to see him unannounced was Lord Edward's contact but it seemed unlikely – he was too smooth, too American. He might be an agent of the new Reich trying to trap him into revealing what he knew and what he intended to do with his knowledge. He sensed the danger he was in and knew he had to get the man out of the flat even if this meant promising things he had no intention of delivering.

Rose, at his most charming, had suddenly started to talk about the glittering career he would have in the Soviet Union if he cooperated and Georg sighed with relief. An agent of the German Reich might have killed him there and then to stop his mouth. It was clear that this man needed him and he smiled and nodded his head to every blandishment. They talked about Lord Louis Mountbatten and Rose asked if he would be accompanying Verity to the polo match at Broadlands. Georg admitted that he would – not, of course, that he was remotely interested in the game but Verity had made it clear that he would be expected to accompany the Mersham party to watch Frank show off his new-found skills. Georg did not mention that his real motive for wanting to go to Broadlands was to see Joan Miller – who, as Hedwig Kiesler, had been his childhood sweetheart.

Rose seemed satisfied but had made it clear that he would expect a favourable answer from Georg when they met at the weekend as guests of Mountbatten. It was an unlikely rendezvous for a Jewish refugee and an American Communist and, for that very reason, was likely to go unnoticed. Just as he was preparing to leave, Rose noticed the Dürer drawing lying on a table. Georg cursed himself for not having thought to hide it before opening the door. Rose immediately saw what it was and his enthusiasm was unfeigned. He asked how it had come into Georg's possession and if he contemplated selling it. In order to end the conversation, Georg rashly said that he might need to. Rose promised to speak to friends in the art world and, when they met, would give him an idea of its likely value.

'It may be worth many thousands of pounds if it is genuine,' he opined.

Stung, Georg said it was certainly genuine and explained its provenance. Rose left feeling pleased with

himself. He had achieved much more than he had anticipated and the sight of the Dürer had excited him. If he
could not own it, he longed to be the agent commissioned
to sell it. Apart from the financial reward, which would be
considerable, it would make him talked about in the art
world.

Georg, on the other hand, was dismayed by this new
threat. He sat with his head in his hands for some time
after Rose's departure and tried to think what it was best
to do. He was not safe. Even here in England he was not
safe. He wished he hadn't let Rose see the Dürer. He even
wished he hadn't proudly shown it to Verity. It wasn't that
he didn't trust her but . . . He decided not to tell her about
Rose's visit. There was too much to explain and he did not
think she would understand. He did not do her justice but
that was the decision he made.

The Mersham party found Broadlands *en fête* and it
seemed that half the county had been invited to watch the
polo. Lady Louis had still not returned from wherever it
was she preferred to Broadlands but, as her husband
appeared quite unconcerned by her prolonged absence, no
one was brave enough to ask embarrassing questions.
Edward saw him take the Duke aside and heard him
mention Frank as they walked out of earshot. If Mountbatten
wanted to make a friend of Gerald, he could not have
found a better way if, as seemed likely, he was about to
praise his son.

On balance, the Duke was forced to admit that Mountbatten was proving a good influence. Polo had given
Frank a new enthusiasm and, under Mountbatten's
tutelage, he had blossomed – not just as a sportsman but
as a young man with a future. Gone was the sulky boy
who liked to puzzle and enrage his father. In his place,
Gerald found he had a son to be proud of. Connie's
anxiety that he might be lured into a 'fast set' and seduced
into a world of loose morals and high spending now
seemed wide of the mark. True he had been on one or two
'benders', as Edward described them, with Stuart Rose

whom Gerald instinctively disliked as an American and a 'pansy' – fortunately, he was not aware that his son's friend was also a Communist – but as Frank had returned from London enthusing about a painter called Picasso and lecturing him on the Quattrocento he supposed it was all right.

What Connie and Gerald had not understood about Mountbatten was that he was ambitious and, once he had an object in view, every pleasure had to be surrendered to gain it. Although he played hard, he worked harder. He liked fast cars and glamorous women but nothing got in the way of his determination to be first in any sporting endeavour he attempted or, more importantly, to rise to the top of his profession. The navy was what mattered most in his life and he was passing some of his enthusiasm for the service on to Frank.

Mountbatten understood more clearly than most politicians – and some of his superior officers – how unprepared the Royal Navy was to meet the new cruisers and battleships Germany was producing at an alarming rate. Many of the navy's impressive-looking ships were out of date, under-gunned and vulnerable to modern German hardware. Mountbatten was waging a campaign to modernize every aspect of the navy from training to equipment. He was particularly worried about the guns on which the navy's destroyers relied and was trying to persuade the gunnery chiefs to buy the Oerlikon which was why his weekend guests included Helmut Mandl and his wife. Under cover of the festivities, Mandl was to meet the admiral who would decide whether or not to purchase the new gun.

Edward had received a cryptic message from Liddell that Mountbatten had also been prevailed upon to invite Heinrich Braken and he had been told in no uncertain terms that this was his opportunity to make Putzi his 'friend'. He had to be persuaded that his future lay in remaining in England and not returning to Berlin. Edward was dubious that he could do any such thing but, all in all, he was rather looking forward to the day's entertainment. He decided it was going to be what his father would have termed 'a rum do'. So many people who would not in the normal course of events be found at a polo match were to gather for a variety of reasons, none of them sporting. Frank had invited Verity and, rather to Edward's surprise, she had jumped at the idea. Of course, she had always had a soft spot for him and Frank certainly admired her. She was also pleased to have something with which to entertain Georg.

Edward realized that he had never got round to telling her about his extraordinary conversation with Georg at Mersham that morning. He had been about to when he had been distracted by her declaration of love for him which had, naturally, wiped everything else from his mind. Georg had begun by asking when he would be able to talk to Liddell. He had sighed heavily when Edward told him that he still had not pinned Liddell down to a definite date but assured him that what he had to say about the secret development of the bomb would be taken very seriously.

'There's so little time!' Georg had groaned. 'If we are to persuade one of the scientists on the team to come to England, we must act now. There's a real chance something can be done in the next few weeks but . . .' he shrugged his shoulders expressively, 'after that . . . who knows? My friend warned me that the SS were increasing security around them and restricting their movements and that was a month ago.'

Edward, to change the subject, told him that he had met Joan Miller at Broadlands and that she had spoken of him.

'You know she is spending this weekend at Broadlands? You will see her if you come to the polo with us.'

'Her husband's a pig – not above prostituting her to Hitler. Bad luck for him the man's a eunuch.'

Edward had never heard him speak so coarsely and it was obvious he was jealous of Mandl, as well as hating him for being a Nazi arms dealer.

'May I ask . . .' Edward said hesitantly, 'were you and Joan . . . great friends?'

'We were lovers,' Georg replied simply. 'But what could I offer her? A Jew . . . a penniless student. She had to marry a rich successful businessman.'

'Does Mandl know you were lovers?'

'He suspects,' Georg said with satisfaction. 'He does not know but he suspects. He hates the sight of me. I look forward to renewing my acquaintance with him.'

He then began what was to Verity a familiar lament.

'I do not understand, Lord Edward, why you English do not comprehend what is happening to my country. You know, one of the guests at dinner last night – Lady Carlyon, I think she was called – asked me if I knew the Goerings! She said they were such "dear people" and told me how her husband had shot a boar on their estate last year. I mean, what was I supposed to say?'

'Nothing, I hope.'

'Remembering where I was – a guest of your brother, Lord Edward, for whose kindness to me I am truly grateful – I did indeed say nothing. But I must tell you I was tempted to pour my wine over her stupid head.'

Edward pursed his lips and was silent. He understood Georg's frustration and he recognized that he was suffering *amertume de coeur* – bitterness of heart – which, if he did not take care, might destroy him.

Verity was being much more tactile than usual – taking Edward's arm, and even his hand, in public. She had insisted on bringing her dog to the polo – perhaps, Connie suggested to Adrian, as a fashion accessory.

'Beauty and the beast?' Adrian offered.

Certainly, in all his liver-coloured magnificence, Basil set off his mistress who wore a charming blue and white cotton dress with a belted coat and a hat so large it almost dwarfed her.

'That hat makes her look like a mushroom,' Adrian muttered to Connie who giggled guiltily. Connie and Adrian, who were getting on very well together, remarked on the change in Verity.

'Something's happened to make her appreciate what she's got in Edward,' Adrian said, pleased but puzzled.

'I know. I ought not to tell you, I suppose, but I believe I witnessed the moment she agreed to marry him.' Adrian looked shocked. 'I didn't mean to . . . I just happened to look out of the window this morning and there they were . . . the two of them . . . in each other's arms. I didn't hear anything. Oh, do stop looking at me like that, Adrian.'

'Sorry! I'm only teasing. So, you think . . .?'

'Yes, I do.'

So she took my advice, Adrian thought to himself in surprise.

'What happened to that German boy she was so taken with at the cricket match last summer?' Connie inquired.

'You heard that Himmler's thugs kidnapped him in Vienna?'

'No, I didn't. Edward never mentioned it.'

'It was awful. I thought he would have told you. Von Trott was kidnapped in front of Verity's eyes and she thought he must have been sent to a concentration camp.'

'But I thought he came from a very good family. Wasn't his father one of the Kaiser's ministers?'

'That's right. He must have been protected from the worst Himmler could do to him because she eventually got a letter from somewhere in the Far East.'

'The Far East?'

'Yes, he's studying philosophy of all things.'

'And so poor Verity was left . . . ?'

'High and dry.'

'I ought to be sorry for her but really . . .'

'So why are you smiling, Duchess?'

'You must call me Connie. I can't gossip with you like this if you keep on calling me Duchess. Anyway, I wasn't smiling – not much, anyway.'

'One can't help feeling that it serves her right for treating Edward so badly,' Adrian said judiciously, 'but, you know, she never means to be unkind. She's just impulsive and honest about her feelings.'

'A dangerous combination! But you know them both as well as anyone – do you think they are together . . . what shall I say . . .?'

'Permanently . . .? Yes, I think so but who can tell? I've given up thinking I know what's happening in my friends' marriages or relationships.'

'You think they might get married despite Verity's principles?'

'I can only say again – who can tell? Verity has always been dead set against the "bonds of matrimony", as you know, but I think she may be mellowing. Have you noticed that she doesn't lecture us nearly as much on social issues as she used to?'

'You don't mean she might give up being a Communist?'

'I won't go that far, Connie. She still has her principles but she's seen enough in Spain to realize that the British Communist Party is now controlled from Moscow and no Party member can question any instruction – however nonsensical or contradictory it may seem. Now, you know Verity. She won't stand for being muzzled. My bet is she'll be thrown out of the Party before long. They don't like her friends, they don't like Edward and they don't like her coming to this kind of event unless she blows it up. I'm just joking,' he added, seeing the alarm on Connie's face.

'Well, the Lord works in most mysterious ways. All I want is for Ned to be happy. Oh look! Frank's bringing over his nice Indian friend. Isn't he good-looking in his polo clothes!'

Adrian, however, was not looking at Frank. 'She's beautiful,' he said with what might almost have been a sigh of regret. 'There's something about a pretty girl in boots and breeches . . . She's a maharaja's daughter, isn't she?'

'Adrian, I'm shocked,' Connie laughingly rebuked him. 'You're a married man, remember?'

'Don't worry! What hope does any of us have when she looks at Frank the way she's looking at him now?'

Frank was in high spirits and talked of the coming polo match with enthusiasm, all the time glancing at the girl for approval. 'I hope it's not going to rain,' he said, looking up at a particularly black cloud.

'Your brother's not playing, I hear?' Connie asked.

'No, poor lamb,' Sunita said with a smile. 'He's in a bad mood, hoping one of us will get injured so he can step in and save the day.'

'Oh, I hope not! Is polo so dangerous?'

'Don't fuss, Mother!' Frank said. 'Sunita will look after me.'

Connie smiled. Any man would want to impress this girl, she thought. She tried to imagine a scene in which Frank told his father he was marrying an Indian and that a grandson, who would one day be Duke of Mersham, would be brown-skinned but she could not make it convincing.

Edward had wanted to witness Georg's reunion with Joan Miller but, as it turned out, he missed it.

'*Lieber Gott! Hedwig! Immer, immer, Hedwig. Nicht wahr?*'

Georg took her hand and kissed it fervently.

'Georg, is it really you? You escaped?'

They spoke quickly in German knowing that they would soon be interrupted. 'Mandl? He is with you?'

'Of course! And he's in a very evil temper. He had a meeting with an English admiral last night who he hoped would buy his guns but he refused.'

'Ah, that is good! I am glad. The British should have no dealings with the Nazis. So now you go back to Vienna?'

'On Monday.'

'Why do you not stay here? I am lonely. You do not love that man.'

'I cannot, Georg. You know I cannot. My child is still in Vienna. Unless I can find a way of bringing her with me . . . I would never see her again if I left her. I asked your friend, Lord Edward Corinth, to help me. He said he would try and think of something but,' she added gloomily, 'I know no one can outwit Helmut. He hates me now but he still needs me. Hitler has asked to see me again. It is said he watches *Last Night in Vienna* very often . . . too often. He scares me, Georg. If I do not please him then . . .'

'*Schnell*! Don't look round but I see Lord Louis coming towards us. Meet me later at the stables during the polo game, if you can. I have something to say to you . . . for old times' sake.'

'*Natürlich, Liebling . . .*' Then in English – as Hedwig Kiesler became Joan Miller again – she introduced Georg to Mountbatten.

'Herr Dreiser, Lord Edward has been telling me about you. We must talk later.' Turning to Joan and effectively removing her from Georg, he murmured, 'Your husband is disappointed, I am afraid.'

'After his talk to your admiral?'

'Yes, I did my best but . . . I have told him to be patient but he says there is no time and that you must return to Vienna. Tell me,' he said, touching her hand, 'is there anything I can do? I would so like to see you again.'

She gave him her film-star smile. 'I am afraid there is nothing any of us can do, Lord Louis. I want to go to Hollywood and be a film star . . .'

'And I can help you,' Mountbatten said eagerly. 'I have friends . . .'

She raised her hand to stop him. 'Instead, I shall return to my child . . . to Vienna . . . to Berlin. We shall never meet again.'

Mountbatten looked put out. 'Come and talk to Herr Braken. Between ourselves, I think he's a little bored. You know him, don't you?'

'Oh yes, I know Putzi,' she agreed wryly. 'You want me to entertain him for you, Lord Louis?'

'That would be very kind.'

Each team consisted of four players with the Broadlands Fencibles – Ayesha, Sunita and Frank under Mountbatten's captaincy – taking on four sailors from the Bluejackets. There were to be six chukkas of seven minutes each and Mountbatten warned Frank that he would find it exhausting. 'You start with a handicap of minus two goals as a beginner but you should come out with something better.'

'What's your handicap, sir?' Frank inquired.

'Seven,' Mountbatten replied modestly.

'Golly!'

'I like to win, my boy,' Mountbatten said, baring his teeth.

Edward – munching smoked-salmon sandwiches and sipping champagne – was talking to Putzi in the marquee. This was not proving as hard work as he had feared.

Delighted at last to be hobnobbing with the aristocracy Putzi was in high good humour. He was telling Edward about Hitler.

'He has a very sweet tooth, as so many Austrians do. He adores those Viennese cakes piled high with sugared cream. I recall once watching him pouring a heaped tablespoon of sugar into a glass of Prince Metternich's best Gewürztraminer! Fortunately, I was alone with him.'

'Hitler's manners are bad?'

Putzi leant forward and Edward caught a whiff of sour breath. 'Between the two of us, Hitler is the best of the pack. That man Alfred Rosenberg – the Jew-hater – he was with us before Hitler became what he is, you understand. Dear Alfred never washed his shirts. He wore them till they stank and then threw them away. He had the taste of a costermonger's donkey. Boorman's no better. I've seen him sniff his own . . .'

Edward, suddenly nauseous, changed the subject. 'You speak such good English because you were in America before the war?'

'I went to New York after I finished at the Gymnasium in 1905. In many ways, those were the happiest days of my life.'

'And you went to Harvard?' Edward prompted.

'I did and I may say I was much teased for being German. The United States may be a mongrel nation but Harvard is Anglo-Saxon, Christian and moral – very like your Oxford and Cambridge, I imagine.'

Edward wasn't sure how moral his Cambridge had been but perhaps it had been rather smugly Christian and Anglo-Saxon. When he came to think of it, there had been only a handful of Jews and . . . But Putzi was holding forth.

'I think I was popular in my four years there. I became president of the *Deutsche Verein*. I am a *Kunstmensch* – I celebrate all that is good in German culture.'

'Indeed,' Edward said fervently, 'and Hitler likes that . . . culture?'

'No, but he liked me. I played the piano for him. He likes being with superior people.'

And you are superior, Edward thought drily. God help the Reich!

'I introduced the Führer to the Wagners – he adores those interminable operas – and to the Bechsteins and the Bruckmanns . . .' He sounded wistful.

'But not any more, I gather?'

Putzi shrugged. 'Now he thinks only of war. I do not like war. I did not serve in the war, you know. Hitler holds it against me, I feel.'

'And the *Anschluss* – did that come as a surprise?'

'Not at all! I remember – it must have been in 1930 – I was with Hitler at Berchtesgaden. He was standing on the veranda looking across towards Salzburg. He said, "Look, Putzi, I was born over there in Braunau on the Inn." I said to him, "Why don't we drive over and see it?" He replied, "We will one day. It's a real shame it doesn't belong to us but they'll come home into the Reich some day."'

Edward was impressed. However foolish and debauched this man was, he certainly knew Hitler intimately and his insights into the mind of the madman who was threatening to bring disaster on a peace-loving world might well be useful.

'You were very successful looking after the foreign press,' he said, hoping flattery would get him somewhere. 'I remember Miss Browne telling me how you helped a friend of hers . . .'

His eyes narrowed and he wiped his hands on his trousers as though wishing to rid himself of something unpleasant. 'I have heard of her. She is a Communist. I do not like Communists, except perhaps that nice Mr Rose.'

Edward was taken aback. 'Stuart Rose?'

'Yes, he has been talking to me about America. I like America – except for the Jews. The American press always ask about the Jews. I say there are not so many Jews in Germany. Why not ask about the ninety per cent who are not Jews – who were unemployed and starving until the Führer rescued them? Ask me about that. Soon there will be no Jews in Germany for the Americans to worry about.'

Joan Miller appeared beside them looking more melancholy than ever. Putzi brightened. 'Ah, *Liebling*! You will excuse me please, Lord Edward? I must talk to this beautiful lady . . .' He took her hand and kissed it. 'Ach! Those days . . . those happy days . . .'

Edward made himself scarce.

7

'Who's that over there?' Edward – relieved to have done his duty with Putzi – was in a corner of the marquee with Adrian.

'That's Peter Gray's niece, Vera. You remember . . .'

'Of course! I was being stupid. I suppose I didn't expect to see her here.'

'Nor did I but apparently Mountbatten invited her. I've just been talking to her as a matter of fact. She said she was amazed to get a telephone call from him asking her down for the night. She said he was really nice about her uncle . . . He wanted to talk to her about him.'

'So he has got a heart!' Edward exclaimed. 'I would never have thought . . .'

'Stuart Rose is a friend of Mountbatten's – he's here too somewhere and it may have been him who suggested it.'

'Rose! He seems to be everywhere and know everyone.'

'You don't like him?' Adrian queried.

'Do *you* like him?' Edward countered.

'I hardly know him but he seems amiable enough. Of course, he wants to get on – become a famous art critic or something. I'm not a bit surprised Mountbatten encourages him. Rose and Peter Murphy are great chums.'

'That man!' Edward said. 'I've heard about him. He's a queer too, isn't he? Is he here today?'

'Murphy? No. He's in Kenya, I believe, on some sort of jaunt. Here comes Vera. Now be kind to her. I know she wants to ask your advice about something.'

Edward raised his hat. 'Miss Gray – how very nice to see you again.'

'Do excuse me, I see a friend over there,' Adrian said tactfully and walked away leaving Vera to talk to Edward alone.

'I had no idea you were a friend of Stuart Rose.'

'Stuart knows everybody in our little world, Lord Edward.'

'The art world, you mean?'

'Yes.' She looked at him, amused. 'Adrian says you don't much care for artists?'

'That's not true. I certainly like *him*.' She lowered her eyes as though she did not know how to continue. 'What is it, Miss Gray?'

'Well, I . . . But, he tells me, you don't like his paintings.'

'I have to be honest, I don't. But it's all in the eye of the beholder, isn't it?'

'I suppose so . . .' She sounded distracted.

'Did you want to say something to me about your uncle's death?' Edward asked gently.

'Yes,' she said, grateful to be brought to the point. 'Two things really. First of all, the doctor at the inquest said he had taken more than three times his usual dose of ergot.'

'Could he have taken too much by mistake – forgotten he had already dosed himself?'

'That's what the coroner thought. The beastly stuff can give you hallucinations and generally confuse and upset you. Maybe he *was* confused and took a second dose.' She did not sound as if she believed it. 'It's horrible stuff. It can even cause dementia if taken for too long a period, the doctor said.'

'You didn't see any sign that he was . . .'

'Losing his mind? No. He was as sharp as ever. Better than he had been, in fact. He hadn't needed ergot for some time, or so I thought. I was very surprised to discover he had started taking it again.'

Edward looked at her in surprise. Reg Harman had said he was forgetful. 'As sharp as ever'? That didn't ring true. 'Could something have upset him – made him anxious?' he suggested.

'It's possible but he would never have told me if there was. His depressions, which for so many years had been unbearable – so bad that sometimes he talked of ending it all – were not nearly so frequent. For a full year he had not had an attack to my knowledge. His work was going well and his paintings were beginning to sell. He had an exhibition planned, as you know? It's rather beastly but the gallery thinks the publicity about his dying . . . Oh, I can't bear to think about it! People are such ghouls – but they say it will help sell the paintings.'

'That is horrible, Miss Gray, but as long as they are appreciated . . . Was there any other reason why his depressions had eased?'

'Just time passing, I think. It's so long since the war, the memories were fading. That's what he said. It even made him feel guilty that he was no longer so haunted – as though he was betraying his dead friends – but I told him he had paid enough.'

'I see. What was the other thing you wanted to tell me?'

'He didn't keep a diary. He wasn't organized in that sort of way but he had a habit of writing notes to himself on the canvas he was painting – in the top left-hand corner usually. Then, when the picture was almost finished, he would paint them out and transfer any notes he still wanted to his next canvas.'

'And you found something?'

'I was just tidying up his studio and getting things ready for the exhibition. I was looking at the picture he was working on when he died and I suddenly saw it.'

'What?'

'A scribble in the top left-hand corner: R – or it could have been M – Tarn Hill – Sat.'

'Hmm! You've no clue, presumably, to whom he was referring.'

'No, I . . . I was just curious – the two things together.'

'Are you suggesting he might have been murdered?' Edward said slowly.

'No, of course not,' she was panting a little, 'but he might have had a terrible shock . . . Like you said – perhaps something *did* upset him. Something I did not know about.'

Edward wondered what had made Vera change her mind so suddenly. Did she guess what was signified by the scribble on the corner of the canvas?

'It's certainly worth taking a bit further,' he said carefully. 'There's not enough to warrant talking to the police. Leave it with me for the moment and I'll put on my thinking cap. If we could find out who he was going to meet – if indeed there was anybody . . . By the way, what was the picture he was painting?'

'It was another view from Tarn Hill. He had painted it dozens of times but he never seemed to get tired of it.'

'How near to finishing it was he when he died?'

'About halfway. He had a very odd way of painting – from the top of the canvas downwards. I've never known anyone else paint that way.'

'I'd like to see it.'

'The picture's still in his studio in Mornington Crescent. I haven't got round to clearing it out.'

'No, of course not. May I come and have a look next week when we are back in London?'

'Please do.'

'Whatever you do, don't paint over the notes on the canvas.' She gave him a look and he added hastily, 'I know you wouldn't but . . . Put the picture somewhere safe when you get back to town. You never know, it could be evidence of something.'

'You don't think I'm imagining things?'

'No, I don't take you for the type of woman who would imagine something was wrong when it wasn't.'

Vera looked relieved.

'Thank you, Lord Edward. You are very kind to help me. I didn't know who else to ask. Adrian suggested I talk to you.'

'Well, I will do what I can to put your mind at rest, Miss Gray.'

Announcements were made that the polo would begin in half an hour and Verity – thinking that she had neglected Georg – went in search of him. As she walked round the

126

back of the marquee, she saw him talking to another man whom she knew to be Braken. She had heard about him but had not met the man and did not want to. From what Edward had told her, Putzi – as they seemed to call him – was a peculiarly noisome individual and she had no wish to get into a shouting match with him while a guest of Mountbatten. However, it intrigued her that Georg would have anything to say to him and, on an impulse, she hid behind a fold of the marquee and tried to eavesdrop. The conversation was heated and, though she was some distance away, she could hear words and even whole sentences when they raised their voices. Although they were talking in German which she still could not speak fluently, she was able to understand much of what she heard. It took her only a few minutes to make out that they were quarrelling over a woman.

Then she heard the name Hedwig. She did not know a Hedwig but, as she strained to hear, she deduced that each was warning the other off. It appeared that both men regarded this Hedwig as his. A quarrel over a woman, Verity thought – how typical of men! The dispute was becoming increasingly heated and she began to think that, if she did not step in, Georg, who was by far the weaker of the two, might be flattened.

Putzi called Georg a dirty Jew and Georg retaliated with a string of expletives at whose meaning Verity could only guess. His normally pale face was red with anger. Then, just as she had made up her mind to intervene, Putzi turned on his heel and stalked off hissing, '*Kommen Sie nie wieder in meine Nähe oder Ich bringe Sie um!*' 'Stay away from me or I'll kill you.' Georg stopped where he was for a few seconds and then marched off in the other direction. Verity caught a glimpse of his face convulsed with fury and decided not to make herself known. It would be embarrassing to have been so obviously eavesdropping on a private quarrel and she had no wish to upset him further. She would let him cool down and then talk to him.

As she walked round to the front of the marquee and joined the crowd streaming towards the polo ground she saw Edward.

127

'Who's Hedwig?' she said, taking his arm.

'Hedwig? Why, that's Joan Miller. Why do you ask?'

'Oh, I'll tell you after the match. Come on, I want to see Frank on a horse. He's so handsome and I'm not the only one who thinks so.'

'Pony, not horse,' he corrected her, enjoying the feel of her arm under his.

The four Bluejackets, smartly turned out on ponies clearly eager to begin, chatted among themselves while swinging their sticks and doing stretching exercises. They wore the famous Royal Navy blue polo shirt with a diagonal red stripe bordered with white and gave the impression of being slightly bored, as if they could not quite understand why Lord Louis had invited them to play against these amateurs, but his word was law. They did not speak much – they had no need, knowing each other's game so well – but occasionally threw amused glances at Frank who was looking tense. Sunita and Ayesha attracted most of their attention. Mother and daughter – though they could have been sisters – were remarkably alike and it was hard to say which of the two was the more beautiful. Sunny bobbed around offering his wife and daughter unwanted advice while Mountbatten was very attentive to Ayesha who seemed to enjoy it.

The sailors joked *sotto voce* about their chances with Sunita but they could see that she only had eyes for Frank. Her attempt to look as much like a boy as possible only emphasized her femininity. Her slim figure was clad in a red silk shirt and white breeches, her legs encased in gleaming brown boots. Her long black hair was tied primly behind her head with a red ribbon. One of the two grooms – whom she addressed as Jim – was helping her on with her helmet, knee pads and gloves while Mountbatten discussed with her which stick she was going to use.

Harry – still annoyed at not playing – was doing his best to rile Frank.

'Do put a sock in it,' Frank said irritably. 'I know you're sore you're not going to be able to show off in front of the women but at least you can enjoy seeing me make a fool of myself.'

Mountbatten noticed Harry was unsettling Frank and told him off in no uncertain terms. Sulking, the boy made off, muttering imprecations under his breath.

Frank had seen the size of the crowd and had an attack of nerves. Why had he persuaded his mother and father to come? Oh God! And there was Verity and Uncle Ned. His bowels loosened and he wondered if he would have to make a run for the lavatory, but the moment passed. They rode on to the ground to a scatter of applause, the umpire threw in the ball and there was no longer time for fear.

The first chukka passed so quickly Frank never even got to touch the ball. The Bluejackets, insolent in their superiority, outmanoeuvred the Broadlands Fencibles to score twice and Mountbatten, losing his temper, swore a naval oath or two and wrenched savagely and unnecessarily at his pony's bridle. Scenting a walkover, the Bluejackets relaxed in the second chukka and Ayesha shot a goal from under her pony's neck which even her exacting captain had to applaud.

By the fifth chukka, Frank thought he had got the hang of it and swung his stick with all the abandon of a novice. Stretching for a stroke he could not possibly make, he hit his captain in the ribs with his stick – fortunately not very hard – and was treated to a dressing-down by the injured Mountbatten. The game was exhilarating and he suddenly found his eye, scoring twice after taking the ball down the ground and popping it expertly between the flags. Then, at 6-8 to the Bluejackets, disaster struck.

Basil, overexcited by the ponies skidding about chasing a ball in front of him, tore his lead from Verity's grasp. He leapt over the low boards which kept the ball in play and disappeared among the ponies' hooves in hot pursuit of the ball. Verity screamed as she caught a glimpse of him charging straight into the path of Sunita's pony. She never had any chance of avoiding the dog and there followed a mêlée of flying limbs – equine, canine and human. Sunita was thrown straight over the head of her pony which, unable to stop, kicked her as it tried to regain its balance.

Basil, terrified by the chaos he had caused, ran across the pitch dodging flying hooves and disappeared into the crowd. At this moment the heavens opened and the rain fell as though a giant bucket of water had been thrown over the struggling players.

Verity, her hands to her face, watched in horror as the two umpires and the grooms rushed to Sunita's aid. Frank, his heart in his mouth, leapt off his pony to join Ayesha and Mountbatten who were already on the ground beside her. There was no immediate sign of blood and it was difficult to know how badly she had been hurt. Mountbatten, cursing the dog and its owner, gently took off Sunita's helmet and was relieved to find that it seemed to have given her some protection.

If this had been a proper match, rather than a friendly, a St John's Ambulance team would have been on hand but Mountbatten had not thought it necessary given the nature of the event. He immediately despatched the grooms to fetch a stretcher and to summon an ambulance using the telephone he had recently installed in the stables. Fortunately, there was a doctor among the onlookers who pushed through the small crowd surrounding the girl. Sunny, in a frenzy, danced about his daughter, splashing himself and everyone around him with mud. Mountbatten angrily told him to calm down.

Everyone waited anxiously, disregarding the rain, until the doctor had finished his examination and judged that Sunita could safely be moved. In truth, she could hardly stay where she was. Umbrellas had been raised over her but provided very little protection against the downpour. The grooms returned from the stables with a stretcher to say that an ambulance was on its way. Sunita was gently lifted on to the stretcher and carried back to the house. Mountbatten, his face now streaked with mud and rain, asked the doctor how badly hurt she was.

'Hard to tell until we get her to the hospital. She's badly bruised where the pony's hooves connected with her stomach and at least one rib and her left arm are broken. She's concussed but how badly I can't tell. The important thing is to discover if there is any internal bleeding.'

Verity was consumed with guilt at having let Basil tear himself from her and cause such havoc. It was no good Edward trying to reassure her or Connie telling her it was just an accident.

'I just couldn't hold on to him. He's so strong and I wasn't expecting . . . Will she be all right? Should I go to the hospital?'

'No one's going to blame you, V. It was just an accident. Polo's a dangerous game. Everyone knows that,' Edward said unhappily.

'Yes, but . . .'

'We can't do anything to help Sunita. There are plenty of people to look after her – her parents, Frank, Lord Louis, Harry – where is the boy, by the way? Let's go and find Basil, shall we? I've no idea where he's got to but he needs a good ticking off. He must learn to behave.'

They walked across the sodden grass – fortunately the rain had stopped as suddenly as it had begun – to where they had last seen Basil and began calling his name and whistling.

'I hope he hasn't gone for miles,' Verity said anxiously. 'There's the main road over there.'

'Let's go towards the stables. He may have hidden himself there. He knows he's in disgrace.'

As they approached the paved courtyard around which the stables were built, they heard a howling noise.

'Is that Basil?' Verity said in alarm. 'He sounds as though he's in pain. I wonder if he's hurt. Perhaps one of the ponies kicked him.'

'Serve him right if they did,' Edward said grimly.

They quickened their pace and soon came to the gate into the stables.

'There he is!' Verity cried, pointing towards the other side of the courtyard. 'What's he doing? He seems to be howling at the moon, except there isn't one.'

Edward's brow furrowed. 'Do you hear that, V? It sounds as though one of the ponies is kicking his stable to bits.'

As they approached, the noise from the stable increased to a steady but violent beating of hooves against wood.

Verity grabbed hold of Basil by the lead still attached to his collar. She patted his head distractedly as the dog wrapped himself around her legs, his eyes bulging and his ears twitching uncontrollably.

'Look at him! He's spooked – no wonder, with that noise. See what's the matter, Edward. Why is that pony going wild in there? It's horrible.' She put her hands over her ears.

Edward peered gingerly through the top half of the stable door, which was open, but pulled back abruptly. The pony was facing away from him, his hooves flying up as though desperately kicking at something of which he was very afraid. But it was not the beating hooves which made Edward retreat in horror. A pile of what for a second he thought were old clothes lay just to one side of the stable door. It was not a pile of clothes he saw when he looked again but the remains of a human being. The head had been smashed to a bloody pulp and the body tossed to one side by the flailing hooves of the terrified animal.

At that moment there were shouts and the two grooms ran up to ask what they were doing.

'You're Johnson, aren't you?' Edward said, recognizing one of the men who had been holding Frank's pony before the match started. 'There's been some sort of frightful accident. We heard the dog howling and the pony kicking his stall. When I looked in, I saw . . . Well, see for yourself. There's a dead body in there – kicked into a bloody mess. It's not a pleasant sight.'

'Christ!' exclaimed Johnson. 'No one ought to have gone in with Button. He had his oats ready for the game and then went lame. Till he's exercised he'll be . . . Oh, Christ!' he repeated, covering his mouth with his hands as he saw what Edward had seen.

'Can you get the pony out without touching the body?'

Johnson nodded. 'Come on, Jim. Stop looking like you're going to be sick and help me get Button out into the yard.'

As the grooms entered the stable, the pony lashed out even more frenziedly and their efforts to calm him seemed to make the animal more violent. Finally, Johnson got hold of his head but it wasn't until the second groom had administered a sedative that the beast quietened and he was able to lead him out past the body.

'There you go, Button,' Jim crooned, stroking his head. 'All right now. There's a good boy. Walk on. Nothing to worry about.'

Once in the courtyard, the pony became docile, whether because he was clear of the corpse and the smell of blood or because of the sedative, Edward could not tell. He closed the stable door and turned back to the pony. As far as he could see, Button was no longer lame. 'Don't wash his hooves,' he ordered the grooms. 'The police may need to examine the blood on them. Where's the telephone?'

'At the other end of the stable block,' Johnson told him, pointing across the yard. As Edward turned to go, he added, 'See here, my lord. It looks as though Button's been drugged. You see the eyes? They're bulging and the pupils ... that don't look right. And the foam round his mouth ... I've never seen the like.'

'You're sure it's not just his fear of the blood? I've heard a horse can go wild if it is taken near a corpse,' Verity asked.

'I wouldn't say so, Miss. Button's been got at – no doubt about it. I'll be damned if he hasn't been given something. It ain't natural. I'll ring the vet and get him to come and have a look.'

'Yes, do that,' Edward agreed, 'but first the police. By the way, Johnson, you didn't hear anything when you came to get the stretcher? I mean, presumably, if you had heard the pony kicking his stall or the dog howling you would have investigated?'

'Of course and we didn't. Mind you, the stretcher is the other end of the block near the telephone and it was raining hard.'

'You heard nothing, then?' Edward repeated.

'The rain on the corrugated iron roofs makes a hell of a racket.'

Edward grimaced. 'Well, no time to lose. I'll go and phone the police while you look after the pony. And, V, take that dratted dog away. We don't want to start anything else.'

133

Verity had the feeling he was calling her 'dratted' rather than Basil and it made her feel even more guilty, as though she had been responsible for the horror in the stable.

'Have you any idea who it is . . . in the stable, I mean?' she asked him.

'It's a man. That's all one can say for sure.'

'You don't recognize the clothes?'

'A dark suit – I'm not sure. It could be Mandl.'

'Mandl?'

'It could be – that's all I'm saying. It's probably someone we don't know.'

He strode off to find the telephone while the grooms continued to walk the pony round the courtyard.

Verity took Basil off to the other side of the courtyard into a barn half-full of hay bales. She attached his lead to a convenient peg and he sank down disconsolately and looked appealingly at her.

'Stay there,' she said sternly. 'You are a very wicked dog. You'll probably end up in a police cell and it's no good you looking at me like that.'

As she went out into the cobbled courtyard, she saw that a tyre from a car or motorbike had left a distinct mark in the mud at the entrance to the barn. She decided to bring Edward to look at it. However, when she walked back to Button's stable, he had still not returned. Curiosity overcoming her disgust, she pushed open the top half of the stable door and peered into the darkness. As her eyes adjusted to the light, she saw the bloody bundle and momentarily retreated. She had seen many horrible things in Spain but it was different seeing death here in the stables of an English private house where everything was so ordered and nothing more warlike than a polo match threatened the peace.

She peered into the stable again. Could it be Mandl? She could not mourn the death of such a man – an arms dealer and a friend of Hitler's whose wife feared and loathed him – but even so, to die in this way was too beastly. She stared intently at the bloody bundle of clothing and then let her eye pass to the straw in which the pony had been standing. She saw something shiny – a cigarette lighter, she thought, but she could not be sure. She was tempted to dash in and retrieve it but, with commendable self-restraint, decided to wait until the police arrived. She was irresistibly drawn back to the bloodied corpse. There was something about it . . . and this time she noticed the shoes. She was almost certain she had seen them before. They were . . . but surely she was imagining it? No, she was certain . . . terribly certain that they belonged to Georg Dreiser.

With a cry of despair she turned and ran towards Edward who was crossing the courtyard having telephoned the police. She flung herself into his arms, weeping.

'For God's sake, what is it? V, tell me, please. What's happened?'

'It's Georg,' she sobbed.

'What is . . .? You don't mean . . .?'

'Yes, I do,' she said, with passion. 'We brought Georg from Austria to save him . . .' She could not speak for a moment or two for the sobs that racked her. 'We thought we were rescuing him from death but we weren't . . . we were bringing him towards it. He hated horses – he told me so. What was he doing in the stables? Georg! He trusted me and now he is dead. Oh God, Edward, tell me I am wrong. Tell me Georg's not dead. That it's someone else.'

But that he could not do.

8

'Someone's got to tell his parents.' Connie looked round the table until her eyes came to rest on Verity. It was Sunday morning and the gloom was almost palpable.

'I'll go to Vienna if they'll let me. I just hope I can get a visa.'

Verity was feeling guilty. No one had said anything but she could feel that everyone – particularly the Duke and Duchess – blamed her for the accident on the polo ground. If she had held on to Basil, Sunita would not now be lying in hospital in considerable pain. Much less reasonably, she felt responsible for Georg's death. She even felt guilty – and this really was absurd – that it was her dog which had discovered the body. It was, as she had said to Edward, as though everything she touched ended badly.

He had told her she was taking too much upon herself. 'There's a sort of arrogance in thinking that any one of us can be responsible for accidents beyond our control. The only person responsible for Georg's death is whoever it was who shut him in the stable with a demented pony and that wasn't you.'

'They'll never let you back into Vienna,' he now said harshly. 'You've got to face that, V. If by some miracle they did, you would be followed the whole time and prevented from seeing or talking to anyone other than Nazi officials. You might actually put Dreiser's parents in danger if you drew attention to them. I will go. I haven't got a choice in the matter. I owe it to him to see if I can help his father get out of Austria. He wanted to bring his parents to England. He can't do that now. It's the least I can do to try for him.'

'Oh, but is it safe?' Connie was suddenly conscious of what she had done. It hadn't occurred to her that her brother-in-law would take on what she had assumed was Verity's obligation.

'Of course it's safe,' Edward said roughly. 'I'm not a Jew or a Communist and since, at the moment, we are not at war with Germany I can travel as a tourist and no one can object. I shall be in a much better position than Verity to help the Dreisers. I have some pull with the Embassy people, and, with Gerald's letter in my pocket offering him a job here, I should have no difficulty in getting them visas.'

Edward was less confident than he made out. If Herr Dreiser had been sent to some sort of camp, it might not be as easy as he pretended. However, he had another reason for wanting to go to Vienna. Georg had told him about his scientist friends at the university and the secret project on which they were working. He might be able to find out something or, better still, persuade at least one of them to come to England. He recognized that this was probably unrealistic but it was worth a try.

'Well, Ned, you must do what you think best,' the Duke said. 'I knew it was a mistake getting involved with Mountbatten. None of this would have happened if Frank had stayed at home.' Edward reddened as this remark was clearly aimed at him. 'To be killed by a polo pony! It would be absurd if it weren't so bloody awful.'

Edward had hardly ever heard his brother swear and realized Gerald was taking it as hard as anyone.

'I still don't understand why Georg had gone to the stables,' Verity broke in. 'I remember him telling me that he didn't like horses and they didn't like him. We were talking about the Spanish Riding School in Vienna and – what are they called – the horses that dance?'

'The Lipizzaners . . .' Edward prompted her.

'Yes. He said he was frightened of everything equine.'

'Ned, didn't you say the stable door wasn't locked?' Connie asked.

'When we got there, it wasn't. In fact, the top half was open.'

'So why didn't Georg just get out when the pony started acting up?'

'I don't know but I can think of several reasons why he might not have been able to. Button might have lashed out and knocked him unconscious before he knew anything about it.'

'We must hope that was what happened,' the Duke growled.

'Or he might have got disorientated and not been able to find the bolt to let himself out if, for some reason, he had pulled it across when he entered the stable.'

'But why was he in there in the first place, Ned?' Connie insisted.

'He might have been avoiding someone or, of course, he might have been lured into what he thought was an empty stable.'

'To meet someone?' Verity asked.

'Yes.'

'Or someone might have lured him into the stable and then bolted the door after him.'

'Oh, Verity, that's too horrible,' Connie expostulated. 'But, anyway, the door wasn't bolted.'

'That same person might have undone the bolt to check Georg was done for,' Edward pointed out.

'I don't believe it!' the Duke said. 'You're imagining things. It was just an accident.'

'I don't think it was an accident,' Verity said pugnaciously. 'I know who killed him.'

'You do?' Connie asked eagerly.

Verity turned to Edward. 'It was your friend Putzi. I heard him threaten to kill Georg over . . .' She glanced at the Duke, unsure how much to say in front of him. 'Over a woman.'

'Over a woman?' the Duke exclaimed.

'They had both been lovers of Joan Miller, Gerald,' Edward explained calmly.

'But – damn it! – she's got a husband.' The Duke was outraged.

'Yes,' Connie said. 'And what about Herr Mandl? Might he not have been jealous?'

'Indeed he might,' Edward agreed. 'Joan never stops telling me how possessive he is.'

'Well, I don't want you getting involved in this, Ned. It's nothing to do with you.'

'I'm sorry, Connie, but it's everything to do with us,' Verity burst out. 'I don't care what you do, Edward, but I am certainly going to try and find out who killed Georg. I brought him here so his death is my responsibility, whatever you say.'

The butler came into the drawing-room to say that Edward was wanted on the telephone. It was with some relief that he followed him out into the hall and picked up the receiver. It was Liddell and he sounded displeased.

'I understand you allowed Dreiser to be murdered before I had a chance to talk to him,' he began, not waiting for Edward to speak. 'That wasn't very clever of you. I hope Putzi is safe.'

'I need to talk to you,' Edward replied, refusing to rise. 'I'm going to Vienna to see if I can bring out Dreiser's parents but there is something else which I can't discuss on the telephone.'

There was a pause before Liddell said, 'All right. I'll come to Brooks's tomorrow at eleven.' He rang off without asking Edward if that was convenient.

Later, as she and Edward were walking by the river, Verity asked, 'Do you think there is any connection between Peter Gray's death and Georg's?'

'Could be – who knows? What will you do while I'm in Vienna? I mean, when are you expecting to go to Prague?'

'Not for a week or two. They're still trying to get my papers sorted out. Shall I do some sniffing about while you're away?' She sounded almost timid as if expecting him to say that she had done enough damage as it was and should let things be until he was back, but he did not.

'Why don't you follow up on Vera Gray? I won't have time to see her now I have to go to Vienna. See what you can find out. Keep an open mind but try to discover if there is any reason to think Gray was murdered and, if he was, if there is any connection with Georg's death. On the face of it, it seems unlikely but two sudden deaths in the grounds of Mountbatten's country house in such a short time is at least one death too many. I told you what Vera said about the notes Gray had scribbled on the canvas. Why not take Adrian with you? She trusts him.'

'And she won't trust me?' Verity retorted with some of her old spirit.

'Not at all. I was going to say that she might talk more freely to a woman. I think there is something else she has to tell us but exactly what I don't know. Her uncle was coming to meet someone at Broadlands and he died full of a drug there was no reason for him to have taken.'

'And Button was drugged?'

'Maybe. He was certainly spooked. Hey! Do you think we have a mad doctor around here somewhere?' Edward laughed.

'Or a mad vet. I say, Edward, do you think it's all right for me to stay on here, even for a night? I mean, I know your brother blames me . . . and Connie . . . I think she'll now blame me for putting you in danger by going to Vienna.'

'I told you – I won't be in any danger and of course they don't blame you for anything. You are always welcome here.'

Verity looked doubtful but bit her lip and said nothing.

'I tell you what,' he said after a moment's thought, 'you're going to visit Sunita this afternoon, aren't you? I'll drive you into Romsey and, while you are dispensing grapes and sympathy to the invalid, I'll drop in on Inspector Beeston and then we'll drive on to London. How's that?'

Inspector Beeston was a large, florid-faced man in his late forties with mutton-chop whiskers and alcohol on his breath.

'You think, Lord Edward, that this Mr Dreiser was killed for his valuable drawing?'

'It's possible. I thought you might like to look at this book. It has a reproduction of the picture by Albrecht Dürer – in black-and-white, of course.'

'You have seen it?'

'Miss Browne has and she recognized it in this book of Dürer's paintings which we found in my brother's library.'

Beeston took off his spectacles, blew on them and rubbed them with a none-too-clean handkerchief. When they were back on his nose, he took the book Edward proffered him and looked at the picture.

'I thought you said, Lord Edward, that the piece of art we are looking for was a drawing? This is a painting.'

Edward gritted his teeth. 'The drawing is a study Dürer made before painting the picture. It was probably part of a sketch-book.'

'No picture of that, then?'

'No,' Edward said shortly.

Beeston removed his spectacles again and chewed one end reflectively. 'And it's only three inches square, you say?'

'But worth many thousands of pounds to collectors or galleries.'

'And you want us to advertise to the galleries and auction rooms that such a picture has gone missing?' the policeman repeated deliberately.

'You could not sell such a work of art without someone recognizing it and inquiring how it came on the market,' Edward said patiently.

Beeston scratched his head. 'To be honest with you, my lord, I would not know how to go about doing that.'

'Perhaps I might be able to help.' Edward did his best not to sound patronizing. 'I have friends in the art world who could circulate the description . . .'

'You have friends in that world? I am sure you do, Lord Edward.'

This man does not like me, Edward said to himself. There was something a touch derisory in the deliberate manner in which he reiterated 'Lord Edward'. He's not going to let me help and the sooner I get out of here the better, he decided. However, he thought he might as well make an effort to find out if the police had discovered anything about either of the deaths.

'As you know, I was there, Inspector, when Mr Gray's body was found. Might I ask if you have decided whether his death was an accident or murder?'

'Murder? Ah! But you are something of an amateur detective, are you not, Lord Edward?' Beeston opened wide his small piggy eyes and, with mock geniality, reprimanded him as he might a naughty schoolboy. 'I am afraid I would not be able to discuss a murder investigation with you, Lord Edward, but, since we are satisfied that it was an accident, I see no harm in putting your mind at ease. The poor gentleman was in the habit of taking some medicine . . .'

The Inspector coughed. Clearly, he could not recall its name so Edward prompted him. 'Ergot.'

'That's the stuff! To help him cope with headaches and all . . . from shell shock during the war.' Beeston tried to look sympathetic. 'To be honest with you, Lord Edward, he was not a well man. He may have committed suicide but there's no direct evidence . . . no note, you understand . . . so for his niece's sake at least, we'll call it an accident.'

'And Mr Dreiser? Was his death in the stables an accident too?'

'We are still investigating,' Beeston said a trifle haughtily and Edward realized his question must have sounded sarcastic. 'I don't mind telling you, my lord, that all these refugees . . . we can't tell what is making them flee their countries . . .'

'The Nazis are killing Jews,' Edward said angrily.

'Maybe so, sir. I know nowt of politics but some, they say, are criminals on the run, if you get me.'

Beeston gave him a knowing look and, for a moment, Edward thought he might actually tap his nose in the approved gesture but he seemed satisfied with a smirk of self-satisfaction.

'But that's quite absurd,' Edward exploded. 'Miss Browne has told you about his background and his parents are most respectable people.'

'I dare say so, my lord. If you can vouch for him . . .'

'And Miss Browne . . .'

'Ah! Miss Browne. Sources have revealed to me,' Beeston said laboriously, 'that she is a Communist.'

'Is that relevant?' Edward asked stiffly.

'Jews and Communists . . . I don't know but that Sir Oswald Mosley doesn't have the right of it. Too many of both in my opinion.'

Edward left Romsey police station more depressed than ever. As he drove to the hospital, he thought about his interview with the Inspector. Was Beeston typical of the police? No, he could not believe that. He knew many intelligent, unprejudiced policemen. Well then, was he typical of the population as a whole? Did most people hold that Communists and Jews were . . . not to be trusted, to put it no more strongly? He very much feared that was exactly the view of 'most people'.

Verity laughed hollowly when Edward reported on his unfruitful interview. 'I don't doubt Inspector Beeston would arrest me for murdering Georg if he could find a shred of evidence. After all, we were first on the scene.'

'Yes, and I was also there when Gray's body was found. Very suspicious!'

Verity had been unsure of the welcome she would receive when she visited Sunita but the girl had quickly put her at her ease and assured her she did not blame her for the accident.

'It's a dangerous game – polo. That's what makes it so much fun. We live such a safe life – not like you – so we have to make our own danger. Silly really, I suppose.'

Sunita had broken an arm and cracked a rib but it could have been worse. Her concussion had not been severe and the ache in her head was beginning to fade.

'She says she doesn't blame me or Basil,' she told Edward as they drove away from the hospital, 'but, of course, I blame myself.'

'Was Frank there?' he asked.

'No, he's in London with Stuart Rose but he's rung up several times and he'll be in to see her as soon as he

143

returns. I really believe they must be in love. Sunita certainly is. It was so touching seeing her blush every time his name came up – and that was every five minutes!'

'A beautiful girl languishing in bed, ill but not so ill that she can't smile at her admirer. I know what it's like,' Edward said smugly.

'You do, do you? Well, I'd just like to remind you how I nursed you when you were shot saving the Duke of Windsor.'

'Come on, V! I don't recall much nursing. You were too busy writing your story for the *New Gazette* and . . .'

'You don't know what I did. I was kicking various backsides so you got the best treatment.'

'I'll give you the benefit of the doubt. So, Frank is in London with Rose? I really can't bear that man. There's something very sinister about him.'

'You're just prejudiced because he's a homosexual.'

'It's not that. I must say I was hurt to hear that Frank has asked Rose to accompany him to his interview for the navy. I would have been only too pleased . . .'

'I don't expect you have to worry about whether Frank gets into the navy or not,' Verity said sourly. 'I mean, I bet Lord Louis has a word with the powers that be. Isn't that the way the world works? I don't suppose the navy is any different from the City or the Law. In any case,' she continued, relenting, 'surely Frank is just the sort of young man the navy's going to need if there is a war. By the way, I got the impression HMS *President* is a ship on dry land. Can that be right?'

'I believe she never moves from her mooring on the Embankment, certainly.' He changed the subject. 'Where are Sunny and Ayesha staying? Mountbatten must be getting a bit fed up with them hanging about at Broadlands.'

'He has been very kind, Sunita says, and they are to stay as long as they want but I don't think it will be more than a few days. Sunita hopes to be out of hospital in the next day or two. Her arm's in plaster, of course, and her ribs still hurt but basically she's on the mend.'

'Talking of Mountbatten,' Edward said as he roared across Romsey's only pedestrian crossing, its Belisha beacon flashing in protest, 'I'm going to ask him if he will let me talk to his grooms. Beeston obviously won't oblige and I am convinced they've still something more to say.'

On the drive back to London, Verity could only think about one thing – Georg's death. She had left Mersham after the briefest of goodbyes to her hosts. On a whim, and taking no notice of Edward's objections, she had decided to take Basil back to town with her. They were both in disgrace and it was time she and her dog made themselves scarce. She had smuggled Basil in to see Sunita and he had licked her hand in puzzled apology.

Uncharacteristically silent as the Lagonda sped on its way, Verity suddenly found her eyes fill with tears. With an angry shake of her head she told herself not to be sentimental. There was work to be done. She took out her vanity mirror and repaired her smudged mascara. Edward had noticed nothing, she saw. He was deep in his own thoughts, seemingly unaware she was even beside him. As the fields gave way to London's suburbs, grief for Georg gave way to anger – anger at fate, anger at herself. She wore her guilt like a cilice, her conscience rubbed raw by her penitential hair shirt. Georg was dead when he should have been safe. Sunita was in hospital with concussion and a broken arm and Edward was preparing to depart on a mission she felt *she* ought to undertake. How much Edward must love her, she thought, if he was prepared to cross Europe on her behalf to give Georg's father and mother the worst news any parent could be asked to hear. She glanced across at him, stern and determined, driving hard and fast like an automaton. She rested her hand on Basil's head for comfort and he nuzzled her.

There was to be an inquest, of course, but, according to Edward, the police had already decided that Georg's death was a tragic accident. Inspector Beeston had not even asked to interview her. It was a relief in some ways but she was outraged that, because Georg was a Jewish refugee, his death was not thought worth a thorough investigation. Beeston's priority, Verity decided, was to keep Mountbatten and his family out of the newspapers. Whatever happened, they must not be soiled by scandal.

Well, she for one and – she knew – Edward for another were not going to let sleeping dogs lie. Georg had been lured down to the stables by someone. It was the last place he would choose to visit in the normal course of events so he must have had a good reason to go there. In her mind Putzi was the chief suspect but how could anything be proved against him? If the police were not prepared to question him, she certainly could not. That meant Edward had to and surely this must be his first task when he returned from Vienna. In the meantime, as he had suggested, she would try to discover what lay behind Peter Gray's death. Just because it did not matter to her as Georg's death mattered, she could approach the problem coolly and rationally.

Edward dropped her off in Sloane Avenue and they parted with hardly a word and a peck on the cheek.

9

As Deutsche Lufthansa wafted him towards Munich from where he would take the train to Vienna, Edward closed his book and contemplated the swastika painted on the wing. It disgusted him to have to fly in such a plane but he had no option. The cotton wool handed out to passengers by the stewardess did little to lessen the noise of the engines which made reading tiring. He had bought a copy of Dashiell Hammett's *The Thin Man* at the aerodrome's bookstall in an effort to look like a tourist but somehow he found he wasn't in the mood for American high jinks. He refused the proffered luncheon basket, preferring the sandwiches Fenton had prepared for him. He shivered slightly despite his coat and gloves and wondered if he was coming down with a cold. He hoped Fenton had packed his Beecham powders.

Liddell had not been helpful or encouraging. He had grudgingly acknowledged that Georg's information about the work being carried out in Germany on developing an atomic bomb might be of interest to government scientists but seemed to imply that Edward should have done more to keep him alive, at least until he, Liddell, had had a chance to interview him. He asked how far he had got ingratiating himself with Putzi and Edward had to confess that he had not got very far.

Liddell shook his head mournfully and dismissed him. 'Don't let me down, Corinth,' he said as they shook hands outside Brooks's. 'Ferguson said you were a good man but still an amateur. Prove to me he's wrong about that last bit, will you?'

He marched off down St James's Street straight of back, head held high, very much the retired army officer, leaving Edward discomfited. *Was* he an amateur? It was true he guarded his independence but he was serious about the jobs he undertook. Anyway, what did it mean to be a professional in the game he was playing? After all, he wasn't some American 'private eye'.

When he reached Vienna, he was bone weary. The whole journey had taken almost twenty-four hours and though – with German efficiency – the plane and the train had been on time and, in the case of the train, comfortable and clean, he had not slept well. The Imperial, however, was more a palace than a hotel and his room was vast and the bed reminiscent of the Great Bed of Ware. He was only sorry that this was not a holiday jaunt with Verity. She loved luxurious hotels, despite her egalitarian principles, and would have shrieked with excitement at the bathroom. He relaxed in the great iron bath, sighing with pleasure as he squeezed the sponge over his head and let the hot water wash away the fatigue. Then he permitted himself an hour's nap before dressing for dinner.

He always felt renewed when he saw himself in the mirror in white tie and tails. He wasn't a vain man but he had a firm belief – never to be put into words – in the superiority of the English gentleman and this was one of his uniforms. In the African jungle or an Indian provincial town, the English gentleman would dress as he was dressed now to partake of his evening meal. It was absurd, even ridiculous, but for a century it had helped preserve the illusion that the British brought civilization to the furthest corner of the Empire.

And now, when the Empire faced danger on every side, it was all the more important to keep up appearances. When he presented his passport in Munich he had been ushered through with a salute while some poor devil jabbering away in a tongue he did not recognize was made to grovel. He hated what the Nazis were doing to decent people with the wrong papers or the wrong accent. Georg Dreiser had escaped this evil regime only to die in England. It made him angry and determined to find his killer but first he had to do what he could to rescue his parents.

He had no particular plan except to go to the Dreisers' apartment and escort them to the British Embassy to get the visa they needed. Liddell had given him the name of his man in the Embassy – Major Ruthven-Stuart – who was designated Honorary Attaché. The ambassador, Sir Michael Palairet, had been withdrawn in protest at the creation of what was now being called *Grossdeutschland* and it seemed likely that the Embassy would be downgraded to a consulate.

The Dreisers lived close to Beethoven's house in the Döblinger Haupt-Strasse. It was a typical Viennese apartment occupying the top two storeys of what had once been a large family house. It was spacious but dark and gloomy. As Edward gave his name and was shown into the drawing-room the following morning by a maid in uniform, his heart failed him. He had a strong desire to turn tail and flee the city while he still had the chance. For some reason, it had never occurred to him that one or both of the Dreisers might be out but, as it happened, both were at home. Frau Dreiser was a petite sparrow of a woman in her late fifties, Edward guessed. Her hair was quite white and she had in her eyes the look of someone who expected the worst. Her husband was stick-like but the loose flesh about his face suggested that he had once been as fleshy as his son. He, too, looked apprehensive and Edward began to appreciate what it must mean to dread every knock on the door.

He began in halting German to explain who he was but Frau Dreiser interrupted him. 'Lord Edward,' she said in good though heavily accented English, 'please, we have many English friends and indeed I used to teach English. Have you come to give us news of Georg? He mentioned your name and we are very grateful for the help you gave him.'

Edward's heart lurched and for a moment he felt unable to breathe. 'I am afraid I have some very bad news . . .'

'Georg reached England safely. He wrote to us. It made us so happy. He said how warmly he had been welcomed by you and Miss Browne.' Frau Dreiser was nervous but had not yet allowed herself to be alarmed. She offered him a glass of *Sekt* as though they were to drink Georg's health.

'No, thank you, Frau Dreiser. I'm afraid . . . Georg was staying with my brother at Mersham Castle when the accident . . .'

Herr Dreiser lifted his right hand as though he would stop him and spoke for the first time and his voice was anguished. 'Georg is dead . . . ?'

'I can't tell you how sorry I am to have to tell you but, yes, he is dead.'

Dreiser took his wife's arm and led her to an uncomfortable-looking gilt sofa. He waved to Edward to be seated. 'Please, Lord Edward, tell us how this could have happened. We thought if he reached England he would be safe.'

'He was at the stables in Lord Louis Mountbatten's house and one of the horses went wild and . . . and I am afraid he was kicked in the head.'

'I don't understand,' Frau Dreiser said. 'Georg did not like animals. He had never ridden a horse. He was a city boy . . .'

'We think he may have been meeting someone . . .'

'Please, Lord Edward, I realize how hard this must be for you but we must know the truth. Are you telling us that the man our son went to meet killed him?'

'It is possible but we do not know yet. Perhaps it was an accident.'

The Dreisers remained silent. Edward wished Frau Dreiser would weep but it seemed her grief was too deep for tears. At last Herr Dreiser spoke again. 'He had enemies. He wrote to us . . . he mentioned . . .'

'He mentioned enemies . . . ?' Edward was alert.

'He mentioned that some people he had known in Vienna were staying nearby at the house of Lord Mountbatten. Hedwig Kiesler, the actress – she calls herself Joan Miller – and her husband, the arms dealer . . .'

'Yes, he told me he knew Joan before she was married.' Edward did not feel able to ask if they knew their son had been Joan's lover. 'Who else might have wanted to . . . to harm him?' Herr Dreiser gave a helpless shrug. 'Excuse me, Herr Dreiser, but if it was not an accident . . . if Georg was killed . . . then we must bring the murderer to justice.'

'To justice . . .?' Frau Dreiser said, her voice sharp with pain. 'There is no justice in this world. My son escapes the Nazis and dies in England where he should have been most safe.'

'Hush, Gretel, *meine Liebe*, we must not give way to our grief. It is the will of God that we must suffer as our people have always suffered.'

'May I see Georg's letter?' Edward asked.

Without a word, Herr Dreiser walked over to a desk, opened a drawer and took out an envelope and handed it over. Edward thought he had visibly aged since he had arrived at the apartment. He took out two thin sheets of paper covered in a spidery hand.

'Is your German good enough to read it?' Herr Dreiser asked with studied courtesy. 'Here, let me translate.'

Taking back the letter he read, '"Dear Mother – I have arrived safely in England and I am staying at the apartment of my friend Miss Browne. Everyone is being most kind but I feel worried about you and Papa and I am homesick. Is Papa now with you as you hoped? Lord Edward Corinth, who I told you about, has arranged for his brother to offer you a job and a little money to work at Mersham Castle. A letter will follow. This should be enough for you to get a visa to follow me here. At least I pray it is so.

'"I saw in London someone I did not expect to be here and whom I fear. I shall not say who it was in case this letter gets you into trouble. I am to meet Lord Louis Mountbatten who, Lord Edward tells me, is a member of the British Royal Family. His house is near that of Lord Edward's brother, the Duke of Mersham, and I understand my friend Hedwig and her odious husband are staying there. Still, it will be good to see her after so long.

'"I wait anxiously to hear that you are on your way to England. Leave while you have the chance. What you gave me is safe. My kind friends here are looking after me and I do not starve! You may not have long. Your loving son, Gorgi."

'Gorgi is his family nickname,' Herr Dreiser said and his face fell as he remembered that he should have said 'was' instead of 'is'. 'We were so proud that our son should be mingling with the English aristocracy,' he added with touching naivety.

'I am very sorry, Herr Dreiser. Sorrier than I can ever say that your son should have died while he was a guest of my brother but this letter seems to prove that he knew he had enemies in England – one, at least. Perhaps Frau Mandl will be able to help identify who Georg was referring to?' Edward hesitated. 'May I ask what it was that you gave him? If it is valuable it ought to be returned to you.'

'You have not found it? It is a small picture – a woman's face sketched by a great master . . . by Albrecht Dürer. We gave it to him because we could not give him money.'

'Ah, yes! He showed it to Miss Browne but we have not found it yet.'

'Do you think it has been stolen? Is that why my son was killed?'

'I don't know, Herr Dreiser, but I intend to find out and return the drawing to you.'

'We thought it would be safe with Georg and he could sell it if he needed to,' Herr Dreiser said sadly. 'If you should find it, do not return it to us. It would only be stolen by the Nazis or, worse still, destroyed. Sell it and use what it fetches to help other Jews more fortunate than our Georg.'

Edward bowed his head in acceptance.

'Forgive me, Lord Edward, but we should like to be alone now.' Herr Dreiser spoke with quiet dignity. 'Perhaps you could come back tomorrow or are you returning to London immediately? It was good of you to come yourself to tell us this terrible news.'

'I have a letter from my brother offering you employment and I will come tomorrow to take you to the British Embassy. As soon as you have a visa, I will help you leave the country. Georg was right: you have no time to lose.'

'Please? You do not think we are leaving?'

'You *must* leave,' Edward said urgently. 'You have no alternative.'

'There is an alternative,' Herr Dreiser said gravely. 'We are part of an organization helping Jewish children to safety. In two weeks, we are escorting a train to the Swiss border and several more are planned.'

'I see. But when you cross the border with the children . . . ?'

'We do not cross the border. We go to the frontier and then, when the children are safely in Switzerland, we return to Vienna.'

'But why?'

'Because they have told us that if we do not return – the escorts – no further trains will be allowed to leave.'

'But . . .' Edward was at a loss for words.

'Please understand, Lord Edward, that once we knew Georg was safe in England . . . or so we thought, we made the decision to stay. We are old. We would find it difficult to settle in a foreign country at our time of life. We can do something useful here. To be in London and know that so many of our friends and families were . . . not so fortunate – that we could not bear. The guilt would destroy us.' He held up his hand. 'Please do not try and persuade us to come with you. You will not succeed. If you wish to be of service, you will make sure there are homes for these children. The Nazis say that only those with addresses to go to in England will be allowed to leave. It will not be long before they prevent any of our people emigrating.'

Edward left, impressed with their fortitude but, when he reached the door of the apartment building, he heard a high-pitched wail from above. The Dreisers' world had been shattered and there was nothing anyone could do about it. His duty was clear: to find Georg's killer and do what he could to bring as many Jewish children as was possible out of Vienna.

Distressed by his visit but grateful that it was over, he felt the need for fresh air and exercise. He strode off, not knowing where he was heading. After twenty minutes, he found himself in what Verity had told him was the Jewish area of Vienna – Leopoldstadt, near the Carl-Theater. Many of the Jewish-owned shops had been broken into and daubed with swastikas. He saw the still-smoking ruin of what had once been a synagogue. He suddenly felt nervous and walked more quickly.

Ever since leaving the Imperial he had sensed that he was being followed. He assumed someone among Austria's new rulers thought he was worth keeping tabs on but he had no fears for himself. He was, however, concerned not to bring further trouble on the Dreisers so he did what he could to throw his pursuer off his trail and thought he had succeeded.

He found himself at the Café Zentral on the corner of Herrengasse and Strauchgasse and remembered Verity telling him about the waxwork of Trotsky which stood in a corner. He went in and was delighted to find that the Nazis had not got round to destroying it. He nodded his head to it and sat down at a nearby table. He ordered an *Einspanner* – one of those coffees the Viennese love so much served in a glass topped with *Schlagobers*, whipped cream – and waited to see who would appear at his elbow. He picked up a newspaper attached to a wooden stick from a rack by the door. It was slow work translating the German and he soon put it down. A young man who had been watching him furtively from a neighbouring table caught his eye and he nodded politely. Seeming to take this as an invitation, he came over and said, '*Entschuldigen Sie bitte, Herr Corinth, störe ich Sie?*'

'*Verzeihung, ich spreche nicht Deutsch.* Or at least not well enough to carry on a conversation.'

The young man looked relieved, perhaps because Edward was who he thought he was, and replied that he spoke some English.

'Who are you?' Edward asked, rather puzzled. It seemed unlikely that this inoffensive boy could be a secret policeman.

'*Ich bin* . . . I'm a friend of Georg's. He is safe in England?'

'I believe so,' Edward volunteered, not wishing to give anything away to a complete stranger. 'How did you know my name?'

'Georg told me you were the gentleman who Fraulein Browne was . . . who would guarantee his visa. I guessed it must be you when I saw you enter the Dreisers' apartment.'

'And your name is . . . ?'

'My name is Gustav.' The young man obviously thought that now they had introduced themselves, they should shake hands, which they did with some solemnity.

'And what can I do for you, Gustav?'

'It is all right. I am not going to ask you for help to leave the country. I am not Jewish.' A charming smile lit up his sallow, melancholy face.

'But you were . . . are a friend of Georg's?'

'He has many friends who are not Jews. So have his parents. That is why Herr Dreiser was released from prison. We have urged him to leave the country but he will not.'

'I know. I, too, offered to help him emigrate but, as you say, he refuses to go,' Edward said shortly. He thought this young man with the sad eyes was honest but he would take no chances. Nothing he said must get the Dreisers into trouble with the authorities.

'So what do you want of me, Gustav?' he repeated.

'Come with me to the university. I have a friend – a scientist – who wishes to . . . who wants to talk to you.'

Edward found that his heart was beating faster than normal. 'It is safe for your friend to be seen with me?' he asked as a little test.

'No one will see you. Shall we go?'

Edward looked at him and tried to gauge whether he was being led into a trap. It was a risk but one he knew he must take. He threw a few *Schillinge* on the table and got up. 'Let us go, Gustav.'

The young man smiled reassuringly. '*Machen Sie sich keine Sorgen. Alles ist in Ordnung . . . alles ist in Ordnung.*' 'Don't worry, everything is all right.' But of course, it wasn't.

Verity and Vera had taken to one another when they had met before and, when she explained on the telephone that Edward had to go to Vienna so she would come in his

155

place, Vera was rather relieved. She found Lord Edward Corinth a touch intimidating. They agreed to meet at Peter Gray's flat in Mornington Crescent. Verity was late – she had got rather lost in Camden, an area she did not know well and did not like. It looked dirty and rundown. Most of the buildings in Camden High Street had been miserable enough when they had been run up in the 1820s and were now little more than slums. As a good Communist, she ought to have been angry at the poverty she saw all around her – and she was angry – but that did not make her want to stay there any longer than she had to.

She found herself standing by a statue of Richard Cobden, the radical economist and MP, and she stopped to examine it. As she stooped to read the inscription, she was accosted by several children who eyed her rather as jackals eye their prey and demanded money. It occurred to her that she did look too smart for the neighbourhood and was attracting attention. Perhaps she ought to have brought Adrian with her as Edward had suggested. She definitely wished she had not chosen the hat with the feather in it – altogether too jaunty.

She surrendered a sixpence and asked directions to Mornington Crescent but the children, pretending they did not understand her, ran off – she hoped not to bring their older siblings to complete her humiliation. Just as she was becoming rather desperate she saw a constable. He advised her that Mornington Crescent was only a few hundred yards away behind the huge, recently built tobacco factory. It was with relief that she identified the house, dilapidated and crumbling at the edges, at the far end of the crescent. She peered at the little tower of bells, each with its own grimy label. The topmost was inscribed Gray so she pressed the bell beside it. Nothing happened though she thought she heard a bell ringing inside the house. After a minute or two she rang again and, just as she was about to give up and go home, she heard the clatter of shoes on uncarpeted stairs.

Vera opened the door looking as though she had been crying – red-eyed and with a smudge on her cheek.

'Oh, there you are. I thought you'd forgotten,' she said crossly.

Verity apologized meekly and explained that she had got lost.

'You didn't take a cab?'

'No, I knew it was near the underground station but I turned the wrong way when I came out.'

'Well, come up then. I was just trying to clear the flat up a bit but I got stuck. I know he'd hate me messing around with his things.'

As she entered the flat, Verity looked around her and tried to catch the personality of the man. In the first place, he seemed to have been both messy and organized. There were paint stains everywhere – on the floor, on the easel, on the few pieces of furniture, even on the ceiling. However, she had the feeling that he would have been able to put his finger on any tube of paint, brush or knife without having to think about it. It obviously upset Vera to be there. Her uncle's presence was almost palpable in the artist's clutter, as though he had only popped out to buy a packet of cigarettes and his footsteps would soon be heard on the stairs. He had already selected some of the paintings for his – now posthumous – show and these were stacked against the walls in neat piles.

'What are you going to do? Move into the flat or sell it?' she asked Vera.

'I haven't quite decided. There's no studio at Lawn Road and it would be lovely to have a place of my own instead of having to go to the Slade but I don't know if I could afford it. Anyway, I've only recently moved into my flat and I like it. There's a community of painters there – quite a few refugees from Germany who we support while they find their feet.'

Vera was not a Communist but she was an active member of the Hampstead Artists' Council which helped bring refugees to London from Nazi Germany. When Verity told her about Georg's death she was horrified.

'To have come so far and to die just when he had reached a safe haven . . .! My uncle would have felt it . . . He hated to hear of violent death. It reminded him of the

157

war. After it ended, he was plagued by depression – well, you already know about that,' she said, rubbing her forehead and wiping more dust into her face as she did so. 'Bad dreams and worse – there were days . . . weeks . . . when I expected him to try and kill himself.'

Verity wondered what it must have been like for her to grow up constantly fearing for her uncle's mental stability. It must, she thought, prematurely age a child.

'Was he ill-treated in those hospitals?' She didn't want to say lunatic asylums.

'Not ill-treated – not deliberately, anyway. They used drugs to quieten him but . . . but they didn't make him better. I think they used patients like guinea-pigs to try out new treatments. You can't blame them, I suppose.' Despite her forgiving words, she sounded bitter.

'But he did get better?'

'Yes, that was odd. Of course, it was partly that time is – how does it go? – "the great healer". But, as this new war loomed, it seemed to change his mood.'

'It made him fearful that history would repeat itself?'

'He certainly hated the idea of another war, as every sane person does. He said he was glad he only had me and that I was a girl not a boy. But . . . I don't know – with something definite . . . something *outside* himself to fear, he seemed . . . not more cheerful exactly but more determined, less introspective.'

'In what way determined? He was too old to fight in the army.'

'It wasn't that. He always said he wished he had been a conscientious objector. At the outbreak of war, he had been as patriotic as anyone. He joined up expecting to be home . . . if not by Christmas at least in a few months. He despised "conchies". It was only later that he understood their point of view and what they had to face . . . how brave many of them were in the face of so much hostility. Women would hand out white feathers to men not in uniform and "conchies" were thought to be little better than traitors.'

'Even though many became stretcher-bearers and medical orderlies?'

'I wish I could explain what I mean. He felt that he and millions of others had been *tricked* into fighting in 1914 but that Hitler was absolutely evil and *had* to be fought.'

'May I see the picture he was working on when he died?'

'Yes, of course. I'm sorry for talking so much but there are so few people I can talk to about him. And with your experience of being in battle . . . you know about nerves and all that.'

'I do,' Verity said with a shiver. 'I can't tell you how relieved I felt when my boss said I wasn't to go back to Spain. I wasn't sure I could face it but at least I wouldn't have been court-martialled if I had refused to go. For soldiers like your uncle . . . they risked being shot.'

Vera brought out from underneath a sheet a canvas of startling beauty. It was a landscape – the view from Tarn Hill he always painted – but it had a freshness which even Verity, who did not know much about art, could appreciate. It was as though the artist was seeing the rolling hills and river valley for the first time but, of course, it was because he knew it so well that he could record it so accurately and with such loving care. It was unfinished and that too helped make it seem a living work – as though the artist was only waiting for the light to improve before setting up his easel again and mixing his oils on the palette with his knife.

'I like it. I really do,' Verity said, feeling inadequate. 'I wish I was knowledgeable about art like Edward and knew what to say.'

'I like it too. I've decided not to sell it. I shall keep it to remember him by. I thought it might make me sad as it was the last thing he did but it doesn't. It makes me remember him being happy which is the way I *want* to remember him.'

Verity peered at the top right-hand corner where Gray had scribbled his notes.

'See?' Vera pointed. 'He used Red Windsor. Here's the tube.'

'M – I think it's an M – Tarn Hill – Sat.' Verity read aloud. 'Have you got a magnifying glass by any chance? I can't make it out. Is it an M or an R? I'm not sure.'

'Yes, there's one here somewhere. Uncle Peter's sight wasn't as good as it used to be and he used a magnifying glass to read small print. Hold on – it should be here.' She rifled around in a paint-stained chest of drawers. 'Ah! Here we are!' She waved it triumphantly. 'He was a very methodical man. He said a painter had to be like a surgeon. He had to have all the tools of his trade to hand so that, when things were going well, he didn't need to break his rhythm searching for a tube of paint or knife.'

Verity took the magnifying glass close to the corner of the canvas. 'You know, I do believe . . .' she said slowly, 'that it isn't a letter of the alphabet at all. I think it is an emblem – I don't know – a flower perhaps. It's just a squiggle. He wouldn't need to be reminded what it was. It was just an *aide-mémoire*. You look.'

Vera took her place. 'I do believe you are right. I think it *is* a flower – a rose perhaps . . .? I suppose I just thought it would be the initial of the person he was meeting.'

'Well, let's say it is a rose. Maybe it stands for a name. Rose is quite a common name. Did he know anyone called Rose?'

'I don't think so,' Vera said, furrowing her brow.

'There was a man staying with Lord Louis Mountbatten . . . Stuart Rose – an American. He's something to do with painting – a critic or a dealer. I was introduced to him but, to tell you the truth, I didn't take much notice. I just remember feeling I didn't like him.'

'I can ask Uncle Peter's friend – Reg Harman. He might know.'

Verity looked round the room. 'There's nothing missing – nothing unusual?'

'You really think my uncle might have been murdered?' Vera asked suddenly.

Verity was immediately apologetic. 'I'm sorry. I didn't mean to alarm you. Why would he have been murdered? But I can't help wondering why he took that ergot when you say he no longer needed it. And then – dying like he did . . . I'm probably just imagining things but it seems . . . not right somehow. I can't explain. Woman's instinct?' she offered weakly.

'Does Lord Edward have doubts too?'

'He does . . . just doubts – there's no evidence, you understand.'

'Woman's instinct?' Vera inquired wryly.

'Not in his case. Look, shall I just go away? I'd hate you to think I was poking my nose into your affairs to satisfy my curiosity and for no good reason.'

'No. I need to find out the truth. Just like you need to find out who killed Mr Dreiser. Ask me anything you like.' She sounded almost defiant. Looking around her, she continued, 'I don't think there's anything missing.'

Verity had a thought. 'Might I look at the case he carried his paints and brushes in? I mean, I suppose when he went to Tarn Hill or wherever, he took his stuff with him in some sort of case.'

'Yes. The police found it and gave it back to me.'

'Is that it?' Verity pointed at a dirty wooden case.

'Yes.' Vera opened it and looked inside. 'It was a Christmas present from my mother I don't know how many years ago. He always used it.'

'It's beautifully made.' Verity was looking at the dozen or so different-sized partitions in which paints and brushes could be safely stored and carried without rattling around.

'You said your uncle was very methodical? Can you see if there is anything missing?'

Vera pulled open a layer of drawers to reveal another beneath it. 'I can't see anything . . . wait a moment. Where's his palette knife? He always used a palette knife. It was one I gave him about ten years ago when the handle of his old one broke.'

'Perhaps it's still on Tarn Hill.'

'Perhaps it is,' Vera said doubtfully, 'but the police said they had cleared everything up very carefully. I'm sure they would have seen it.'

'It's definitely not in the flat?'

'I don't think so. He always kept it in this box.' She lifted a few objects listlessly.

'Is that it – under the table?' Verity knelt down and picked up a battered-looking knife.

'Fancy that! That's it all right. How could it have got there, I wonder?'

'It must have fallen out of the box.'

'But I haven't opened it since it was brought back from Tarn Hill.'

'You're sure?'

'Quite sure!'

'So he went to paint on Tarn Hill and forgot to take his knife.'

'He was getting rather confused . . .' she began and then stopped. She looked at Verity uncertainly.

10

'I made one useful friend in Vienna – an attaché at the British Embassy called Ruthven-Stuart,' Edward told Verity. They were in St James's Park exercising Basil who was relishing the new and exotic scents. Verity continually had to tell him not to pull on his lead but he took absolutely no notice.

'A thoroughly nice man, I thought. We went for a long walk in Grinzing to admire the view. We stopped at a *heuriger* overlooking the city – an inn where the Viennese go on fine Sundays to drink wine from local vineyards. We shared a jug of rather sour white wine and devoured a plate of smoked meats because the exercise had made us ravenous. He told me about Vienna in happier times – how he loved the opera. For a *schilling* one could get a seat in the gods, he said, and hear Bruno Walter or Knappertsbusch conduct *Der Freischutz* or Wagner. I wish I had spent time there when I was younger.'

Verity was amused by Edward's nostalgia for a place he had never known. She had rarely seen him give way to anything like sentimentality.

'But you saw the swastikas hanging from every public building?' she said brutally. 'The Communists were the only party to put up a fight and they're now all in camps or dead. Better dead, I expect.'

'I did see the swastikas, yes, and the Jewish shops with their broken glass and hateful slogans daubed on the doors. That's what made me sad. Can Vienna survive the war? Does it deserve to? The bombing . . .'

'I should worry about London first,' Verity said grimly. Trying to change his mood, she went on, 'This Ruthven-Stuart from the Embassy. . . why were you talking to him?'

'I was talking about what we could do to help get the Jewish children out of the city. There's a train planned for two weeks on Tuesday. Of course, the authorities may cancel or postpone it but I said Mersham Castle would take as many as could be fitted on the train, at least until they could be found English families to take them in.'

Verity felt she had been wrong-footed but was glad of it. She had suspected him of taking on a spying job for Churchill or some secret government agency but decided she had done him an injustice. She could not know that her suspicions were justified and that Edward had also been talking to Ruthven-Stuart about spiriting out of Vienna a scientist working on the German atomic bomb.

'You haven't told me if you have decided to marry me or not,' he said attempting to sound casual.

'Well, you haven't offered me a ring on bended knee,' she riposted. Then, seeing he might reasonably interpret this as a 'yes', she added, 'I've already told you – I can't think about us until we have got to the bottom of why Georg died. I feel his ghost urging me on. I'm sure you have an apt quotation from Shakespeare to annoy me with.'

'"Thy bones are marrowless, thy blood is cold. Hence, horrible shadow!"'

'*Hamlet*?'

'*Macbeth.*'

'I've told you before, you're over-educated. Basil! You're pulling my arm off. You take him for a minute, will you, Edward? So, what happened when you went back to say goodbye to the Dreisers?'

'Nothing. They had nothing to add. It was almost as if . . . how can I put it? . . . that Georg had died when he left Vienna. They knew then that they would never see him again, on this earth at least. To hear from me that he had died before them was a shock, of course. I told you I heard

Frau Dreiser's cry of pain, and I won't ever forget it, but it was as if they had ceased to expect death to do them any favours. They asked me to see that he was buried as a Jew and of course I said I would. I believe he ought to have been buried within twenty-four hours but until the police release the body . . . And they were unhappy when I said there would have to be an autopsy. Apparently, that can be seen as defiling the body.'

'Oh, Edward! It's too sad. I think we must live in the worst age of man. The Dark Ages.'

Edward took her arm and thought, This must be what it's like to be married, walking in the park arm in arm, talking over problems.

'I say,' he said, pulling himself together with an effort, 'let's make some notes. Suspects, motives . . . that sort of thing. I feel we know quite a lot but nothing seems to fit together.' He sat down on a bench and Verity, surprised but not unwilling, sat down beside him. Basil resignedly lay down at their feet, panting. Edward took out a note pad and his fountain pen. 'Let's take Gray's death first. "What, is't murder?" – sorry!' he said hurriedly, seeing her face. 'I promise not to quote from the bard. You think he was killed in his studio and taken up to Tarn Hill with his painting kit to make it look as though he had died there – and of natural causes?'

'I do but I admit the evidence is very slight – just the mystery of the palette knife and the unusual amount of ergot in his blood.'

'Your hypothesis would be more convincing if Gray *hadn't* dosed himself with ergot. That alone might have made him forget his own name, let alone his knife. In any case, I would be readier to accept that he had been killed in his studio and his body transported to Tarn Hill if it had been found beside his easel. Why take his body down the hill – leaving the painting behind – and drop it on Mountbatten's front door? Too difficult and too complicated.'

'You believe he walked to where he died?'

'I do but it would be useful to talk to the doctor who did the post-mortem. He might have views on it.'

'So, he left his knife behind but set up his easel on Tarn Hill at his usual spot. Then he walked down to Broadlands and died?'

'That's about the size of it, V.'

'Do you think he was meeting someone who was staying in the house?'

'Seems likely.'

'Stuart Rose was the only guest of Mountbatten's with artistic leanings and if I'm right in deciphering the squiggle on the canvas as a rose . . .'

'We need to talk to him but let's keep an open mind. Gray might have wanted to talk to someone else about something else . . . something from his past. He might even have wanted to talk to Mountbatten himself. Or the squiggle might just be a squiggle and mean nothing at all.'

'Where do we begin, then? Can we be sure his murder – if it is murder – is linked to Georg's?'

'No, but we'll know more once we've interviewed our chief suspects – Mandl and Joan . . .'

'We don't really suspect her, do we?'

'She may have unwittingly caused his death,' Edward said slowly.

'And the other suspects?'

'Putzi, Rose. . .'

'I suppose you'll end up doing most of the interviewing,' Verity said sulkily.

Edward took out his gold case, offered her a cigarette and took one for himself. As he leant towards her to light her cigarette, she thought – not for the first time – how good-looking he was. She liked his long nose and strong chin. There were wrinkles around his eyes which she was almost sure had not been there three years earlier and it made her wonder if she too was visibly ageing. The thought made her nervous.

'Not at all!' he said, expelling a lungful of smoke. 'You talk to Rose. He's one of your lot – a Party member, I mean. I think he'd open up to you more than he would to me. He is the only suspect who could have a connection with both Georg and Gray.'

'Art, you mean? He might have stolen Georg's Dürer

and as a Communist . . .' She stopped. 'But why might he have killed Gray?'

'I have no idea,' Edward said, shrugging his shoulders, 'but he *was* an artist. As for Georg, perhaps Rose cheated him over some deal to sell the Dürer but I agree it's not convincing. Anyway, you question Rose and I'll take on the egregious Putzi.'

'Good idea. I know I'd lose my temper and get nowhere with that man. He probably wouldn't even speak to me.'

'Right! Let's think about Georg for a moment. If we assume it was murder . . .'

'Of course it was!'

'V! Didn't I say we need to keep an open mind? The police don't think it was murder.' Verity scowled but said nothing so he went on, 'However, if we take his death as murder, we can probably narrow our suspects down to someone who knew Georg in Vienna or Germany before he came to England. I gather he had travelled in Germany but not elsewhere in Europe, or at least not recently. No one who met him for the first time in England would have had a motive to kill him except Rose – to steal his Dürer. And that's one fact we can't ignore – the Dürer has vanished.'

'It's not in his suitcase or anywhere else obvious,' Verity agreed.

'Correct. So why might Mandl have killed Georg? He and Joan were lovers before, and maybe even after, she married Mandl.' Edward was becoming excited. 'Probably Mandl knew about it – he doesn't look the kind of fellow who would *not* have researched his future wife's love life. We know he was very jealous when she became infamous for appearing naked in that film of hers.'

'*Last Night in Vienna*.'

'So, when he saw Georg at the polo, he lost his temper . . . No, that can't be right. He would have been mad to kill him because of some past romance. All that was history.'

'He might have seen them together and decided it wasn't history. In any case, on top of any personal motive Mandl might have for wanting Georg dead, we know that – as a Nazi – he would not have hesitated to remove a Jew who got in his way,' Verity suggested. She had another idea. 'Perhaps Georg threatened him with something which might have scuppered his business dealings with the navy?'

'Scuppered indeed – a suitably naval metaphor! But I confess I am dubious. I think Mandl's hopes of selling guns to the Royal Navy must already have been dashed by the time of the polo match. I must ask Mountbatten if that was the case . . .' He rubbed his forehead as he often did when he was thinking hard. 'But this is just wild guesswork. One thing we can assume – since you heard Putzi quarrel with Georg and stalk off in the opposite direction – he could hardly have been the person Georg was expecting to meet at the stables.'

'No, that must have been Rose. I think Georg asked Rose to sell his precious drawing for him . . .'

'And Rose decided to kill him for it. Then he could have sold the Dürer as its owner. After all, as far as Rose was aware, no one – except Georg's parents – knew he had the painting so Rose would have nothing to fear.'

Verity considered. 'I don't think he would have dared. Rose must have guessed he would show it to me. After all, Georg was staying with me. It would have been natural . . . Or – what about this? – Putzi might have followed Georg to the stables and killed him as he waited for Rose to turn up.'

Edward nodded. 'Remember, V, in his letter to his parents Georg talked about an enemy he had seen in London whom he would not name for fear of his parents getting into trouble. Since he had mentioned Mandl in the letter, he could not have meant him.'

'But he could have meant Putzi,' Verity said excitedly.

'Yes. As far as Georg knew, Putzi was an intimate friend of Hitler and therefore a dangerous enemy.'

'One thing is certain,' Verity said with decision, 'neither Putzi nor Mandl would contemplate sharing a woman with a Jew.' She grimaced. 'These people disgust me! Maybe, as you are always implying, Communists are less than perfect but the war against Fascism has to be fought and for so long we were the only . . .'

'Get off the soapbox, V.'

'Sorry.' They stopped talking for a moment, trying to get to grips with what might have happened to Georg.

Verity broke the silence. 'You said from the beginning that Mandl was fooling himself if he really thought the Royal Navy would buy guns from a Nazi when the political situation is so critical. He can't really have believed the British Government, or even the Admiralty, would have bought arms from a man like him. Now, if he had been Swiss . . .'

'I agree, but he may indeed have been fooling himself. These sort of people are cunning but not necessarily intelligent.'

'And Joan Miller?'

'Can't think of a motive unless she mistook Georg for her husband. She certainly wants *him* dead. The trouble is, I can't believe she would know enough, or be cool enough, to inject something unpleasant into a horse.'

'Frankly,' Verity admitted, 'I can't see Mandl injecting a pony with some noxious substance either. I can imagine him shooting Georg or hitting him on the head with a polo stick but this was such an odd way to kill a man – so complicated.'

'We ought to talk to the grooms,' Edward agreed. 'Maybe one of them was paid to do it. I wonder if the police are following that up? I'll telephone Inspector Beeston. Perhaps he already knows who murdered Georg. I wish he was more cooperative.'

'What about the vet who examined Button?'

'Yes, I must try to talk to him as well. He gave me the brush-off when I tried to ask him a few questions while he examined Button just after we found Georg's body.'

Verity, not wanting to be side-tracked continued, 'You told me that Putzi is thinking of seeking asylum here.'

'V, I told you that in complete confidence.'

'Well, suppose Georg knew something about him which would have made the authorities think twice about offering him asylum? The last thing Putzi would do is get involved in something like murder. That wouldn't endear him to them.'

Edward knew from Liddell that, whatever the man's crimes, if the British Government had a use for him, they would take him. They wouldn't let a little thing like murder stand in the way of offering him asylum. However, he thought it best not to mention this.

'There's a lot of work to be done,' Verity said doubtfully. 'And you may not be around much longer?'

'I just don't know. I'm in limbo at the moment. If I can't go back to Vienna, I want to go to Prague as quickly as possible. Things are moving so fast.'

'I feel somehow, V, that if this is ever to be solved, it has to be solved in the next few days. The Mandls will soon be back in Vienna and out of our reach. Goodness knows where Rose and Putzi will be but they probably won't be accessible to us . . .'

'And I need to know Georg's murderer has been caught before I leave. I failed him when he was alive. I can't fail him now he's dead.'

'I know, V, and I feel the same way.' Edward hesitated for a moment. 'At least we don't have to suspect Sunny or Ayesha.'

'I can't see them murdering anyone,' Verity said decisively. 'And in any case, Sunny was watching Ayesha and Sunita play polo. Putting aside Putzi for the moment, my chief suspect is Rose. I don't like him. I find his charm quite creepy. And I wish Frank wasn't so taken with him.'

'I don't like him either,' Edward agreed. 'The moment I heard he was a friend of Bernard Hunt, I was suspicious of him. But you can't accuse someone of murder just because he's a bit too charming. Not even if he turns out to be an art thief.'

'He knows too many people. There's a Jewish saying Georg taught me which seems to apply to Rose – "He dances at two weddings." He's a Communist but seems to be at ease with out-and-out Nazis like Mandl and Unity Mitford. I told you Rose and Unity Mitford were both at that dinner I went to?'

Edward thought wryly that Verity was the pot calling the kettle black when it came to dancing at weddings but kept the thought to himself. Instead, he said teasingly, 'You mean Joe's party when Churchill turned out not to be the bogeyman you had imagined?'

'That one, yes,' she replied, refusing to be drawn.

'And,' Edward said meditatively, ' he was also at that awful club I went to with Putzi and the Mandls later that same night. I agree with you, he does know too many people. Still, I think Mandl's our chief suspect. At least we know he was there when Gray's body was found, if we take it the two deaths are linked.' His face clouded. 'The fact is that we don't have a shadow of a case against anyone yet. Perhaps we are getting too suspicious in our old age . . . in my old age,' he corrected himself, catching her scowl. 'Perhaps Gray died a natural death. We may never know. It's a nuisance that Inspector Beeston is such a dead loss. Only the police can *make* people answer questions they don't want to. Still, I'll see if I can persuade him to tell us what he has found out. I'll also talk to Mandl, Putzi and Joan. You corner Rose and I think you should pursue your friendship with Vera Gray. Oh, and talk to Reg Harman – Gray's friend from the old days. See what you can dig up. I have a hunch there's something in Gray's past we don't know about which has a bearing on his death.'

'I thought we women were supposed to have the hunches?'

'And, V, why don't you go and see your old friend Richard Leist at the Redfern? Show him the Dürer picture in the book we found and tell him about Georg's drawing. He's a senior figure in the art world and he'll know how to alert his colleagues that they may be offered a stolen masterpiece. The trouble is it's so small it will be easy to smuggle out of the country.'

He looked at her thin, eager face and felt his stomach turn over. 'Darling V,' he said impulsively, 'I do love you. I know . . . I know, I've promised not to badger you to marry me until we've cleared up this mess so let's get going.'

Verity looked at Edward intently. 'Yes, wait until we've nailed Georg's murderer. I like investigating with you but I wish it didn't have to be Georg who died.'

Edward looked at her sharply. It wasn't quite the put-off he had been expecting. He was about to say something more when Basil leapt out from under the bench in hot pursuit of a poodle which had just walked past in what he must have considered an insolent manner.

Reg Harman had no telephone but Vera had written to ask whether he would talk to Verity about her uncle. A day or two later, Verity had received a battered postcard bearing a photograph of the Grand Hotel, Broadstairs. In a spidery hand the old man had written that he was normally at the Slade on Thursdays and Fridays between eleven in the morning and three in the afternoon. Taking this as consent, Verity had made her way to Bloomsbury and found him without difficulty. He was perched on a wobbly stool looking critically at a portrait, the work of a young man notable for his shock of bright red hair. Harman greeted her distractedly and it was some time before he remembered who she was and why she had come.

'My name's Ben,' the young man said, smiling. 'I doubt Reg'll ever get round to introducing us. In fact, he probably can't. He frequently forgets my name.'

'Nonsense, dear boy! I know perfectly well who you are but, it is true, my old brain does play tricks on me.'

'Is Mr Harman your teacher?' Verity asked.

'I'd hardly say that,' he replied affectionately, smiling at the old man. 'I listen to his anecdotes of times past and the great painters he has known and he tells me I'm not a patch on Gertler or Augustus John.'

'I can't pretend to teach these boys,' Harman said, taking the remarks in good part. 'They never listen. They think they know it all. I tell them to go to the National Gallery and copy the great masters but they take no notice.'

'He's fearfully out of fashion,' Ben said with a chuckle, 'so we have to keep it a deadly secret that he's tutoring us.'

'Blasted child,' Harman murmured, patting the young man's head and smiling. 'This lady is . . .' he scratched his head, 'a friend of Adrian Hassel.'

'I know Adrian. I say, are you *the* Miss Browne – Browne with an "e"?' Ben said, excitedly. 'He talks so much about you.'

Verity blushed. 'Nice things, I hope.'

'Awfully. He says you are the bravest and the best of the war correspondents and he can't think how you haven't been killed yet. Oh! How beastly. I didn't mean . . .'

'I take it as a compliment. Now, may I borrow your tutor for half an hour?'

'Of course!' said the irrepressible youth. 'You want to grill him about Peter Gray. The whole place has been talking about it. Do you think he was murdered? Damn – there I go again. Sorry, Miss Browne. I hang my head in shame.'

He did so and Verity laughed, feeling old enough to be his mother. 'Did you know Mr Gray?'

'I met him once. A great man, but not – what shall I say? – not friendly, like Reg here. However, I think he'll be remembered after we're all dead and gone. Don't you agree, Reg?'

Verity saw that the old man enjoyed being treated as an equal and called by his first name.

'I do indeed. Now, get on and do what I told you. The ears are quite wrong and why the streak of blue in his hair?'

They went to a small café nearby which Harman told her was much frequented by the students and Verity ordered coffee and cake.

'What is it you wish to know, Miss Browne?' Harman inquired as he stirred the watery-looking coffee the waitress had brought. Verity was suddenly aware that he was not the vague and gentle old fellow he pretended to be. His shrewd eyes beneath white bushy brows were taking her in and judging her. 'You think my old friend was murdered? The police don't.'

'I don't know if he was murdered but we – Lord Edward and I – think the police don't want to investigate the possibility in case they embarrass Lord Louis Mountbatten.'

'Hmm. That's probably true but I don't think he was murdered and I don't like you worrying Miss Gray. It does no good to raise questions in her mind which can't be answered. She's had enough heartache already, poor child. Peter was a very good painter but he wasn't an easy man – particularly after his wife died.'

'Vera was still a little girl?'

'Yes but she grew up quickly. Had to. There was an old aunt or something but she died or left – I expect Vera's told you all this – and then she had to cope on her own.'

'With the shell shock?'

'Yes. I was a conscientious objector. Went to prison for it,' Harman said proudly. 'And would do so again. What did the war do to those brave men who joined up in 1914 so eager to serve their country? Peter was badly affected but he was by no means the worst. "Basket cases" they called them! Lives destroyed for nothing. That's what I call murder. And now we have to do it all over again. What a waste! That young man you saw just now . . . I can't bear to think of him lying dead in France . . .' He wiped what might have been a tear from his eye. 'I'm sorry, what were we talking about?'

'You were saying that Vera looked after her uncle.'

'That girl's a saint,' he said vehemently, chewing his upper lip. 'We all tried to help – his friends, you know? But the burden fell on her young shoulders and she bore it without complaint.'

'When did he start painting the view from Tarn Hill?'

'When his wife died. When Betty died . . .' he repeated mournfully.

'So he painted the same view hundreds of times during . . . what? Twenty years?'

'Like Monet and his water lilies.'

'Did he ever tell you why?'

'He didn't tell me but I knew.' Harman hesitated. 'I should have told you when Lord Edward asked me after the memorial meeting why Peter might have walked down to the farm buildings at the bottom of Tarn Hill but I thought it was too private a thing to tell strangers. Perhaps I was wrong. His wife was brought up in that farmhouse. He courted her there and he told me they often walked up the hill to contemplate the view . . . It was the epitome of peace for him, if you can understand.'

'Home and beauty,' Verity muttered.

'That sounds trite,' he rebuked her. 'I would go so far as to say he painted his soul in that view.'

'The painting! I must look at it again!'

'Which painting?' Harman asked, startled.

'The one he was working on when he died. I thought I had looked at it but now I realize I didn't see it at all. Goodbye, Mr Harman,' Verity said, rising and almost knocking over her untasted coffee. 'You have been most kind and I think . . . I think you may have explained why Peter Gray died.'

'What?'

'I can't say anything more until I've seen the painting again. Goodbye . . . and thank you.'

Putzi was being evasive and Edward was finding it more and more difficult to hide his irritation. He didn't want to go back to Germany . . . he thought his life would be in danger . . . but his son Egon was there. He wanted to stay in England . . . or go to America or Switzerland . . . He needed money . . . he was homesick . . .

The meeting was taking place in his suite at Claridge's and Putzi had made it clear that he expected the British Government to foot the bill. Edward was trying to explain that 'nothing will come of nothing' and he had to decide whether or not he was going to work for the British. The implied threat was that he might otherwise be bundled off back to Berlin where it was more than likely he would be sent to a camp or shot.

Putzi was claiming not to be anti-Semitic. 'Unity Mitford, you know her?' Edward said he had met her. 'She does not like Jews and I have told her to shut up about it. She's always boring me about Jews. She's a Jew-baiter and she hates Americans. But I have to keep on her good side, you understand? She is a great friend of Hitler's.'

His attitude to Hitler veered between slavish devotion and petulant protest. He said he hated Goebbels who had poisoned Hitler against him.

'They say you slept with Joan Miller when you were in Berlin,' Edward suddenly threw in to see what reaction he would get.

Putzi looked sly. 'She is a very beautiful woman. Do you not think so, Lord Edward?'

Edward had to master a strong desire to kick him. Instead he said, 'Did you have Herr Mandl's permission to sleep with his wife?'

'He wanted me to speak well of him to Herr Hitler.'

'So he *did* give you permission?'

Putzi tapped his squashed nose with a finger. 'There are some things which do not need putting into words, are there not?'

Edward, by this time reckless in his dislike, asked, 'Did you mind that you were sharing her with a young Jew – Georg Dreiser? Is that why you killed him when you saw him at Broadlands?'

'I do not know what you mean, Lord Edward. Are you trying to be offensive? Why should I kill this man I had never heard of?'

'I did not see you watching the polo.'

'Joan and I had one or two things to say to each other so we walked about talking of old times.'

'Did you go near the stables?'

'The stables? Why? Ah, I remember! That was where the poor man met his end, wasn't it? I think we did go near the stables,' he added insolently. 'I remember the smell of the horses. I do not like horses.'

'Did you see anyone near the stables?'

'No, but we were rather wrapped up in each other.'

'So wrapped up in each other that you did not hear the pony kicking against the stable door?'

'What is this, Lord Edward? Are you a policeman? Are you going to arrest me?' He smiled and Edward wanted to hit him. He managed to control himself.

'No, I am not a policeman but I would like to find out who killed Georg Dreiser. Like you, Herr Braken, he came to England as a refugee from the Nazis and was killed – probably by someone who knew him back in Vienna.'

'I am not a refugee,' Putzi responded, stung by the comparison with a Jew. 'I may choose to stay here but not if I am to be treated with . . . with contempt. Do your superiors know how you speak to me? I could help your government but why should I when you call me a murderer?'

'I didn't call you a murderer,' Edward said, back-tracking hurriedly. He had a vision of Liddell's fury if he got to know how the interview had gone. 'I just want to find out who killed Georg Dreiser. We do not permit anyone to be murdered in England without doing our utmost to bring the murderer to justice. I gather it is different in Germany.'

Edward heard himself insult Putzi with horror. He was no good at diplomacy, he realized, if it meant you had to smile with villains.

Putzi looked at him with undisguised amusement. He had won a sort of victory and he knew it.

In a very short time, Frank had become intimate with the American, Stuart Rose. They drove down to Marlow to dine and dance at Skindles in a 1932 Delage – a super-sports version of the four-litre D8 – not Rose's but 'borrowed from a friend' as he put it airily. Skindles was expensive – gin and tonic an exorbitant ninepence – but it was fun to mingle with the *jeunesse dorée*, dine off oysters and champagne and dance into the small hours before racing back through the night to London.

They went to art galleries and parties – Rose seemed to know everyone – but at no time did he talk politics or make a pass at him. It was as though he looked on Frank as a perfect specimen of a particular type of upper-class English boy – unfamiliar to him and therefore of consider-able interest, to be studied as an example of a species. He knew that the one thing which would disgust the boy was a hint of anything of a sexual nature.

Connie was not entirely happy about this friendship but she had come to the same conclusion as had Edward – that if she tried to come between them it would only make

Frank more eager to be in Rose's company. And there was no doubt he was learning a lot. Eton was as philistine as any other English public school and Frank was lamentably ignorant of the visual arts and hardly less so of music and drama. Rose took him to the theatre and then, afterwards, backstage to meet the actors. It was a new world to Frank and he revelled in it.

Sunita was recovering and urged him not to mope at her bedside but it hurt when he regaled her with stories of parties and other jollities from which she was excluded. He seemed – naively – to think she would not be jealous when he told her of meeting Noël Coward and dancing with Gertie Lawrence. 'But she's old enough to be my mother!' he exclaimed when she said something about it.

'But do you miss me sometimes?' she asked timidly. And he would explain that he would much rather be with her than at Skindles and she put on a brave face determined not to appear to be 'chasing' him.

Sunny was also unhappy. He did not like the way his host flirted with his wife but he was reluctant to have a row and Mountbatten would not hear of them leaving Broadlands or Sunita recuperating elsewhere.

'Where would you go?' he demanded of Sunny. 'She's not well enough to travel. Take her to the South of France next month but stay here at least until the end of April.'

Sunny reluctantly acquiesced. At least Lady Louis had returned but Ayesha still seemed to spend a great deal of time in Mountbatten's company. Sunny trusted his wife absolutely – of course he did – but he could not help but be jealous.

Verity thought it was by accident that she bumped into Rose in Sloane Avenue. She had Basil with her and was going to walk him in Kensington Gardens. Rose lifted his hat and asked if he might accompany them.

'It's such a wonderful spring day,' he said. His accent was noticeable but difficult to pin down and she asked him where he had grown up. To her surprise, he said Baton Rouge.

'I thought that if you were a Southerner you'd speak like this,' she said, attempting a Southern drawl.

'I left home soon as I could. I was real happy to be gone,' he said demonstrating how 'Southern gen'lmen' really spoke. 'I've spent most of my life on the east coast and quickly learned to lose my home-town roots – voice and all.'

'Why did you leave?' He looked at her and she blushed. 'I mean just because . . . because you don't like women?' she finished unhappily.

'But I do like women,' he contradicted her. 'Just – not for sex.'

Verity blushed again to her annoyance and said quickly, 'I don't suppose they like Communists in Baton Rouge either.'

He laughed and she looked up at him. He was really very attractive.

'No, durn it – they sure don't,' he responded in a rather good James Cagney voice.

'But you are a Communist?' she persisted.

'Hey, let me take hold of the dog. He's too big for you – too big for London. He almost knocked over that baby carriage.'

'We call it a perambulator.'

'Oh, sure – a pram, I remember.'

Verity was still waiting for an answer to her question. 'If you are a Communist, you're a very odd one.'

'Because I like fast cars and good restaurants? I don't think you have any right to criticize.'

'I wasn't criticizing – just asking. So you yearn after the revolution?'

'Something like that, I guess,' he replied gaily. 'In fact Owen Coombs is a friend of mine.'

'Coombs!' Verity said, startled. 'Oh, I see. That was why you "bumped into me"? He said a Party member would contact me but it never occurred to me that would be you. You want to tell me what to do?'

'Not the case, I assure you,' he said hastily. 'It's very useful for the Party to have Comrades who can mix well in all areas of our corrupt society.' He smiled to show he was half-joking. 'We have Comrades in every department of government both here and in the United States. In the art world, movies . . . wherever opinions are formed and there are people with the power to change things. The danger is . . .'

'That we get to like the capitalist world too much . . . ?'

'Even that doesn't matter if we are prepared to obey orders – even if we don't like them or understand them.'

'And I don't take orders?'

'The Party has not asked anything difficult of you yet, so Mr Coombs tells me, but there will come a time when you have to choose . . .'

'Mr Rose,' Verity said, her feathers ruffled, 'I don't know who you really are and I certainly don't intend to take orders from you.'

'Not orders – advice.'

'I don't intend to take your advice either. I make up my own mind and what I witnessed in Spain has led me to doubt whether the Party is the same one I joined in 1934. I rather think it is now merely an arm of the Soviet Union.'

'The Soviet Union is the Communist Party militant and Stalin is its spirit.'

'That must have been how the Jesuits spoke of their Church in Queen Elizabeth's time.'

'We are crusaders of a kind.'

'Not in my book.'

'Then you may expect an uncomfortable time ahead,' Rose said, raising his hat.

'Before you go,' Verity said, taking Basil's lead from his hand, 'can I ask a question?'

'As many as you like,' he said courteously.

'Did you kill Georg Dreiser?'

'Dreiser?' He seemed genuinely surprised by the question. 'Why would I do that?'

'I don't know why. Perhaps he asked you to sell his Dürer drawing. Did you think, Why share the money with a Jewish refugee? No one knows he has it so I'll kill him and steal it.'

He looked shocked. 'Miss Browne, those are very harsh

words. Is that really how you see me? No, I did not steal it and I certainly did not kill him.'

'But he did show you the drawing at the stables – during the polo?'

'He did and I had to tell him it was a fake – a valuable fake – nineteenth-century probably but not worth anything like what he thought.'

'So you gave it back to him and left?'

'I did. I left him alive.'

'So where is the Dürer now?'

'I have no idea. It would be tragic if it has disappeared for good.'

'Even if it's a fake?'

'A nineteenth-century fake might still have things to teach us and if it was copied from Dürer's sketchbook – now lost to us – it would be invaluable.'

Verity looked him in the eye. 'I don't believe you.'

'That it would be invaluable?'

'That you did not steal it.'

'That is your privilege, Miss Browne, but I should tell you that – if I hear you make any such accusation against me in public – I shall not hesitate to sue. I have the beginnings of a reputation in the art world on both sides of the Atlantic and it would not be good for me if your wild allegations got around. I hope you understand me.'

Her heart pounding, Verity let Basil pull her away. 'And I should get that dog trained,' he shouted after her, 'before it kills someone.'

11

Joan had managed to slip away from the hotel while Mandl was at the German Embassy. She said he was in an evil temper. Having – predictably – failed to sell his new gun to the Royal Navy, he had proceeded to insult Mountbatten, accusing him of wasting his time. Now, he was in bad odour with the Embassy for attempting to do business with an unfriendly power. Goering had asked to see him as soon as he returned to Berlin and Mandl knew he would have to buy his way out of trouble by presenting the great man with some very expensive gifts. Altogether it was the worst possible outcome from what he – somewhat naively – had considered a perfectly normal sales trip.

'Mandl's going straight to Berlin so I will have two days – perhaps more – before the gate closes on me.' Joan had finally decided to leave him and go to America but first she had to get her child out of Vienna.

They discussed the plan Edward had suggested. It was dangerous but the past weeks in England had allowed her to look at her life dispassionately.

'If I stay with Mandl, he will lead me a life of misery. He will prostitute me to ingratiate himself with powerful Party officials until I start to lose my looks and then he will beat me. I shall be allowed to make a few second-rate propaganda films and then I will disappear. I'm still young with a career ahead of me if only I can get to California. You will help, Edward?'

'I shall do my best, Joan, but it is a very great risk – for you, I mean.'

'And for you. This may damage you if you get a reputation for being a reckless adventurer.'

Edward blanched. 'Don't worry about that,' he said bravely. 'Just do what we have agreed.'

'I will and . . . and thank you,' she said, leaning over to kiss him on the cheek. 'You are a good man. In two or three years you will come to Hollywood as my guest.'

'I hope so,' he smiled. 'By the way, it doesn't look as though I am going to get an opportunity to ask Mandl if he killed Georg. Do you think he did?'

'Poor Georg,' Joan said, her face clouding. 'He was such a gallant young man and so intelligent. You know why I found him so attractive?'

'Because he loved you?' Edward hazarded.

'You are right,' she said, surprised at his acuity. 'Of all the men who lusted after me, he was the only one who loved me for myself. Every night he came to the theatre and how could I resist him . . .? We both knew we had no future together. He was poor. I was poorer. I needed a rich protector – or at least I thought I did.'

'Did Mandl kill him?' Edward repeated.

'Out of jealousy? I don't think so. Georg was of no account to Mandl. Why would he risk an important arms deal by killing a Jewish refugee who was no threat to him?'

'He's possessive. You said so yourself.'

'He is. I am not saying he could not commit murder. He probably already has for all I know. But I don't think he ever knew Georg and I had been lovers and even if he guessed it . . . well, it was some time ago.'

'And you didn't see Georg at Broadlands? You didn't have a rendezvous?'

She was silent. 'Because of all you are doing for me, I owe you the truth. We did see each other briefly and he asked me to meet him at the stables during the polo.'

'And did you go?'

'I went and . . .'

'And . . .?'

'And we talked.'

'That was all? You just talked?'

'We kissed.'

'You made love?'

'No! Of course not! Anyway, we were interrupted.'

'Someone came? Who was it?' Edward asked excitedly.

'I did not see.'

He sank back in disappointment. 'You did not see?'

'I ran away. I thought it might be my husband. But I smelt him! He was smoking a Camel. Not Mandl's brand.'

'How do you know it was a Camel?'

I know because I smoke them myself when I can get them.'

'I thought you smoke Sobranies?'

'For the effect,' she said, smiling and looking for a moment like a young girl. 'When I try to believe I am Greta Garbo.' She giggled. 'Now I must go. Goodbye, dear Edward.'

As she stood up, a sudden gust of wind made her reach to secure her hat. On an impulse, he pulled her towards him and kissed her on the lips. Still clutching her hat, she responded. Then, gently pushing him away, she laughed and said, 'Really, Edward, I did not think you could be so . . . so dashing – *romantisch*. What would your little girl say?'

Edward felt a pang of guilt. 'It is bad of you to tease me,' he managed. 'It was just a kiss, nothing more.'

'I hope it was something more,' she said, 'but take care. Those people over there are looking at us. The English are so easily shocked.'

'They are jealous. But you must go. We shall meet in a week's time.'

'God willing,' Joan said, suddenly serious.

He raised his hat and watched her walk away from him – well aware that his eyes would be following her. She was, he thought ruefully, a beautiful woman and he did not regret his kiss but it was – how had she put it – 'his little girl' whom he loved. How Verity would hate that description!

'Lord Louis told you that I wanted to ask a few questions about the death of my friend, Georg Dreiser?'

Edward had found the grooms mucking out the stables at Broadlands. They seemed happy to take a break from their work. He and Verity, with Basil in tow, were back at Mersham determined to finish the investigation.

'Yes, my lord. I hopes as you don't think we had anything to do with it. The police . . .'

'No, please don't misunderstand . . . I am merely trying to get it all straight in my head. His parents . . . you know,' he said duplicitously, 'they want to know what happened. Quite natural. You can imagine how they feel. They thought their son was safe in England and then this. The irony is that he didn't even like horses. He was afraid of them.'

'Then why was he here, my lord, at the stables?'

'Well, there's the question, Jim. We think he must have been meeting someone. You didn't see anyone hanging around . . . any of Lord Louis' guests, for instance?'

'Not then, my lord.' It was the older man, Alfred Johnson, who spoke. 'We was at the polo with the ponies. It were only when we heard the young lady screaming and the dog barking that we came runnin'.'

'But when you came to telephone for an ambulance and fetch the stretcher, you said you didn't hear anything?'

'No, sir, we was too far off, like, and in too much of a hurry,' Jim answered.

'And the rain was fair drummin' on the corrugated iron,' Johnson chipped in.

'But you had seen someone hanging around the stables before that?'

'Not hangin' around as you might say,' Jim corrected him. 'Lord Louis likes to take his guests on a tour of the stables to look at the 'orses.'

'Was that on the morning of the polo match?'

'No, sir. The day before.'

'I see. Lord Louis took all his guests to see the ponies?'

'Not all. Some ladies don't like it.'

'But the German lady, the film star . . .?' Edward trusted Joan would not mind being called German.

'Aye, she were there. She were a looker, eh, Alf? I'm sorry, my lord.' Jim checked himself.

Edward grinned to show he wasn't a prude. 'So – forgive me for asking this – no one asked you to . . . to do anything? I mean, I know you wouldn't . . .' He stopped, seeing their faces.

'Lord Louis' a very generous master and we'd never do anything unless he ordered us to,' Johnson said disapprovingly.

'No, of course not . . . of course not.' Edward, seeing the suspicion in their eyes, realized he had been clumsy.

'Like, we wouldn't be talking to you if the guv'nor hadn't said to,' Johnson continued, almost insolently.

Edward was being told, firmly enough, that if any tricks had been played that day, they knew nothing about the perpetrator.

'When exactly did Button go lame?' He felt the grooms relax.

'Not until the morning of the polo match. He were all right the night before.'

'What caused it?'

'Who knows, my lord?' Johnson said. 'He may have knocked his leg . . . No obvious cause, but it does happen.'

'No one could have done it on purpose . . . lamed him, I mean?'

Johnson shook his head. 'No, there was no cut or anything – no mark. Why should they? He ain't a racehorse.'

Edward thought for a moment and tried again. 'Were you surprised that Button lashed out at poor Mr Dreiser?' He was certain the grooms had something to tell him but he couldn't seem to find the right question.

Johnson scratched at an armpit. 'He is a stallion . . .'

'That's quite rare for a polo pony, isn't it?'

'They're mostly mares – yes, my lord.'

'And are stallions more skittish . . . more difficult to control . . . more excitable?'

Johnson looked at Jim before replying, 'Mebbe, my lord, mebbe, but Button was quiet enough.'

'So what could have upset him?'

'He'd had his oats because we thought he would be ridden and he heard the other ponies go . . . he might have been upset.'

'But you wouldn't have expected him to lash out?'

'Not but the man *did* something. He didn't like horses, you say? Mebbe he unsettled him in some way.'

Edward tried another tack. 'They found a cigarette lighter in the stable.'

'It weren't ours,' Johnson said quickly.

'No, of course not and we don't think it belonged to the dead man either. But it shows someone went into the stable. There was no sign of the straw being burnt . . .? I mean, the smell of smoke might have panicked Button.'

'If there *had* been a fire . . .' Johnson agreed, 'but there were no sign of anything like that.'

Edward was ready to give up but said on a whim, 'Is it an old wives' tale or should a woman not handle a stallion when she's . . . you know, when it's her time of the month?'

Jim guffawed and Johnson looked at him with contempt. 'I never heard that, my lord. We doesn't like girls round the stables, leastways, if they ain't going to ride the animals but I never heard . . .'

'No, no. Forgive me! Such silly stories get around.' Edward gave up. He would get nothing out of these two. 'Well, you have been most kind. Just one of those mysteries, eh? An accident . . . a freak of nature.'

'Mind you,' Johnson said, relenting slightly now the inquisition was almost over, 'I did smell cigarette smoke, now I come to think of it, when I was taking Button out of the stable. But I didn't think anything of it. Mebbe you're right, sir, and there were someone messing about. To be straight with you, I don't think as though Button would go mad like that without a reason.'

'After you'd brought Button out of the stable, I remember you saying you thought he might have been drugged.'

'I was mistaken, my lord,' Johnson said firmly. 'Mr Rush – the vet, see – he said there were no sign of drugs.'

'And you believe him?'

'Certainly, my lord.'

'But something upset him?' Edward tried one last time.

'I thought I heard a motor . . .' Jim said hesitantly.

'When was this?' Edward asked sharply.

'When we was running back with the stretcher.'

187

'But you said you heard nothing?' Edward's voice betrayed his exasperation.

'I thought nothing of it,' Jim said, obviously wishing he had kept his mouth shut.

'You heard a car?'

'A motorbike, more like. I didn't take no notice.'

'You think someone was riding a motorbike through the yard?'

'I think so. Riding off 'cos he heard us coming.'

The vet – a man by the name of Godfrey Rush – boasted a huge handlebar moustache of which he was clearly inordinately proud. He obviously resented having to answer Edward's questions but Mountbatten was a power in the land and could not be denied.

'So there was nothing odd about Button kicking out like that?'

'No, I . . . it can happen. Something must have disturbed him . . . frightened him. A bird or, indeed, the man himself . . . Dreiser, was that his name? A Jew . . .'

'What has that to do with it? You think Jews smell bad?'

'No, of course not! Don't misunderstand me, Lord Edward. I just thought that, being a foreigner, he might not know . . . about horses.'

'He didn't like horses. They frightened him.'

'There we are then! Button may have smelt his fear. And the blood … Horses go wild when they smell blood and can't get away.'

'Yes, but there would have been no blood until he started kicking out.'

The vet said nothing but stroked his moustache. Edward tried again.

'Did you think the pony had been interfered with – drugged?'

'Drugged? No, it never crossed my mind.'

'I saw the pony as he came out of the stable. The groom – Johnson – he thought Button had been drugged. His eyes were bulging and he was foaming at the mouth. By the time you got there, he was calmer.'

'I got there as quick as I could.'

'I'm not blaming you. I'm merely saying that, when I saw Button, he seemed in distress.'

'Distress?'

'Shaking – breathing heavily – sweating . . .'

'That can be put down to hysteria. The pony had sensed a strange presence – had kicked out – smelt blood and . . .'

'So you are saying the pony couldn't have been drugged . . . injected with something?'

'I don't say *couldn't* but there was no evidence that he had been interfered with. The groom had administered a mild sedative, that was all. I don't know what you are trying to prove but I think you must accept this was a tragic accident. Anything else is pure speculation. No one would believe you . . .'

Edward realized the interview was at an end.

'No one would believe me,' he said aloud, as he got into the Lagonda and swept away from the little house with its tiny garden and the man with the handlebar moustache. Rush was right, damn it – no one would believe him and he wasn't sure he believed it himself. On the other hand, Joan had said that someone had smoked a Camel in or near the stable and Stuart Rose smoked Camels. He remembered when he had first met him in Mountbatten's drawing-room, he had offered him one. Moreover, whoever it was had lost his cigarette lighter – the kind Camel gave out to advertise their product, the kind with which Rose had lit his cigarette. Had it fallen into the straw during some sort of fight? And then there was the motorbike. Who had been riding a motorbike in the stables around the time Georg had died? He remembered something Verity had mentioned and he had forgotten. She had seen the distinct mark of a car or motorbike tyre in the mud.

Joan, Putzi and Rose had all been to the stables. Was one of them a murderer? He shook his head. He felt he almost knew . . . but not quite . . . soon, but not yet.

Sunita was dressed and sitting in an armchair reading a

book when Frank came to visit her. She had been feeling depressed but the sight of him made her spirits soar.

'Frank! How lovely to see you. How was the party last night?'

Frank looked uncomfortable. 'Not too bad but, to tell you the truth, I'm getting a bit fed up with that crowd.'

'You mean Stuart Rose's crowd?'

'Yes. They're fun but . . . but they don't *think* about anything except pleasure. They're not serious.'

'Isn't Stuart serious?'

'He's all right, I suppose. He's taught me a lot about art,' he added, as though trying to be fair. 'The fact of the matter is, I don't really like the man. I think he's a fairy for one thing.'

'A fairy!' Sunita repressed a smile.

'You know – not natural.' Frank sounded embarrassed.

'You don't mean he's . . . you know – at you?'

Frank blushed. 'Nothing like that. I just mean he's amusing enough but I don't want him to think he's my friend.' Sunita felt momentarily sorry for the man Frank was dismissing so brutally. 'Anyway, why are we talking about him? I want to know about you.' He sat on a chair next to her and took her hand.

'The doctor says I'm getting better and it'll do me good to leave this place. In fact, we're going soon. I can't wait! I was worried that my father and mother were outstaying their welcome. Lord Louis has been kindness itself but it's time to go. I can see Pa is very restless.'

'Why don't you all come and stay at Mersham? My mother would be so pleased.'

'That's kind of you, Frank, but we're going to Paris to see some cousins. Then I have to go back to school. I can't bear the thought of it. I feel I'm grown-up. It's so babyish having to think about lessons and rules and all that rot.'

'It's just one more term and then you'll be free.'

'Will we . . . do you think we'll see anything of each other when . . .?' Sunita asked timidly.

'Of course! We love each other, don't we?'

'Yes, but . . . they'll never allow us to . . . they'll say it's a schoolgirl crush . . . they'll say we're too young.'

190

'Darling girl, listen to me. We're not children. I love you and you love me. Nobody can stop us marrying.'

'Marrying? Oh, Frank, of course they can stop us marrying. I don't know, perhaps we *are* too young. You'll get bored with me. You'll meet someone else.'

'I'm not joking,' Frank said, uncertain whether he had been or not. 'I want to marry you, Sunita. You are the only girl for me. I don't want to meet someone else – not if I have you.'

'You're a sweet boy,' she said with an effort, trying to be mature. She put out a hand – tentatively – and stroked his face. 'I do love you. I tried not to but . . .'

'But what?' He sounded irritable as though, once he had made his declaration, she ought to have accepted it without demur.

'But I might be a drag on you. They'll think I set out to trap you.'

Frank got up and strode about the room. 'You didn't, did you?'

'Of course I didn't!' She sounded shocked – even insulted.

'Well then, what does it matter what people say? We love each other. That's all there is to it. I wish people would stop saying I'm too young.'

'Don't be cross! I have to think for both of us. If we got married, what would it be like?' she said seriously. 'You'd regret it. In a year or two, you'd fall in love with someone else and I'm not sure I could bear that.'

He came back to sit beside her. 'Stop telling me I'll fall in love with someone else or I'll start believing you. Do you love me?'

'You know I do but I don't want to ruin your life – our lives! Can you imagine what your father and mother would say if you told them you were going to marry an Indian girl? They would be horrified. You've got to marry someone from your own circle who'll give the Duke an heir . . .'

'My father likes you!'

'He's very sweet but I can see he views me with suspicion. And rightly so – what would he say if he could hear our conversation?'

'I don't care what he says,' Frank said, getting up again to light a cigarette. 'I'm not marrying to please him but because I love you.'

'How many girls have you said that to?' Sunita said, watching as Frank blushed. 'There! You are too honest to deny it. I'm not the first girl you've asked to marry you and I won't be the last.'

'Damn it! Oh sorry, Sunita – I know you hate swearing – but you can't do it.'

'Do what?' She looked at him, her face pale, her eyes wide with anxiety.

'Drive me away. I may be young but I'm not an idiot. I know what I have in you. I'd be mad to let you go.' He knelt down beside her, took her hand and stroked it. 'Yes, all right, I have thought I've been in love before but this is different. You ought not to doubt me.'

'Sorry. Am I interrupting something?'

'Oh, Verity, it's you,' Frank said, momentarily put out. 'If you must know, I was asking Sunita to marry me.'

'Golly, what bad timing! I'll walk about a bit and come back in ten minutes and congratulate you, shall I?'

'I told him he practises on all the girls,' Sunita said, trying to sound light-hearted.

'Do you, Frank? I wonder if Edward proposes to other women?'

'I'm following your example, Miss Browne,' Sunita added with forced gaiety. 'I've told him I'm not planning to get married.'

'I'm thinking of changing my mind,' Verity said coolly.

'You are?' Frank was amazed and failed to disguise it. 'Good show! I say, won't the old boy be flummoxed when Uncle Ned says he's marrying you and I tell him I'm marrying Sunita!'

'What larks, indeed,' Verity said acidly. 'You mean neither of us is suited to joining the famous Mersham clan?'

'No, I didn't mean that!' He saw with horror how his words might be interpreted.

'We know what you mean,' Sunita said, coming to his rescue. 'I think you had better leave us now, Frank, so we can have a girls' talk. I think I need Miss Browne to advise me.'

Frank opened his mouth to speak but Verity stopped him. 'Go!' she commanded.

'I'm going. I'll just say this, Verity, I leave my future in your hands and you'd better not let me down!'

Sunita waved her plaster cast at him threateningly and he left with as much dignity as he could muster.

12

Verity and Edward had driven down with Basil to Mersham to go through with Connie and Gerald the preparations to receive the Jewish children who would be housed and cared for there until they could be found families prepared to take them in. To Verity's surprise, the Duke was whole-heartedly behind the venture. He had felt so useless in the face of so much suffering that it was a positive pleasure to have, at last, something to do – to make a difference, however small, to the dispossessed. It was what his brother would have done had he been alive and the sense of inferiority he had felt after a lifetime in the shadow of the dead hero was made a little easier to bear.

When they left for Croydon to catch a flight to Zurich Connie had surprised Verity by hugging her almost as if she was apologizing for any unkind thoughts she had harboured.

Edward had tried to get permission from the authorities in Vienna to accompany the train on its journey through Austria but the Nazis refused. The idea of an English lord witnessing this shabby act of mercy was not one they could contemplate. They also sought to hide what they were doing from the ordinary Viennese. They rightly believed that the solid citizenry of that great city had no wish to be disturbed by scenes of extravagant and often noisy grief. Why should they have to witness distraught parents parting from their children – probably for ever? It wasn't their fault or, if it was, there was nothing they could do about it and it was better to pretend it wasn't happening. So it was decreed that the train would leave Vienna at three in the morning and would reach the border about seven o'clock.

On the Swiss side of the border, Verity and Edward, along with a reception committee of refugee agencies and Swiss welfare bodies, huddled in the cold and talked quietly of the arrangements which had been made to feed and reassure three hundred terrified children – many of whom could not speak a word of French or English. The Swiss and French governments had declined to take any more refugees from *Grossdeutschland*. The Swiss wanted to preserve their neutrality and the French were unwilling to give the German authorities any excuse for taking action against French passport holders in the new Reich.

The children were to be whisked to the coast across two countries with the minimum of delay and offloaded on to ferries to take them to their new home. It was a lot to ask of children who had already suffered so much but it had to be done. Verity and Edward chatted with British representatives of the Movement for the Care of Children from Germany and the British Committee for the Jews of Germany about the urgency of the situation. This was to be the first of many trains from Vienna and Berlin and they agreed there would be lessons to be learnt. They would have their work cut out if their escort duty was to be judged a success.

When the children reached England, two hundred were to go to reception centres – holiday camps in the summer months – where they would be looked after until homes could be found for them. Mersham was to take the remaining hundred and Connie had marshalled the neighbourhood to help look after them. Nothing like this had ever been attempted before and only time would tell if the preparations were adequate. At Verity's urging, the *New Gazette* had started a fund for the children and Lord Weaver had personally promised ten thousand pounds.

The stationmaster informed them that the train had arrived at Feldkirch, the last station inside Austria, and was waiting there – he didn't know why. An hour passed and still no train appeared. Someone said the train was being searched. Somebody else said it had broken down. Another hour passed before there was a faint sound of wheels on metal track and smoke was seen.

It was one of the most distressing sights Verity could remember witnessing – and she had seen a few – when, at last, the train came to a halt. The children – aged from five to fifteen – were almost all in tears. Each had a label tied round their neck bearing a number which corresponded to their permit to leave the country. When asked what had caused the delay at the border, one of the older girls said that every child had been made to open the one pathetic suitcase the Viennese authorities had allowed them to take with them and anything new or of any value had been stolen by the border guards. The children had not been given anything to eat or drink and, as the lavatories were already overflowing, many of the smaller children had wet themselves or worse.

Without meaning to, the older children – aware of the danger they were in – conveyed to the younger ones their fear of being taken off the train and sent who knew where. The three adults who had been allowed to travel with the children had been made to leave them at the border and return to Vienna. Edward was unable to discover if the Dreisers had been permitted to accompany the train. None of the children seemed to know the names of the adults who had come with them to the border.

Among the older children, tears quickly turned to smiles when the voluntary workers – mostly Catholic but some Jewish – handed round hot cocoa and sandwiches. The smaller children, bewildered and asking for their parents, were hard to console and clutched the hands of older brothers or sisters with desperate strength while those without anyone at all retreated into their own private misery.

Verity and Edward – alarmed by what they had taken on – did their best to help sort out the children going to Mersham. They were to board another train bound for Boulogne where they were to take ship for England. All the time, Edward was looking for one particular child and finally found her twisting her plaits with one hand and sucking her thumb with the other. It was Heidi, Joan Miller's child. But where was Joan?

Edward looked at his watch. 'She should have been here hours ago,' he fretted. 'I hope she managed to escape from Mandl. I don't know what we'll do with the child if she doesn't come soon.'

At that moment, a chauffeur-driven car drew up and Joan rushed out, furs flying, her usual icy calm replaced by blind panic. She saw Heidi at once and ran over to pick her up. The child seemed only moderately pleased to see her and Edward heard her ask, '*Wo ist Papa?*'

Before Joan could answer – though what answer she could have given Edward did not know – a taxi drew up and Mandl appeared beside them.

'Papa!' cried the little girl in delight as she struggled to release herself from her mother's embrace.

'*Heidi! Komm'mein Mädel!*' Mandl called to her.

'Stay with me. We are not going with your father,' Joan said, clutching the little girl to her.

'Why can't I go to Papa?' demanded the child. 'I want to be with Papa – not with you.'

At these words the courage seemed to leave Joan, and Edward thought she might faint. She dropped Heidi who sped off to join her father. He picked her up and cuddled her. As he turned to go, a look of triumph crossed his face. Joan's expression conveyed to Edward her agony and his heart went out to her. He moved toward her to give her what comfort he could. Mandl noticed him for the first time and said in English, 'So this was your doing? You thought you could outwit me and steal away my baby? Never!'

He spoke with such passion Edward finally understood what Joan had meant when she called him possessive.

'Mandl! Let the child go. She ought to be with her mother,' he replied as calmly as he could.

'With this whore? *Diese Hure . . .?*' he answered, nodding contemptuously towards Joan. 'Never! You are an interfering *Schwein* and I ought to kill you, but not in front of my little one.' He stroked Heidi's head and kissed her. 'You English – so arrogant, so *viel besser* . . . It is my comfort that my guns will soon reduce your . . . *eitel Selbstzufriedenheit* – your smug self-satisfaction will turn to awe and terror at the might of the German nation in arms.'

Hearing the word gun, Joan seemed suddenly to wake from her trance. She opened her handbag and, for a second, Edward thought she was looking for a cigarette. Instead, he saw she had in her hand a small silver pistol.

She said as though it were a groan, 'Mandl, give me back my child.'

He turned and, as he did so, she shot him. Only, as he was holding the little girl to his chest, the bullet, instead of hitting him, entered the back of Heidi's head. At first, Mandl did not realize what had happened. The little girl did not cry out but he felt her shudder and then go slack in his arms. As he adjusted his hands to support her head, he felt the warm blood ooze stickily over his fingers and cried out in sheer disbelief. Joan made as if to go to her child but stumbled and fell to the ground. As she put out her hand to break her fall, she dropped the gun. So innocent-looking, more like a toy than something that could kill, it slid across the platform and fell on to the tracks beneath the still-steaming train.

Three days later Edward and Verity were walking by the river. Mersham was alive with the cries of children enjoying themselves, playing croquet and ping-pong or those secret games the rules of which adults can only guess at. A few lay crumpled on the grass, still shocked and dazed, unable to come to terms with their sudden removal from all that was familiar. However much they tried to comfort them, their English guardians could not explain to the little ones why they had been parted from their mothers and fathers. Verity, who was not very good with children, found herself hugging one little boy, rigid with grief, whispering to him the sweet nothings Adam – her lost German lover – had taught her when they had lain in each other's arms. She had no idea whether these endearments were appropriate but they seemed to soothe the child.

'I think this has really opened Gerald's eyes to what Hitlerism means in reality. I've heard much less of how Hitler is misunderstood and a peace-lover at heart.'

'Yes,' Verity agreed, 'and have you noticed how much he likes having the children here?'

'You think he feels he's doing something, however small, to right the wrong done to them?'

'Yes, but I think it's simpler than that. He enjoys having the castle full of young people and all those stiff formal rooms echoing to the sounds of children's voices.'

'I think you're right, V. The thing is with Gerald – though I'll kill you if you quote me – is that he has very little imagination. He understands intellectually what is going on in Germany – he reads *The Times* – but he can't grasp the enormity of what is happening to the Jews. Having these children here under his roof brings it home to him – literally.'

They walked on in companionable silence. When they were out of sight of the castle, Verity put her arm through his.

'Do you blame yourself for what happened to little Heidi?'

'Of course I do,' Edward said roughly. 'If I hadn't interfered she would still be alive. I knew in my heart I ought not to have got involved with Joan. She's trouble.'

'You did your best. You couldn't have known that Mandl would find out what was going on. He bullied the poor old nanny to tell him. She was the weak link.'

'I know that but . . .'

'But what? If we didn't try to help people because we were afraid of making matters worse, we would never have got these children out of Vienna.'

'That's different. You know it is. These children had no future in Nazi Austria. We had to do what we could for them. But Heidi had nothing to fear.'

'Dear Edward! Remember how you chided me? You too have a tendency to blame yourself unreasonably. Your conscience is very tender. It's one of the things we have in common – at least I'd like to think so but it does make life uncomfortable.'

'We should be uncomfortable. Why should we be comfortable in a world where violent death is the norm?'

'So, if it's the norm, why do we care when individuals like Georg die violently?'

'We care in order to keep ourselves human. I've told you before, V, it's what I hate about Communism as much as Fascism – the idea that the "common good" is something to which individual men and women have to be sacrificed. Once we label groups of people, we dehumanize them. Surely you can see that?'

'Of course I do but sometimes you have to label people, as you put it. Lloyd George gave the pension to "old people". To everyone – not just those who deserved it. And every child ought to have enough to eat and a sanitary place to live.'

'You know what I mean,' Edward said gruffly.

Ever since that moment at the Swiss border when Joan Miller had killed her child, he had been sunk in gloom. Fortunately, there had been so much to do getting the children across an angry English Channel and then by charabanc to Mersham that he had not, until now, had time to indulge his appetite for self-punishment.

Verity decided she had to distract him.

'You know, I think I've discovered why Peter Gray died. It wasn't very difficult.'

'You have?' Edward lifted his head and looked at her with something like interest.

'Yes. It was all in the picture.'

'The one he was painting the day he died?'

'Yes. He'd painted almost the same picture – or at least the same view – time after time in every kind of light, in good weather and bad. So I had to ask myself why. Or rather I asked Reg Harman. He said that, apart from Vera, the only woman he had ever loved was his wife.'

'And she had died soon after they married?'

'Yes, of influenza like so many others.'

'And the view was special because . . . ?'

'It was where they had courted. Betty – his wife – had

been born and brought up in the farmhouse at the bottom of Tarn Hill.'

'I remember it. It's on the Broadlands estate.'

'That's right. And I discovered' – she could hardly keep the triumph out of her voice – 'that Mountbatten was about to knock it down to build new housing for his tenants.'

'I think I see. Gray heard about this and . . .'

'It made him depressed. The perfect view, which summed up everything that had been good in his life, was to be changed, desecrated. He started taking ergot again – I'm only guessing here – to overcome his depression. It made him ill – forgetful . . . worse – it gave him nightmares.'

'Still guessing?'

'No. I tracked down his doctor. He confirmed that Gray was being visited with bad memories of the war – memories he thought he had put behind him – and he feared for his mental health.'

'So you think he committed suicide by taking too much ergot?'

'One can't know for certain but I think that on the day he died he was on his way to talk to Mountbatten – to beg him to leave the farmhouse as it was.'

'Mountbatten never said anything about meeting him.'

'I don't think he did meet him. In fact, I don't believe he had any idea that Gray wanted to remonstrate with him. I think Gray saw the activity below him, guessed Mountbatten was having one of his house parties and decided on the spur of the moment to beard him in his den and beg him not to spoil his view.'

'On the spur of the moment? I think I remember you saying the note he made on the canvas was either an R or a squiggle or a . . .'

'An M! Of course! It wasn't a spur of the moment decision. He was gearing himself up to go to Broadlands. That's why he forgot his palette knife. He wasn't intending to paint that day.'

'So why did he take his paints and the picture?'

'As a talisman? To focus on what he was in danger of losing? Who knows? Perhaps it was just automatic. He reached for his paintbox because he always took it with him to Tarn Hill.'

Edward was silent. 'Yes, I think you've cracked it. Are you going to tell Vera?'

'I think I owe her that.'

'And Lord Louis?'

'What's the point? If I'm right, it's still not his fault.'

'You know, old thing,' Edward said, cheering up slightly, 'it's rather a relief to think that Gray wasn't killed.'

'Don't call me "old thing",' Verity corrected him automatically. 'Makes me feel like an armchair.'

'Sorry, but Gray . . .'

'The war damaged him and the influenza killed his wife.'

'Yes, but . . . Well, do you think that perhaps Georg also died accidentally?'

She furrowed her brow. 'I'm beginning to think we'll never be able to prove anything else.'

'Let's look at the facts,' Edward said and Verity was glad to hear his voice lift. 'There's no question someone lured him down to the stables. He wouldn't have gone there of his own volition. The lighter in the straw was a Camel and the first time I met Rose he gave me a Camel and lit it with his Camel lighter. I remember it vividly.'

'But there are hundreds and hundreds of Camel cigarette lighters. They give them out to publicize the brand.'

'Granted, but probably not round here.'

'And Georg wanted to sell the Dürer through Rose.'

'Or at least get it valued by him.'

'And there's no sign of it so we can assume Rose stole it, knowing he'd get away with it.'

'If Georg was dead,' Edward agreed. 'He either found him dead and took the opportunity to steal the picture or he killed him.'

'How?'

'By exciting the horse – but how could he have done that? I can't imagine he knows anything about horses. He's not the type.'

'Perhaps the pony – a stallion, overfed and skittish – was frightened by someone or something . . . by Georg and lashed out. Perhaps it *was* an accident. But you remember how I told you I'd found a clear print of a car or a motorbike tyre outside the barn on the far side of the stable yard?'

'And one of the grooms told me he'd heard a motorbike when they went to get the stretcher for Sunita. Oh God, V!' Edward said, rubbing his forehead. 'I think I know who must have been riding that bike.'

'Not . . .?'

'Who else could it be?'

'What'll you do next?' Verity asked anxiously.

'I'll have to ask him, won't I?'

'Now?'

'I think we need to clear it up, don't you?'

'Let me alone! My husband is only in the next room.' Ayesha's eyes flashed and Mountbatten let go her hand.

'I was only trying to say . . .'

'It was all a mistake,' she broke in. 'I ought not to have allowed it.'

'Don't tell me it was all my fault!' he said scornfully.

'I'm not saying it was your fault, Dickie. I wanted you and . . .'

'And I wanted you! I still want you, damn it. Forget about Sunny . . .'

'Of course I can't forget about him,' she countered fiercely, managing to keep her voice low. 'I love him. I ought not to have given way. He'd never forgive me.'

'But why not?' Mountbatten sounded puzzled. 'You've done your duty. You've given him a son and a daughter almost as beautiful as her mother. Why should he mind you having a little fun?'

'That's what you call it, is it, fun?' Her eyes were bright with contempt. 'I was just a casual plaything? What would you call it? A bit of fluff? A bit on the side?'

'No! Well, I . . . yes!' he stuttered. 'We want each other. What harm does it do as long as Sunny doesn't know?'

'Dickie! You're quite without scruple. Of course it matters. Or rather it matters to me. And it would matter to Sunny. You may have different rules with Edwina but to Sunny . . . to us, it matters . . . being faithful. Can't you understand?'

'No, I can't,' Mountbatten hissed. 'I want you, Ayesha, and I don't understand why it's suddenly all so different. I thought Sunita . . . I thought it was a golden opportunity . . . that's why I insisted on you staying at Broadlands.'

'Oh, Dickie! You really don't understand, do you? You're missing some cog we call conscience. To you Sunita's accident was just an opportunity to have me at your mercy. No! Don't touch me! It's finished. Please, you must understand. I can never be alone with you again. I ought not to have . . .'

Mountbatten looked at Ayesha with incomprehension and then disgust.

'Go then! Go as quickly as you can and take your brood with you. I thought you cared for me but I see I was wrong.'

'Dickie, please! Don't let's part as enemies. I'm grateful for what you did for us . . . for Sunita . . .'

Mountbatten, without a backward glance, stormed out of the drawing-room. Sunny put his head round the door and said lightly, 'All finished then, my love? Shall I tell the servants to get on with the packing?'

Ayesha looked at her husband and saw that he knew exactly what had taken place but had trusted his wife to put an end to it.

'I love you, Sunny. You know that I'll always love you, don't you?'

'I do,' he replied. 'You don't have to tell me.'

'I have to tell myself,' she said quietly. But Sunny had already gone to tell the servants to prepare for their departure.

They drove the by now familiar few miles to Broadlands and Edward parked the Lagonda by the stables. Of course there was no sign of Verity's tyre print.

'Look, there's my friend Johnson,' Edward said. 'Hello there, we're not burglars!'

'No indeed, my lord. I'm glad to see you, sir.' Johnson scratched his head with a muddy finger. 'The fact is, when Jim and I were mucking out Button's stable, we found something. It may be nothing but . . .'

'Show me.'

'Come into the tack room. I put it in a drawer.'

'In a drawer! So it's not very big?'

The bridles, saddles, boots and the age-old scent of horse gave the tack room a character all of its own. Edward had hunted as a young man and it all came back to him now – crisp winter days riding across ploughed fields in pursuit of an elusive fox. He regretted that he had become so city-bound and decided there and then that, before war broke out and the shutters came down, he must have a summer and a winter of healthy exercise.

'Here it is,' Johnson said, taking an old biscuit tin out of a drawer and passing it to Edward. Cautiously, he prised open the lid and found inside the fragments of a small picture.

'I'm afraid Button must have stepped on it. There's nothing much left.' Johnson sounded apologetic.

'You were right to show it to me. I think these may be the remains of a drawing which belonged to the man who died.' They were so badly damaged it was difficult to see precisely what they were and he passed the torn and muddied scraps to Verity.

'Is it the Dürer sketch?' she asked doubtfully.

'I think it must be but only a scientist could tell us for sure.' Edward sighed heavily. 'We've allowed a priceless work of art, which could have thrown light on the working methods of a great master, to be destroyed. The world has lost something of great beauty from everything I've heard of it. I feel very much to blame. Well, at least we didn't accuse Rose of stealing it. We would have looked perfect asses.'

'I'm afraid I did,' Verity confessed. 'He said he would sue me if I repeated it.'

Edward laughed. 'Ah well, no harm done. I hope it gave him a jolt – he's altogether too smooth for his own good.'

'If the police had done their job properly, they would have searched through the straw and found it,' Verity said censoriously. 'I only hope Rose was right and it was a nineteenth-century copy.'

'Let's hope so,' Edward agreed. 'I'll take this, if I may, Johnson. Can you spare the tin? Perhaps the experts at the National Gallery can do something with it.'

On their way to the house, they put their heads into the garage where Mountbatten stored his collection of motor-cycles.

'I must suggest he keeps this door locked. Some of these machines are worth a lot of money,' Edward said.

'I wonder if Mountbatten would let us borrow a couple of them. Do you remember when we rode those two Triumphs at Haling? I suddenly have a great desire to ride one of these beauties.'

'I seem to remember, V, that I discovered – after the event – that you didn't have a driving licence.'

'Well, I do now.'

Edward was not listening. He was examining the wheel of the Rudge. 'It has certainly been ridden recently. Look at the mud on it.'

'Well, let's get on with it then.'

It was with a heavy heart that Verity and Edward asked the butler if the Maharaja and Maharini were in the house.

'They are taking tea with his lordship in the drawing-room,' he informed them.

Edward's heart sank even further. It looked as though Lord Louis would have to be told.

'Could you ask your master if he could spare us a minute, please?'

They were shown into the drawing-room and greeted warmly by Sunny and Ayesha, though both seemed rather strained. Lord Louis introduced his wife. Edwina was standing by the window and looked as though she could not wait for her guests to leave but was polite enough to Verity and Edward.

'Miss Browne,' she said, with the clipped intonation of the aristocrat, 'I am very glad to meet you. I read your reports in the newspaper. I admire you for doing a man's job and doing it better than most men could.'

Verity was surprised and pleased.

'You think there will be war?' Lady Louis asked without further small talk.

'I am sure of it,' she replied.

'I know it is wrong to say this but I will not be so very sad. Dickie will be able to prove that his navy can defend us. I shall find war work of another kind.'

Mountbatten said, half apologetically, 'It will be like the last war in one respect – while the men are fighting, the women will have to take over on the home front.'

'Not only on the home front . . .' Lady Louis stopped herself and contemplated Edward. 'I can see you have come with some news, Lord Edward.'

'We shall leave you, now,' Sunny said, rising from his armchair and addressing the Mountbattens. 'I cannot tell you how grateful we are to you both for the way you have looked after us. We are departing in an hour or two, Edward. I was going to telephone you. Our stay here has been so much longer than we anticipated but our hosts have been very patient.'

Sunny seemed relieved to be leaving, Edward thought, and he wondered if there had been some row or misunderstanding between the Mountbattens and their guests. Certainly, Ayesha and Mountbatten were making sure they did not catch each other's eye.

'Don't go for a moment, Sunny,' Edward said abruptly. 'What I have to say concerns you.'

'Concerns me?' Sunny echoed.

'And Harry. Is he outside?'

'He's at the stables, I believe,' Ayesha said, looking a little alarmed.

Mountbatten, obviously intrigued, asked if Edward wanted him summoned.

'I think it would be for the best, if you don't mind.'

For ten minutes they tried to talk of other things. Lady Louis seemed genuinely interested in Verity who blossomed, as she always did, under sympathetic questioning. No one else said much.

At last, Harry appeared looking rather dishevelled in riding boots and breeches.

'You wanted to see me?' He scowled at the assembled company. 'I've been riding,' he added unnecessarily.

'Yes, Harry,' Sunny said. 'Lord Edward apparently has something to say which concerns you. Are you clean enough to sit down without muddying the furniture?'

Harry looked at Edward balefully and threw himself down on an upright chair.

Verity thought he had a good idea of what was coming and felt almost sorry for him. It reminded her of being summoned to the headmistress's study on one of the many occasions when she had been caught misbehaving.

Sunny looked first at his son and then at Edward in consternation. 'I say . . .' he began.

'Is it about the man who was killed in the stable?' Harry interrupted.

'Yes, I'm afraid it is,' Edward answered.

'It was a terrible accident. That's what the police have concluded,' Mountbatten said although there was a hesitation in his voice.

'I think it *was* an accident,' Edward began slowly, 'but an unnecessary one. Georg Dreiser – the man who was killed when Button went wild in his stable,' he added for Lady Louis' benefit, 'was a Jewish refugee. He came out of Austria with nothing of value except a small drawing which he believed was from Albrecht Dürer's sketchbook.'

'Dürer?' She repeated in astonishment.

'Yes, it was – or at least Georg and his parents thought it was – a preliminary sketch for a painting of a young girl which is now in the Kunsthistorisches Museum in Vienna. I have not seen the picture myself but from reproductions it is obviously a masterpiece.'

'So the drawing was very valuable?' Mountbatten asked.

'Indeed. If it proved to be a genuine sketch by Dürer, it might have been worth many thousands of pounds.'

'You think it wasn't genuine?' Lady Louis inquired.

208

'I'm no expert. Stuart Rose thought it could have been a nineteenth-century copy.'

'Stuart?'

'Yes, Lady Louis. Rose was a guest here when Mr Dreiser was staying with my brother at Mersham Castle. Hearing of Rose's reputation as an art expert, Dreiser brought the drawing with him to Broadlands on the day of the polo match.'

'How do you know this?' Mountbatten barked.

'Rose told me that Georg had shown it to him,' Verity said.

Mountbatten nodded his head for Edward to continue.

'But what has this to do with Harry?' Ayesha could not restrain herself from asking.

'I shall tell you,' Verity continued. 'Rose and Dreiser had agreed to meet at the stables during the polo. Georg did not like horses but he guessed the stables would be deserted while everyone was watching the match. He knew he had something very valuable but he wanted to keep it secret until he had decided what to do with it. Rose presumably planned to talk to his friends in the art world and find out what the drawing was worth.'

'Georg went to the stables after he had had a brief altercation with Herr Braken. Braken, or Putzi as he's called,' Edward explained to Lady Louis, 'is a friend of Hitler from when he was a nobody . . .'

'Hitler still is a nobody!' Verity could not resist commenting.

'But now he has offended his master and is contemplating offering his services to the British Government or the Americans. Verity happened to overhear Putzi threatening Dreiser – telling him to stay away from Joan Miller.'

Lady Louis raised her eyebrows. 'They had both had affairs with her,' Edward added, having no wish to go into any detail in Harry's presence. 'Georg's reaction – predictably – was to seek out Joan and together they walked down to the stables talking of old times. Georg said he was lonely and asked Joan to resume their relationship. She refused.

'Then they heard someone coming – or rather Joan smelled the cigarette Rose was smoking. She made off and Georg had his meeting with Rose. Rose examined the drawing and told Georg – this is according to Rose – that it was a nineteenth-century copy and nothing like as valuable as he imagined.

'My first thought was that Rose killed Georg to get his hands on the drawing. Even a nineteenth-century copy would be worth something and, of course, if it turned out to be genuine ... well, that was worth killing for. I was wrong. Johnson, one of the grooms, later came across the remains of the sketch – by now totally ruined – when he was mucking out Button's stable. Here it is.'

Edward opened the tin box and passed the contents to Mountbatten.

'So why did Dreiser go into Button's stable and what drove the pony so wild that he lashed out at him?' Mountbatten asked.

'That's the question and I admit I was foxed until Verity reminded me that she had seen a tyre print in the stable yard and one of the grooms said he had heard the sound of a motorbike when they rushed back to get a stretcher for Sunita. Georg also heard it and, not wishing to be found there skulking, dodged into Button's stable. He probably had no idea it was occupied until he closed the door. It would have been quite dark in the stable.'

He stopped and turned to Harry whose sulkiness had given way, Edward thought, to a mixture of rage and fear. 'Harry, I know you did not mean to cause Georg's death but it was you, was it not, who rode the noisy Rudge into the stable yard and unsettled Button?'

Harry remained mute. Sunny opened his mouth to say something but, before he could speak, Mountbatten barked an order.

'Come on, boy, it's time you made a clean breast of it. You heard what Lord Edward said – you are not being blamed for Herr Dreiser's death. You couldn't know he was hiding in the stable but, if what he says is true, you ought to have come forward as soon as you heard what had happened and admitted to taking the Rudge without my permission and riding it where you ought not to.'

Mountbatten had all the authority of an officer over a naval rating and it seemed to do the trick.

'I didn't mean to. I was bored and fed up because I wasn't playing polo so I thought I'd borrow the Rudge. It was so exciting the last time, when we found the dead body, but then I only rode for a few seconds and it was all over so quickly. I wanted to see what it was like over rough ground.'

'That was so bad of you, Harry,' Ayesha said, her eyes filling with tears.

'No, it wasn't,' Mountbatten snapped. 'It's what any boy would do. It's what I would do in those circumstances.'

Harry brightened. 'Would you, sir?'

'You should have asked my permission – but we'll say no more about that. So what happened? Where did you go?'

'I rode right up the drive and round the back of the house and through the stables . . .'

'It didn't occur to you that you might frighten the horses?'

'I thought they were all up at the polo ground.'

'You didn't see anyone near the stables, I suppose?' Edward asked.

'No, sir. I had no idea Mr Dreiser was there. Of course, when I heard what had happened, I realized it must have been me who frightened Button.'

'Why didn't you tell us?' Mountbatten demanded.

Harry hung his head. 'I knew I ought to have done, sir. I *meant* to but . . . I was a coward. I thought I might go to prison. I didn't want to shame my father.'

'Now look here, Harry,' Mountbatten said, not un-kindly, 'we all make mistakes. We all do things we don't mean to and find our actions sometimes have unforeseen and unpleasant consequences.' He coughed as though he had just thought of some of these. 'The only thing that matters is that we face up to them. You ought to have come to your father or to me and told us what had happened. In the long run, as you have now found out, it is much worse when you don't speak up frankly, like a man.'

'I know, sir. I am very sorry. It has been weighing me down. I wanted to tell someone but then it was all too late and I couldn't. I'm not a murderer, am I?'

'Come here, Harry,' Sunny said. 'Lord Louis is quite correct and I expect any son of mine to behave like an English gentleman and a future ruler of Batiala, but no, you are not a murderer. Isn't that right, Edward?'

'Certainly, but it would have saved us all a great deal of worry if you had told us what you had been up to. Miss Browne and I felt particular responsibility for Mr Dreiser because, as you are aware, Harry, we were instrumental in bringing him over to England from Vienna. You know why we did that?'

'Because the Nazis are putting the Jews into prison camps?'

'That's right. We thought – and I know you will agree – that those of us who are fortunate not to be persecuted for our race or religion ought to help those who are.'

Verity thought he sounded rather pompous but forgave him.

'Yes, sir.' Harry hung his head.

'Now, what I would like to suggest, if your father agrees – and this is not a punishment – is that you help us with the next trainload of children to arrive from Berlin or Vienna.'

'I would like that, sir,' Harry said, his eyes shining. 'And, what's more, I could get some of my friends from school to help.'

'That would be an excellent idea!' Mountbatten agreed.

'I'll talk to the headmaster,' Sunny said.

'Will I go to prison?' Harry said, once again a worried small boy.

'No, indeed,' Edward said. 'I don't think there is any need to tell Inspector Beeston, do you, sir?' He looked across at Mountbatten.

'No. I don't see what good it would do. Beeston thinks Dreiser's death was an accident – which it was. It will only confuse matters if we explain how the accident came about. In fact, I suggest that all of us keep absolutely quiet about Harry's misdemeanour. He has learnt a lesson – that's the important thing. Telling the world about it won't bring Dreiser back to life. I don't think we even need tell Frank and Sunita. It's over and done with.'

13

'And it would have embarrassed Mountbatten,' Verity
said wryly as they discussed on their way back to
Mersham why there had been no proper police investigation into Gray's death. 'Talk of unforeseen consequences! If he hadn't decided to convert that farmhouse
into houses for estate workers, Gray might still be alive.'

'You can't blame Mountbatten for that, V.'

'I don't, but there is an irony there. We have looked into
two strange deaths and found that both of them were – if
not accidents – certainly the unintended results of
someone's actions.'

'So what?' Edward said dismissively. 'We can't ever
know what the future holds. When Georg introduced
himself to you at that ridiculous *thé dansant* in Vienna, who
could have said where it would lead?'

'And if you hadn't persuaded Joan to get her child out
of Vienna on that train, she might still be alive today,'
Verity said, stung into responding. Edward's face fell. 'I'm
sorry, I shouldn't have said that,' she added, immediately
contrite.

'No, I deserved it.'

'How long do you think Joan will be in prison?'

'I don't know. The Swiss authorities were surprisingly
understanding. I'm going back for the trial, of course. I
think she wants to be punished, but it was, once again, an
accident.'

'She meant to kill Mandl. I think you are too lenient.'

'Perhaps I am. As I get older, I find I am less and less willing to condemn. The one thing she didn't mean to do was to harm her child. Think what she is suffering. How did Wilde put it? "Yet each man kills the thing he loves."'

'Unintended consequences . . .' Verity said thoughtfully.

'The war will bring plenty of those – if we can ever nerve ourselves to fight. I keep thinking that even this spineless lot of halfwits who pretend to govern us can't humiliate themselves further but they always find some excuse to retreat and surrender.'

'Well, if Hitler takes the Sudetenland, even Chamberlain will have to do something.'

'I wish I thought you were right, V.' Edward was silent for a moment and then took a deep breath. 'You said that, when we had cleared up the mystery surrounding Georg's death, I could ask you to marry me.'

'Did I?' Verity sounded surprised.

'Yes, you did. Don't pretend you don't remember. I'm going to ask you one last time. If you refuse me I'll know you mean it and I promise not to bother you again.'

Verity looked startled and opened her mouth to protest – to delay the inevitable – but Edward gave her no time. He knelt in the muddy grass, ignoring the fact that he was ruining a perfectly good pair of Harris tweed trousers.

'Verity – darling – will you marry me? I promise I won't expect you to change. You can be as bloody-minded as you like, run halfway across the globe and get yourself into the most frightful jams and I won't complain – or at least not much. I would prefer you not to take other lovers but even then . . .'

'Edward!' Verity sounded genuinely shocked. 'If I married you, I certainly wouldn't feel free to take lovers . . .'

'However much you might want to?' Edward completed her sentence.

'No . . . yes . . . oh, please, get off your knees. You look absurd and you're making me feel uncomfortable.'

'Not as uncomfortable as I feel. But I'm not getting up until you give me an answer, drat it!'

The 'drat it' was precipitated by a trickle of water running down his leg into his sock.

'Well . . .'

At that moment, Frank and Sunita hove into view. 'I say, Uncle Ned, are you all right? Have you tripped or something?'

Sunita put a hand to her mouth to hide a smile. Edward struggled to his feet looking thoroughly put out. 'Damn you, Frank, what do you want? Sorry, Sunita – you don't mind me swearing at my nephew, do you?'

'Not at all,' she giggled. 'I expect I shall be doing the same quite soon.'

'What do you mean?' Verity asked suspiciously.

'The fact is,' Frank said, unable to hold back the news a minute longer, 'I have asked Sunita to marry me and she has agreed. Isn't that wonderful? She is the best and most beautiful girl I have ever met and I love her to bits.' He pulled her to him and kissed her.

'Please, Frank, behave,' Sunita protested, though not convincingly, Edward thought.

'My dear boy . . .' he exclaimed, his heart sinking at the thought of the ructions which were sure to follow this announcement. 'That's wonderful! Isn't it, V? Have you told . . .?'

'Wonderful!' Verity echoed, reaching out to embrace them both.

'Do you think my father will cut up rough, Uncle?' Frank broke away, looking worried. 'Sunita thinks he won't allow it but I've told her he'll be delighted. After all, he's the most frightful snob and she is the daughter of a maharaja.'

'And an old friend of mine,' Edward reminded him. 'Sunita, I'm delighted, truly. Frank's a good boy but he'll lead you the most frightful dance, I should imagine. But why are you telling me when you haven't yet spoken to your parents, Frank? I mean I'm most flattered but . . .'

Frank grimaced. 'Well, the thing is, as I say, the pater ought to be really pleased but . . .'

'You want me to help you break it to him? Is that it? And what about your father, Sunita? Have you asked his permission to marry this ne'er-do-well? He might have objections.'

'He'll do whatever he thinks will make me happy.' She smiled and Edward had no doubt that she was right.

'Can we get it over with, Uncle?' Frank suddenly looked like a worried little boy.

'Oh, God! Now? I suppose I had better go with you. I won't be a minute, V. At least I hope I not. Wait for me, will you? I must have an answer . . .'

'Take as long as you need,' she said, laughing. 'I have to do some thinking anyway.'

'I'll stay with you, if I may,' Sunita said. 'You see, Frank,' she explained, 'if your father refuses his consent I don't want to be humiliated by having to hear him say he doesn't think me good enough.'

'Of course you're good enough!' Frank expostulated. 'What's so special about the Dukes of Mersham? From what I've heard, the first one was little better than a pirate and at least two have had their heads chopped off.'

'Yes, but that was centuries ago. They've all been frightfully respectable for ages.'

'Well, if Pa does cut up rough, we'll elope. He can cut me off without a shilling for all I care. I love you and that's an end to it.'

Edward could not prevent himself trying to imagine Frank surviving on whatever he could earn or cadge from his uncle and shuddered. 'I shouldn't really say it but I rather doubt Gerald *could* cut you off – so much of Mersham is entailed.'

'You mean you can't *not* be a duke if you are born to it?'

'Oh hell!' Edward exclaimed. 'This is worse than when I was at Eton nerving myself to dive into an icy river. Come on, let's get it over with.'

The Duke looked at his son and Edward thought one hardly needed Freud to interpret the war of emotions reflected in his face. Connie, too, though she had anticipated this moment, was pale and not entirely at her ease.

'Aren't you a bit young to be getting married?' Gerald managed eventually. 'And, Ned, why have you got mud all over your trousers? Did you fall over?'

They were in the library. The Duke had been sleeping behind *The Times* and Connie was finishing some embroidery when Frank burst in, Edward in tow.

'I thought you were urging me to get married the other day.' Frank sounded aggrieved.

'You really love this girl?' Connie asked.

'Mother! Don't call her "this girl". You are talking about my future wife.'

'Sorry, darling. Sunita. I mean, you have thought you were in love before . . . that American girl on the *Queen Mary* . . .'

'This is quite different. I can't understand you both. Sunita is . . . she's quite wonderful.'

'She's charming,' Connie agreed quickly. 'Has she talked to her parents about this . . . about this engagement?'

'Not yet. We thought we'd tell you first.'

'Well, I think both of you should talk to them.'

'You do like Sunita?' Frank asked anxiously.

'We like her enormously and when we get to know her, I am sure we will love her. She's a delightful girl.' Connie was eager to reassure her son. If Sunita was to be her daughter-in-law, she must never be reproached for making disparaging remarks about her. 'We only want to be sure *you* are sure.'

'I'm quite sure!' Frank said firmly and Edward felt proud of him. 'She's rich, if that's what you are worrying about. And a maharaja is a sort of king – much higher in rank than a duke, you know.'

Edward, seeing that his brother was about to contest this remark, broke in. 'Please, Frank, you know this isn't about money or rank. It's about your happiness. I'm right, am I not, Gerald?'

'Quite right. What I would like to suggest is that you have a private engagement and if after . . .' He thought about saying a year and then, knowing that this would not wash, changed his mind. 'If, after six months, you are both still certain you want to get married, then let's make it all official.'

'I think that's fair, Frank,' Edward said and his brother looked at him gratefully.

'There's a war coming . . .'

'I still think you should do what your father asks,' Connie said. 'During the last war there were so many quick weddings – shotgun weddings they were called – before the men went to the front and many of them did not last.'

'Well,' Frank said dubiously, 'I suppose it's all right. Shall I ask Sunita to come in so you can tell her?'

'Of course!' Connie responded faintly.

'I'll go!' Edward decided it was time he retired. He had done his bit and now it was up to father and son to thrash it out between them.

He went back to Verity, relieved that things had gone as well as they had, and told Sunita she was to join Frank in the drawing-room.

'It's all right then?' Sunita opened her eyes wide.

'It's all right but they'll make you wait a few months before it's official. I'll let Frank tell you.'

'You're a darling, isn't he, Verity?' Sunita said, hugging and kissing him.

Edward went pink with pleasure. 'Run along. You're not marrying me but Frank's a very lucky boy. I am quite sure he doesn't deserve you.'

When she had gone to discover her fate, Verity said, 'It's such a lot of nonsense. What does it matter who Frank marries so long as he loves her? Why do they have to wait? The English aristocracy needs new blood so that, after the war, when it's relieved of all its wealth and privileges, it can cope.'

'That's all very well, V, but being a duke . . .'

'Fiddlesticks! If Gerald had cut up rough . . . well, I know Connie wouldn't . . . but if Frank isn't allowed to marry Sunita he'll run off and marry someone quite unsuitable just for . . . not spite, but you know what I mean – on the rebound. Someone like that American woman who told us all about sex . . . the one who worked for Dr Kinsey.'

'Sadie?' Edward shuddered. 'I agree. Don't harangue me. I'm on Frank's side. I have no regrets about bringing them together.'

'Another of those "unintended consequences" we were talking about. If you hadn't met Sunny on the road like that . . . If his Rolls had been more reliable . . .'

'She's beautiful, sensible and just the sort of girl he needs. She'll make him an excellent wife. Does that satisfy you?'

'And, one day, a good duchess – if there still are duchesses,' Verity added. 'I'll tell you what, Edward,' she said, turning to look him in the face, 'you've probably forgotten but, before we were interrupted, you asked me to marry you.'

'I hadn't forgotten,' he said gravely.

'I *will* marry you but only when Frank marries Sunita. I couldn't marry into a family whose head objects to his son marrying a rich, beautiful girl – the daughter of a maharaja no less – just because she's got brown skin.'

'V!' Edward protested weakly. 'No one's objecting to anything.'

Verity took no notice. She was on her hobby horse and she refused to get off. 'I'm sorry, Edward, but I mean it. Look on this as a sort of test. You fancy yourself as a negotiator, so negotiate this. Then I'll marry you – but not in a church, of course.'

Edward closed his eyes for a moment. Weren't proposals of marriage supposed to be met with timorous cries of pleasure and gratitude on the girl's part? Why did Verity have to be the one who saw it as a challenge to her sense of self?

'Do you love me?' he asked at last.

'That's got nothing to do with it. I *do* love you,' she said, relenting a little. 'You know I love you but marriage is a different kettle of fish. You know how suspicious I am of it. If you can prove to me that it works, then I'll marry you. Otherwise I will be your concubine. That's such a lovely word, isn't it?' She smiled the smile he so loved. 'And you haven't got too much time. I'm off to Prague in a few days and goodness only knows who I might meet there.'

220

'V!'

'Just joking, silly!' she said, putting her arm around him. 'I love you and I'll be proud to be your wife. It's not something I ever thought I'd say but . . .'

Edward pressed his lips to hers, stifling any further protestations or qualifications.

'I'm going up to London to see a man about a dog,' Edward said facetiously at breakfast the next morning.

Verity lifted her head from her cornflakes. 'Will you give me a lift? My father's in town and wants to see me. I don't know how he knew I was here but I've just had a telegram from him.'

Verity very rarely saw her father who was a busy lawyer but when he summoned her, she always came running. Edward wondered if she would tell him about his proposal – even ask his permission to marry. He knew better than to voice his thoughts.

'And Joe wants me to come in to the paper to discuss my new posting,' Verity added.

'Two excuses to leave us?' the Duke said with ponderous good humour. 'You want to escape the children? You know the spotty one – I think he's called Emil – has broken the Ming vase in the hall? Mind you, I never liked it.'

'Not escape the children exactly. I hope you don't think I'm running away from my responsibilities but . . . Well, I can't do much here.' Verity managed a smile. 'Connie, you've got a good team to look after them until they can be placed. You don't need me, do you?'

'No, dear. You go and do the job you are meant to be doing. It's much more important than being a nursemaid.'

'Now you are making me feel guilty. You know they've got another train planned – did I tell you, Connie? Don't worry!' she laughed, seeing her face. 'They're not coming here. The *New Gazette* has really got behind the *Kindertransport* as it's being called. You remember when Joe organized that ship to bring refugees from Spain? He sees this as a natural follow-up. His readers love it – feeling generous – and the circulation has shot up.'

'Don't be cynical, V,' Edward put in.

'I'm not. I'm a realist. Joe can get the *New Gazette* to do good deeds but there has to be some sort of reward.'

'So, you're coming with me to London?'

'Yes please.' Verity knew she must not outstay her welcome and, without Edward to protect her, Gerald might give her one of his fierce stares which she found so disconcerting. Connie, she noticed, kept on looking at her oddly, as though suspecting she had something to announce and not understanding why nothing was said. 'Joe telephoned yesterday to say everything is almost ready for me to go to Prague. Apparently, things are really beginning to hot up there.'

'You'll be quite safe in Prague, my dear,' the Duke said comfortably. 'Hitler will not invade – take my word for it. He's got enough on his plate absorbing Austria into his *Grossreich* or whatever he calls it.'

Edward saw Verity wrestle with her need to correct him and was glad to see that she was able to restrain herself.

The Duke's complacency and the fact that he had made what passed for a joke suggested to Edward that his brother was reconciled to Frank's marriage. Sunita had accepted with good grace the Duke's request that she and Frank had a secret six-month engagement before anything was announced publicly and they had gone off happily to tell Sunny and Ayesha.

In the Lagonda, on their way to London, Verity leant over and put her hand on Edward's knee. He jerked the steering wheel and almost hit the kerb.

'I'm such a cow, aren't I, Edward? Any decent girl would be tickled pink to be asked to be your wife. I just use it as a weapon to beat you about the head. I want you to know that it means a great deal to me . . . it means *everything* to have you beside me. No, don't interrupt! I want to say this while I can. I love you and the proof is that I will marry you – since it means so much to you – even though I always swore I wouldn't marry. You are the only man I trust and that's important because, as I have found out, love without trust means nothing. I'll do my best to make you happy but, if I fail, you must never think it was because I didn't love you. Don't say anything!'

Edward was silent but he was deeply moved. This bellicose, awkward, courageous girl had decided to marry him against all her principles. It was enough. He had won through.

Guy Liddell looked at Edward over the top of his spectacles and then looked back at the papers on his desk. Edward was reminded, as Verity had been reminded in Mountbatten's drawing-room, of uneasy interviews with school authorities. It was in just such a way his housemaster – m'tutor, as he was known to the boys in his care – had studied his report before sealing it for despatch to his father. Since the old Duke never referred to them in his presence and, Edward was inclined to think, never even read them, he was able to approach these inquisitions without due concern. This was different. If Liddell approved of what he had done he might be offered a permanent berth in the department. If he was judged to have failed, he would have to look elsewhere for war work when the time came.

Liddell took off his spectacles and stared at Edward. The little moustache on his upper lip quivered and his eyes were icy. It was hard, Edward thought, to imagine him dancing or playing the cello yet he had been told on the best authority the man in front of him was more than proficient in both activities. No, he looked like a thousand other ex-officers, which only went to prove the old axiom that one could not judge a book by its cover.

'In America!' Liddell jabbed at the paper on his desk. 'Braken has thrown in his lot with our cousins across the water. How do you account for your failure, Corinth?'

'I did what I could. I did not like the man but we got on well enough.'

'You didn't like the man? What has that got to do with anything?' Liddell asked angrily. 'Your job was to get him into our fold and you failed.'

'You told me not to suck up to him too obviously. You said I ought to make him want to join us but not bribe him.'

'You think he was bribed?'

'You told me Braken was a snob. He may be a snob but what he wants more than invitations to grand country houses is money. The Americans have more of it than we have. It's as simple as that.'

'Who offered him money? Who handled him?'

'It is in my report, sir. Stuart Rose who, I was informed, was of no account – because he was a Communist and a homosexual – turned out to be an agent of the American intelligence service. Braken found Rose and what he had to offer more attractive than anything we could offer him.'

'You seem very cool about your failure.'

'I am a realist. I can only do what I can do. Sometimes it works out, sometimes it doesn't.'

'Is that the way you judge your unfortunate interference in the marital affairs of that arms-dealer fellow?'

'I very much regret what happened. Mandl is an out-and-out Nazi. He had a better gun to sell than we have – Mountbatten says so and I believe him – but there was no possibility of the British Government doing business with him. What happened to Joan Miller was a tragedy but it had no effect on what I was doing for you.'

Liddell grunted but said nothing for a minute. He turned over several pages of the document on the desk in front of him.

'This is better. You found a way of spiriting the nuclear scientist – Fritz Lange – out of the country before anyone in Vienna noticed.'

'Ruthven-Stuart's a good man, sir.'

'But it was you who set it up.'

'I had help from an Austrian patriot.'

'Don't be so infernally modest, man,' Liddell said with the hint of a smile. 'You won't get much praise from me so you might as well enjoy whatever comes your way.' Edward held his peace. 'Rutherford says he's been an eye-opener. He had no idea the Germans were so advanced. Well done – good work! We're pleased with you.'

Liddell really did smile now and Edward allowed himself a slight nod of acceptance.

'What do you make of Unity Mitford, by the way? You saw she was arrested in Hyde Park the other day for causing a disturbance at a Socialist rally? She was wearing a swastika and shouting Fascist slogans.'

'Mad and bad but no real danger, I would say. Miss Browne says she fancies she's in love with Hitler. She's just a silly girl – nothing worse.'

Liddell went back to grunting. Then he said, 'Anything else to report? What about the death of that Jew your young lady brought over? Was that just an accident, as the police decided?'

'At first, I thought it might have been murder but, in the end, I came to the conclusion that it *was* an accident. I did not like the way the police came to that decision without a proper investigation – just because he was a Jew and so as not to annoy Mountbatten and bring him unwelcome publicity.'

Liddell grunted. 'I don't think you are being quite fair. Beeston's an oaf, I grant you, but he wouldn't say something was an accident if he knew it wasn't.'

'I beg to differ, sir.'

'And Mountbatten? What's your assessment of him? Is the man a charlatan?'

'Not at all. He may be a little vain but he's no fool and as a result of his efforts, some important modifications have been carried out to naval gunnery. He may not have much imagination but he's very thorough. I give him full marks for determination. He could have wasted his life away as a playboy but he's set on making it to the top of his profession. Mr Churchill thinks he has it in him to do it on his own abilities.'

Liddell grunted again but this time his grunt sounded surprised. 'You're very sure of yourself, Corinth.'

'You asked for my assessment, sir,' Edward said, feeling rather hard done by.

'Yes, yes,' Liddell agreed impatiently. 'Well, that's all then, Corinth. Good work – keep it up.'

'Does that mean you will give me other assignments?'

Liddell looked at him and Edward thought there was a suspicion of a twinkle in his cold grey eyes. 'Would you like that?'

'I would, sir. In the event of war, I shall be too old to join the army without making an ass of myself. I would like to be of use to my country some other way, if that's possible.'

'It's possible,' Liddell said with a brusque nod. 'You'll just have to wait and see.'

'But there's not much time. War may be declared sooner . . .'

'There'll be no war for another year at least,' Liddell said decisively. 'Take my word for it.'

Verity was made to wait. Lord Weaver's secretary explained that the great man was discussing with the editor the government's surprise decision to spend eleven million pounds on new aerodromes but Verity was sure that it was his way of putting her in her place. She might be one of Fleet Street's star foreign correspondents and his particular protégée but that did not mean she was indispensable.

She was in a fever because she was dining that evening with her father at the Ritz. It was such a rare treat – he was always so busy and, of course, Verity was now so often abroad – that she wanted to look her best. She had to have her hair done. She had managed to get an appointment with Ray at four and she knew he hated clients being late. He would take his revenge with painful tugs and twists but he was still the best hairdresser in London.

It was ten past three before the editor came out of Weaver's office, throwing her a glance of undisguised dislike. She had never got on with his predecessor and had been full of hope when Michael Henderson was appointed. She had heard good things of him and, under different circumstances, they would probably have got on well. The problem was that Henderson thought he could rewrite her reports. She was adamant that he could not do this and had appealed to Weaver who came down in her favour. As a result, Henderson refused to have anything more to do with her and tried whenever possible to spike her stories.

'Verity! My dear – I hope you haven't been waiting long,' Weaver greeted her disingenuously. 'You know what a gasbag that man is. By the way, he doesn't seem to like you much. Recommended you be fired. No need to look like that. I wouldn't fire you. Annoying my editor gives me too much pleasure – it reminds him who's the boss around here.' He smirked and Verity tried to smile. 'Now, I haven't a lot of time, I'm dining with the Prime Minister tonight.' He could never resist bragging to his staff of the circles in which he moved.

'Well, I hope you will tell him not to betray Czechoslovakia – at least not until I've learnt the language.'

Weaver chuckled. 'You don't need to learn the language. They all speak German, some French and a few speak English. You'll be all right.'

'They wouldn't have me back in Vienna?'

'Wouldn't hear of it! You must have been doing something right. I've never heard Ribbentrop be so rude about anyone. In any case, Vienna's a backwater now. You have to be one step ahead of Hitler. The Sudetenland is next, mark my words.'

'Will we go to war over it?'

'Over a few German-speaking Czechs joining the Reich? Certainly not.'

'But if he takes over the whole country?'

'He won't – not yet, at least. He's still got a lot to do in Austria.'

'Jews to kill?' Verity asked ironically.

Weaver was unperturbed. 'I was sorry to hear about your Jew. Sounded an interesting man. What a bizarre way to die. Talking of Jews – your idea of getting us involved in the *Kindertransport* was inspired. *New Gazette* readers have been writing to us in their hundreds expressing their outrage at Hitler's heartlessness and many are sending cheques and postal orders. And the photographs – very moving. This is the way to mobilize public opinion. A single photograph of a weeping child holding a teddy bear is worth a hundred of Winston's speeches. That reminds me, he was talking to me about you the other day. He seems to think highly of you though I'm not sure why. I don't know what you said to him at that dinner party. I thought you hated his guts. I counted on there being an almighty row.'

'If that's what you wanted, I think you made a mistake inviting Unity Mitford, Joe. Next to her, Mr Churchill seemed a moderate.'

'So you are open to argument! I never would have thought it.'

'Don't tease, Joe. Of course I can be persuaded to change my opinions. I hadn't met Mr Churchill until that evening and he wasn't anything like I expected. He ought to be in the cabinet.'

Weaver looked at her in genuine amazement. 'Well, fancy that! Our most notorious Communist makes common cause with the man who broke the General Strike! You'll be telling me next you're going to marry Edward.'

Verity tried not to blush and decided to make a determined effort to keep to the less dangerous subject of Churchill. 'I'm not saying I agree with everything he does and says but, as far as the one big thing is concerned, he is right and almost every other politician is wrong.'

'Hmm! Well, I'm going to throw you out now.' He touched a bell under his desk. 'You are flying from Croydon on Thursday. You go via Paris. Best not to go anywhere a German agent might kidnap you.' He saw the look of disbelief on her face. 'You can say I'm talking poppycock – I probably am but stranger things have happened. Think of what happened to your friend von Trott. By the way, have you heard anything from him?' He did not wait for an answer. 'You count your lucky stars you got out of Vienna alive. It's not only Henderson who hates your guts.'

Weaver's secretary came in to say his car was waiting and to hand over to Verity her letters of accreditation and other necessary documents.

'Can I give you a lift?' he flung at her but, before she could ask him would he mind dropping her in Sloane Square, he had disappeared. She smiled at the secretary, whom she knew well. 'I'd best get used to finding my own way, I suppose!'

By eight thirty she was in the Ritz being handed a note from her father. 'A hundred apologies,' it read, 'but something has come up and I have to fly to Paris tonight. Tried to get you on the telephone but no answer. Have a very expensive dinner on me – with a friend if you have one. What about that nice man Corinth you treat so badly? Know you'll understand. The same in your profession, I don't doubt. Your loving father.'

Verity crumpled the sheet of paper in her hand and asked the attendant to return her cloak. With as much dignity as she could manage, she got into a taxi and returned to Cranmer Court. She sat on the edge of her bed cursing her father and all the men who had let her down. She then thought of Edward and burst into tears. She picked up the telephone and dialled his number. Of course she would marry him – the one man who had never let her down. It was Fenton who answered. His master was engaged and could not be disturbed. Was there a message? She said there was not. If there were, it was not one she could relay to Edward through his valet.

Feeling exceedingly sorry for herself, she lay on the bed, still in her Chanel dress, and cried like a little girl for the mother she had never known until, eventually, she slept.

14

As Edward reached the steps of Albany, he noticed a young woman. She had her back to him and was engaged in conversation with one of the porters. She turned and, to his surprise, he saw that it was Vera Gray. He was still in good spirits after his interview with Liddell so he raised his hat and greeted her cheerfully.

'What are you doing in this part of the world, Miss Gray? Were you coming to see me?'

It crossed his mind that she might have developed an interest in him, which would be embarrassing, but when she spoke he realized this was not her motive in seeking him out.

'I feel awful coming to see you unannounced, Lord Edward, but I thought I would take the chance that you might be in. I've just been visiting the Royal Academy.'

'I'm delighted to see you. Come in and have a cup of tea or something stronger. I'm sure we deserve it.'

He ushered her into the drawing-room and set about making cocktails – a ritual of shaking and rattling he much enjoyed. He was talking lightly of trivial matters – asking about preparations for her uncle's exhibition and how her own work was progressing – when she stopped him with a gesture and an odd noise somewhere between a sob and a gasp.

'The truth is, Lord Edward, I have something to confess.'

'To confess?' Edward repeated, at a loss to know what she meant. 'What is there to confess? If you mean about your uncle . . .'

'I do mean about my uncle, yes.' There was something desperate in her tone of voice as though she had nerved herself to say what she needed to say and could not bear to be prevented from speaking.

Edward poured out the cocktails, wondering whether whisky might not have been more appropriate, and sat down opposite her.

'Now tell me what's bothering you. Have you discovered something among your uncle's papers to distress you?'

'No, it's nothing like that. The fact is . . . I wanted to tell you that I killed him.'

'My dear! No! I simply don't believe it. You were the most loving niece a man could wish for. A daughter could not have cared for him better. What possible reason could you have for . . . for doing that?'

She put her cocktail down heavily on the table beside her chair, spilling much of it. She did not notice what she had done and continued to stare at Edward in mute horror.

'There was a moment when I thought you had guessed why I did it. I killed him because I could not bear it to happen all over again.'

'For what to happen all over again?' It came to him in a flash. 'You mean his depressions?'

She nodded her head slowly. 'Not so much depressions this time but . . . well, at first he became forgetful. He forgot to eat or wash.'

'He was still painting.'

'How can I make you understand? He used to take his painting kit up to Tarn Hill and do exactly the same picture he had done before.'

'But that was a tribute, or at least I thought it was, to the place where he had been happy – where he courted his wife.'

'It began like that but towards . . . towards the end he did not know why he was painting that picture – except

231

that it was the only one he *could* still paint. You see, he had done it so many times before that he didn't need to think about it. His body took over.'

'You mean he was going senile?' Vera nodded. 'Did you take him to a doctor . . .? Surely he wasn't old enough to go senile?'

'The doctor said it was probably brought on by his breakdown during the war but I blame it on the ergot. He said my uncle would soon need full-time nursing and that I ought to make arrangements. I told him I couldn't afford it. The doctor said, cool as anything, that it was my job. I was to be his nurse. I asked about putting him in a home. He said that, if I couldn't afford nurses, I wouldn't be able to afford a private hospital. I asked if there were any public ones and he looked at me as if I had asked for an abortion. He said coldly that no one would put a man like my uncle in a public hospital if they had ever seen inside one.'

'So you killed him rather than see him deteriorate?'

'I killed him to save my own sanity,' she said bitterly. 'I am so selfish! I just couldn't face twenty or even thirty years trapped with someone who didn't even know his own name . . . someone whose every need I had to see to . . . someone who could not even go to the lavatory on his own. That was what the doctor said I was faced with.' Her voice became shrill as she relived her panic. 'It wasn't as if he was an old man and, you see, my childhood was given over to looking after him. You can't imagine what it was like. I was his slave. I always had to be at his beck and call. When he was in one of his depressions, I was the only one who could soothe him. Twice I came back from school to find he had cut his wrists. When he was himself, he was the kindest man imaginable but, at the back of my mind, I always feared the black dog – that was what he called it – would come and spoil everything. And it always did.

'As a child, the burden of it almost drove me mad. I couldn't pay attention at school. I was naughty and even wild. The teachers despaired of me. I had very few friends and those I had I did not dare take home. As I got older, I saw my life slipping away. I had no boyfriends. Well, I didn't mind that so much, but I wanted to paint and

I couldn't. I was stifled. I was always anxious, always looking for signs that the black dog was coming. Oh dear! I can't explain it to someone like you who has never had to be at anyone's beck and call. It's a prison without bars but a prison nonetheless.'

'What were the signs that your uncle was going to have one of his depressions?'

'He would be angry for no good reason. Normally, he was the mildest of men. He stopped sleeping, and then he would have these nightmares.' She shuddered. 'You don't want to hear all this. You must think I'm just trying to make excuses for what I did.'

'These nightmares,' Edward persisted, feeling instinctively that Vera needed to talk about what she had suffered, 'what form did they take?'

'I would hear him groaning in his sleep. You can't imagine how frightening that was. Then the next night he would be shrieking. I would go and try to wake him but it was surprisingly difficult. Sometimes, if I woke him too suddenly, he became violent.'

'He would hit you?'

'Not deliberately. He would be dreaming he was at the front and his friends were being blown to pieces all around him. He would punch the air – as if he was fighting to escape some net.'

'And when he woke?'

'Then he would cry. In some ways that was worst of all. As a child, to find my uncle weeping like a baby . . . I would feel so helpless . . . so sad.'

'And during the day?'

'I would go off to school and, while I was out of the house, I knew he would be thinking about killing himself. He could not bear the idea of going to bed and suffering those nightmares again. He tried drink but that did not work. He hated whisky and, if he tried to make himself drunk, it just made him more suicidal. The only thing which helped then was ergot but, as you know, it has side effects. It gave him hallucinations and he couldn't paint. In the end, I think the ergot brought on his dementia but, at the time, it was better than nothing.'

'Weren't there any friends you could call on?'

'When I was very young there was Auntie May, as I called her – though I think she was really a cousin of some sort. She couldn't cope with me or Uncle Peter. After that, there were some friends . . . painters for the most part, like Reg Harman. But they had their own lives to lead and my uncle was reclusive by nature. He made it difficult for his friends to help him.'

'He didn't teach or anything?'

'He tried teaching but, unlike Reg, he wasn't good at it. In the end, the Slade more or less sacked him.'

'But things got better and then you were able to move to Lawn Road?'

'Yes, as a new war loomed, Uncle Peter – in an odd way – became happier. He stopped having nightmares of the trenches. I thought he had recovered and it was all going to be all right. For the first time I had the freedom to live my own life, paint my own pictures. I have never been so happy as I was in my little flat – my own living space. Virginia Woolf said that all creative women – sorry, does this sound pretentious – anyway, she said we need a "room of one's own" to escape domestic life for a few hours and she was right.

'I knew it could not last but it was so brief . . . so very brief.' Vera hung her head and mumbled. 'I had been out of the cage for such a short time and suddenly – talking to that awful doctor – I realized that I would have to move back to the flat and look after him – maybe for years. I might die before him. I just . . . I just thought I couldn't do it. I think of myself as a strong person but I knew I couldn't go through with it.'

'You couldn't have found someone to help you . . .?'

'I told you, there was no money and anyway, I would have felt guilty not looking after him myself. After all, he was a real artist and I'm . . . I'm a nobody. People would have said that he took me in as an orphan. Now it was my turn to care for him.'

'So what did you do?'

'Well, the weeks went by and I became more and more desperate. In the end, I decided to give him ergot – there

234

was plenty left – a dose big enough to kill him.' She faltered for the first time and Edward saw the tears running down her face. 'I thought I would take him up to his favourite place and let him die where he was happiest. And so that was what I did. Only I forgot the palette knife he always used and Miss Browne found it in the studio.'

'I remember. But why didn't you tell her that you had opened his paintbox and the knife must have fallen out?'

'I know. I ought to have said that but I could not do it. I just told the truth – that the box hadn't been opened. I must have been a bit mad. You know, I think I half-hoped I would be found out. I didn't want to get away with it. I knew I shouldn't be allowed to get away scot-free.'

'But your uncle was found at the bottom of Tarn Hill, almost on the Broadlands drive?'

'I thought I had given him enough ergot to kill him but I was wrong. He was woozy when I got him into the car. If he had been unconscious, I couldn't have manoeuvred him.'

'And so when you left him . . .?'

'By then he was unconscious. I thought he was dead. I kissed him and walked away. I knew he would be found before too long.' She shuddered. 'I couldn't have allowed him to lie out there all night.'

'But he wasn't dead?'

'No, he must have come to – oh, it's too awful to think about – and staggered down the hill and died where he was found. I'm a murderer, aren't I? Tell me I am wicked? Tell me I should be hanged?'

Edward looked at Vera aghast. Tears were running down her cheeks but she did not wipe them away.

'So why did you mention the notes on the canvas? Why did you draw attention to the fact that your uncle had taken ergot unexpectedly?'

'I don't really understand myself. I suppose I thought you suspected there was something wrong and I wanted to distract you.'

'And you were successful. Verity and I thought the notes had to be connected with someone at Broadlands – possibly Mountbatten himself.' A thought crossed

Edward's mind. 'Did you do those squiggles on the canvas?'

'No, no! He did them and I really believe that he was upset at the thought of my aunt's home being destroyed. I think, in his muddled way, he did want to talk to Lord Louis about it. That was what he *was* trying to do when he walked down the hill that last time. He was getting so forgetful, as I said, he made notes to remind himself . . .'

'But I think there was another reason why you suggested there was something strange about your uncle's death. I think you wanted to be found out. You wanted someone to know – to ease your conscience. You wanted to be punished.'

Vera hung her head like a naughty child. In a low voice, she said, 'I thought of you as my nemesis. It was so unfair, I know. I thought that if you found out the truth . . . and forgave me – or did not forgive me – I would have – what's the word? – *expiated* my sin. It was very wicked of me. . . to try and transfer my guilt to you. I suppose, if I was religious, I would have confessed to a priest.'

'But I *didn't* find out the truth,' Edward said bitterly.

'You didn't want to,' she murmured.

Edward was silent. He was not God. He was not nemesis but he did distinguish – as the law did not – between murder done out of malice – greed, envy, hatred – and murder brought on by despair. He thought, wryly, of the legend beneath the Mersham coat of arms – *Aquila non captat Muscat.* Eagles don't catch flies. He suspected there must be other instances where children, driven to the edge of madness by the burden of looking after senile parents, resorted to snuffing out a life. Such deaths seldom if ever came to be investigated by policemen and condemned by judge and jury.

He knew he ought to be angry that it was so but he preferred to think that there was often mercy in the killing and mercy should be shown to the killer. As Shakespeare put it, 'the quality of mercy is not strain'd. It droppeth as the gentle rain from heaven,' by which he meant, surely, that mercy should not be governed by inflexible human laws.

They sat in silence for several minutes until he could restrain himself no longer. 'Oh Vera! Why did you have to tell me this? What am I supposed to do? There's no evidence to convict you of murder except your own confession. Yes, if you were convicted of murder, you would indeed be hanged. It is the mandatory sentence for murder. The Home Secretary might reduce the sentence to life imprisonment but how could you ever bear that? Your defence counsel might argue that, when you left your uncle on the hill, he was still alive so you had not actually killed him, but the fact remains that you *meant* to kill him and, in the end, he did die as a result of the ergot you gave him. However, unless you decide to repeat it to the police your confession is of no interest to anyone except those who care about you. I have no intention of repeating what you have told me to the police. That is for you to do, if you so wish, but I beg you to keep silent and find some more constructive way of dealing with your guilt.'

Vera looked at him, haggard and pale. 'At first I thought that I could deal with it – my guilt. I had my freedom and would pay the price for my wickedness having to live with the knowledge that I had committed the worst sin against the person I loved most in the world. As the days went by, I realized I could not. I had to tell someone. It was as simple as that. So I told you. I am so . . . so sorry to have burdened you with it. '

She made to get up but Edward stayed her.

'Vera,' he said, laying his hand on hers. 'No one who knows you can doubt that you are a good person. You acted out of desperation. You had been deprived of the childhood which was yours by right and suddenly you were faced with the fact that, once again, you would have to devote the best part of your life to caring for your uncle. No sane person would say you are a cold-blooded murderer.'

'But that is what the law would say.'

'It would,' Edward said grimly, not wanting her to be in any doubt of the danger in which she lay. 'And, what is more, you would be pilloried by the newspapers – misunderstood and caricatured. It doesn't bear thinking about.'

'My God! What am I going to do?'

'You alone can decide. No one can make the decision for you but the fact that you had to tell me what happened suggests to me that your conscience will lead you out of the morass. You must do something or you may punish yourself some other way.'

'Suicide? I have thought of that. Don't think that I haven't,' she said vehemently.

'Your death will help no one and I can't believe it would be what your uncle would want. He had seen enough pain and suffering.'

'So what do I do?'

'It's not for me to tell you but I have a suggestion,' he said slowly. 'The Germans have an expression, *Trauerbeit* – the labour of mourning. The coming war is going to bring a world of suffering. Why not devote as much time as possible to helping refugees? Perhaps, in that way, you will be able to make peace with yourself.'

Vera's face cleared a little and she looked at him with something like hope in her eyes. 'Refugees?'

'Verity and I have helped bring over and settle a trainload of Jewish children from Vienna. Other trains are planned but the organizers are desperately short of competent people to help.'

'Children are coming on trains?' she sounded bewildered.

'Yes. The British Jewish Refugee Committee has been formed to organize what they call *Kindertransport* – trains and planes to rescue children from almost certain death in the camps which the Nazis have set up. Would that be a way forward for you?'

Edward spent another hour talking Vera through the tragedy in her life and he was very weary when at last she left. They had not felt like eating but now he found he was hungry. Although it was nine thirty, he thought he would see if Verity was in her flat. He had dialled her number before he remembered that she was dining with her father. He was just about to replace the receiver when, to his surprise, she answered. She sounded as though he had woken her.

'You're not at the Ritz with your father . . .?'

As matter-of-factly as she could manage, she told him how she had been stood up.

'Meet me at Gennaro's and we can weep on each other's shoulders,' he urged her. 'No need to dress.'

Had he known Verity was going to pour out her anguish at her father's ability to absent himself whenever she needed him most, he might not have been so ready to take her out to dinner. He had had about as much as he could take of fathers and daughters, uncles and nieces. However, he listened patiently as she told him how isolated she felt – how badly she had missed a mother's guidance as a child and, worse still, when she had first gone out into the world as a young girl. She spoke about her passionate love for her father and how she had been so proud of him. How she had tried to understand why the good causes he espoused had always taken priority over her. She remembered a school play in which she had the starring role. He had promised to be there but his seat had remained empty and when, taking her curtain call, she had looked for him, he was not there. How she had trained herself not to care – or so she thought – that he forgot to collect her from her friends' houses and never remembered her birthday unless she reminded him. It became a sort of joke between them, only it had ceased to make her laugh.

When she was quite done, he told her about Vera.

'Oh God! Edward, you must be exhausted!' she cried. 'You ought to have told me to shut up. How could I have burdened you with my problems with my father when Vera . . . oh, that poor girl! You know, I always thought there was something odd going on. That day I met her at her uncle's flat, she was doing her best to appear normal but there was something . . . I couldn't put my finger on it. Of course, what she told you explains everything.'

'Do you think we were foolish not to have worked it out without her having to tell me?'

'I don't see how we could. She had no motive for killing her uncle – or none that we could have known about. But, thank God, we never spoke to anyone about our version of events.'

'Particularly that ass, Inspector Beeston.'

'No, thank goodness!'

'Darling V! Tell me again that you'll marry me. I somehow can't quite believe it. Say you haven't changed your mind.'

Verity closed her eyes and then opened them again as if she had been praying although as a paid-up member of the Communist Party of Great Britain and an avowed atheist this was unlikely. She put her hands into his across the table and said simply, 'I will marry you, Edward, if you still want me.'

A week later, Edward found himself in a gloomy north London synagogue listening to a rabbi recite Kaddish. He prayed for the soul of Georg Dreiser and for his parents, probably in some hideous concentration camp by now. Then he prayed for Verity, who had left for Prague, and for their marriage.

'Don't look at me like that!' she had ordered when he kissed her goodbye. 'I won't be in Prague for very long. The Germans will march into Czechoslovakia and I will be thrown out. I am trying to be thrown out of every country in Europe.' She joked but her voice cracked. 'I am the albatross – the bird of ill-omen. I move to the sound of marching boots and I dance to the goose-step.'

'V!' he chided her. 'Don't go all gnomic on me. It's not like you to be so gloomy.'

'Georg's death has shocked me more than all the deaths I saw in Spain.'

'Why? Because you think it was our fault?'

'No. I know it wasn't our fault but I feel it as very close to me. Georg was the first person I thought I had a chance of saving and I failed. And now I won't be at the synagogue to pray for him.'

'You don't believe in prayer.'

'No, but I'm not always logical as you well know. Pray for him for me, will you, Edward?'

Before setting out on her long journey across Europe, Verity had spent the night in the arms of her lover. They had eaten a last supper of bread and cheese and drunk a last bottle of wine in the bed which smelled of their entwined bodies. The flat in Cranmer Court – still largely unfurnished – was an adequate refuge, so anonymous it seemed to concentrate all their longings inwards, one upon the other.

After they had eaten, they lay in the darkness and tried to sleep but there were too many thoughts to pursue in each of their minds to make it possible. Edward stroked her, feeling her flutter under his hand like a bird. She clung to him with all the passion of a child at her mother's breast, wanting to tell him what he already knew – that she was frightened of her appointment with destiny. She had been in danger so many times and escaped death when others close to her had not. Perhaps her luck was finally running out. Perhaps she would end up in some squalid Nazi prison camp. She tried to still her rising panic. She knew that in the morning light she would see things more clearly. She would not be afraid. She would be dry-eyed as she kissed Edward goodbye but, in the darkness, she could give way to night terrors and be comforted.

'V, darling, you're shivering. Are you cold?'

'I am a little cold, yes.'

'Shall I warm you again – the way you like?'

'But it's the middle of the night . . . Don't you want to sleep?'

Edward did not answer but cradled her to his chest. She was so small! How could such a sparrow fly so far from him? He felt her breath warm against his mouth. He kissed her and felt, rather than saw, her tears.

'Hey, don't cry, my darling,' he murmured. 'We'll part in the morning but only for a little while. I shall come after you in a month or two and bring you home.'

'But, Edward,' she protested, suddenly happy, 'I'm a hard-bitten, bloody-minded reporter – not a child to be carried off to safety as soon as the going gets a little rough.'

'Of course you are, my darling, but you are also going to be my wife and that gives me the right to protect you.

It's a right I have desired for so long and now you cannot deny me.'

'I won't deny you anything,' she promised him.

'Oh, V!' he cried, entering her as though into a new life. 'Come to me, my darling girl! I love you very much. You will never be alone again, however far away you are from me.'

And when it was all over and they were satisfied, they slept and were comforted.

The rabbi had told Edward that the Kaddish was in essence a reminder of the greatness of God rather than what a Christian might think of as a mourning prayer.

'You see,' the old man said, 'the great Rabbi Meir consoled her husband for the death of their two sons with a prayer which likened their dead children to precious objects God had lent them for a while and now demanded they return. So, when a loved one dies, we say, "The Lord gave and the Lord took back. Blessed be the name of the Lord."'

It seemed cold comfort to Edward and he felt uneasy praying standing up and with a hat on his head. He studied the English translation of the ancient Jewish prayer and, as the words echoed in his mind, they brought him a kind of understanding.

'He who creates peace in heaven, may he bring peace for us and for Israel,' the rabbi intoned.

Georg had not found peace in his beloved Austria, nor in England. Perhaps he was at peace now. Edward hoped it was so. He solemnly swore to the spirit of Georg that he would do his utmost to bring life and hope to the children in the trains shuffling their way over dangerous borders to a kind of safety. They, at least, must feel the quality of mercy.

He closed his eyes and offered up a moment of quietness – what his friend the Reverend Tommie Fox had told him was called a hesychasm – as he silently repeated words from the twenty-third psalm. 'Yea, though I walk through the valley of the shadow of death, I will fear no evil for thou art with me.'

He sighed. *Sursum corda*. Lift up your hearts! He offered up a prayer for Verity's safety in Czechoslovakia and for Frank, who might soon be fighting Nazism on another battlefront. He hoped there was a God to hear it.

As he left the synagogue, words from *Measure for Measure* – perhaps Shakespeare's bleakest play – came to mind. They seemed in some mysterious way to fit the time and the place.

> Mortality and mercy in Vienna
> Live in thy tongue and heart.

Historical Note

The first *Kindertransport* refugee train left Berlin for England in early December 1938, some months later than I have it in the book, for which I hope I will be forgiven.

After *Kristallnacht* (the Night of Broken Glass) on 9 and 10 November 1938 when 367 synagogues were destroyed and the windows of all the Jewish shops left in the Reich were shattered, the British Jewish Refugee Committee appealed to the British Government to admit any Jewish children up to the age of seventeen from Germany and what had until the *Anschluss* been Austria. After a debate in the House of Commons this was agreed and, as a result 10,000 children were saved from the concentration camps. The last train departed from Berlin just two days before war broke out on 3 September 1939.

For more information go to www.kindertransport.org